GRIMOIRES OF THE GALÈRE

or

~Magic Gone Amiss~

A Glass Cauldron Mystery
Book One

By T.L. Woodliff

T. L. Woodliff

MORE BY THIS AUTHOR

GLASS CAULDRON COZY MYSTERIES

Book 1: Grimoires of the Galère-
Magic Gone Amiss

Book 2: Familiars of the Galère- PART ONE-
Magic will be Messy

Book 3: Shaman and Warrior of the Galère-
Histories of the Galère Chapter One

Book 4: Familiars of the Galère- PART TWO-
A Magical Stop, Drop and Roll

Book 5: Sacred Grove of the Galère-
Histories of the Galère Chapter Two- Coming June 2019

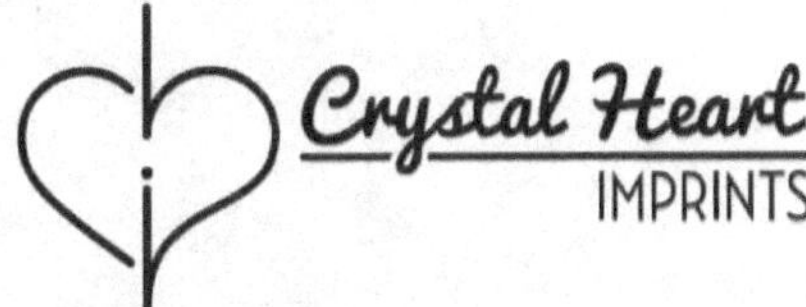

T. L. Woodliff

For My Springfield Galère
To all of you, with all my love

PHOTO CREDITS:

Woman With Flowers- Alphonse Mucha

Summer- Alphonse Mucha

Art Deco Girl in Blue- Brita Seifert

Victorian Beauty in White by Atelier Sommerland

Reveire- Alphonse Mucha

TERMS:

Galère- a gathering of a group of motley characters who share a common interest

Enscored- past tense of *enscore;* a sentient being under magical control by another

Ensorcelled- a non-sentient item that is controlled by a creature of magic

Sidhe- the Fae, fairy or magical beings who move between realms of reality

MEMBERS OF THE GALÈRE:

Mist Butler (Amethyst)- One of the four, main witches and our usual story-teller. I (the narrator) am allowed to tell a story or two in this adventure, but usually, you'll be following Mist. Mother of Jade. Owner of the *Axe & Stovepipe.* Sister to Slate. Element is Fire.

Crystal Thapa- One of the four, main witches. Mother to Aaron and Eva. Author. The oldest and wisest of the group. Element is Wind.

Mica Durand- One of the four, main witches. She's a well-known artist to the city of Springfield, and the surrounding area. (Wait 'til you see what she does with abandoned spittoons!) Element is Water.

Amber Greene- One of the four, main witches. The youngest by far, closer in age to Crystal's children than to any of the other witches, but it makes no difference. Her gift with plants cannot be denied. Her Element is Earth (no surprise, that.)

Slate Butler- You'll learn his title in another story. Brother to Mist, engaged to Liam and business partner to Cole. A lawyer by trade, but the Fates have something else he'll need to learn (and quickly.)

Liam Lindsey- He too has a title that is yet to be revealed. He's engaged to Slate, though he already considers Slate's family his own. Works in media relations for the Illinois EPA.

Jade Butler- Seventeen-year-old daughter to Mist, and niece to Slate and Liam.

Cole Thompson- Slate's business partner. Looks like a Greek god and knows it.

Nic Berhane- Assistant Manager at the *Axe & Stovepipe*. Celibate, spiritual, busy reshaping his life.

Eva & Aaron Thapa- Twins. College students. Children of Crystal, and prone to getting things done.

Jasper Greene- Brother to Amber; owner of *Eighth Circuit Brewery;* totally embraced modern primitive movement. Has eyes for Mist, but she's (weirdly) oblivious.

PREFACE

The eras of The Witches come and go. In between these ages, Gaia, the Earth Mother, pours that potable energy into the seers, shamans, mystics and energy-workers that have always been among us.

The Fates, three sisters with keen third-eye-sight and a collective taste for order, maneuver the lives of women they believe most suitable onto intertwined paths so that should Gaia command a new era begin, the witches have already been gathered while still blind to their potential. Always thinking ahead, these Fates.

But even the most attentive immortals will sometimes lose focus. The bloodied chaos of the twentieth century left them exhausted. The Fates pulled back, only a little, to seek rest and heal their wounded souls after the slaughter of millions left them raw and ruined in spirit.

They looked away.

And in that moment, the banished returned to the lands of Gaia, and the Fates are already three steps behind.

The new era begins, battle plans lay out on a chess board that reaches into many realms. And the new witches? Well, if they can survive the first weeks, there just might be a chance for them in this game of the gods.

They are given no choice- learn, and learn fast.

CHAPTER ONE
Mist

"**T**his is brilliant." I watched Amber lift her bathing suit high overhead before she snuggled under the jet sprays of the hot tub. She threw the item behind her with a loud laugh as it vanished over the roof gable, followed by that smirk only the young can get away with. The steam caused her short, reddish-brown hair to curl about her round face. She grabbed her glass of wine and, with a salute, finished half of it.

"Hey!" Crystal was still struggling to follow Amber's lead and maintain some sense of modesty. "That's to be sipped, you desecrating imp." She scowled before vanishing from sight, rising up from the bubbling waters a moment later like a sitting Statue of Liberty. Draping her suit on the edge of the tub, it slid to the plastic floor covering, or rather, roof covering, with a *slurp* sound.

She settled back with her long white hair edged in lavender streaks plastered everywhere and then focused her infamous scowl on me. "Exactly whose bright idea was it to make clothing not an option for the wine tastings, Mist?"

"You, my friend, are the one who joined this thing called the Naked Wine club. We here," I cast my free hand in a circle to include all four of us in the hot tub, "simply wish to support you in this endeavor." I took a small sip of the three-year-old, affordable cabernet that was in the most recent batch from the wine club. "And it's just better when sitting in warm bubbles."

"So warm," Mica sighed, slipping under for a moment.

"I would like to point out," Crystal began as she swirled her wine glass beneath her nose, "the name refers to the distance between the wine taster and the vineyard, not the distance between the wine taster and their clothing."

"And I would like to point out that I am keeping my swim shorts on, thank you. Nice aim, Amber."

A chorus of "Slate" went up, along with raised glasses as my brother came around the rooftop gable, his eyes covered with one hand, and holding Amber's bathing top in the other.

"Is everyone decent?"

The immediate response was a unanimous shout of "Never!" as the glasses came back down. Crystal leaned her head back with a throaty laugh and Amber smiled mischievously as Slate made his way to join us. Before I could say anything to protect my baby brother, Mica spoke up.

"Not a word, Amber. He's not for you."

"Moi?" She couldn't quite grasp an innocent voice as she took another long draught. It was an old joke. We were complaining about our ridiculous dry spells in the boyfriend category when Crystal, who claimed she was done with all men forever, suggested we put our heads to better pursuits. One of those was to explore chasing tasty wines instead of tasty men.

The other was to try our hand at solving an old mystery in our history-rich part of the country where Abe Lincoln rose to fame. I'm not quite sure when Crystal's wine club evolved into a crow's nest-hot tub-sans-clothing event, but so far, it worked. When Amber joined last fall, she seemed a perfect fit, even if, at twenty-two, she was the youngest by almost a decade and barely old enough to sample the wines. She had yet to embrace the word 'sample,' though.

"Yes, you." Mica nodded to Amber as she poured Slate the

last of the cabernet. "One down, two to go." She placed the empty bottle on the small table behind her before changing her mind and nestling it on the floor among the extra towels. Of all of us, she seemed the most concerned about things tumbling off the roof even though the hot tub had been built-in during the building's move and reconstruction. And it was almost completely hidden from any peering eyes.

That was important- this large residence was built when Abe Lincoln loaned money to a friend to buy his family a home and as such, it's important to the city. The council members were more than supportive when I bought the crumbling house to restore it.

Oh, and I also moved it five blocks up the road so it would be right across the street from the historical park where good ol' Abe's home still stands. The city council had been beyond accommodating, so the hot tub needs to stay way below the radar. It was put it by an expert construction worker Mica knew, and it followed all codes, but we didn't want to draw any eyes. Mica was afraid something would fall down right when a council member walked by or entered the café on the first floor and I'd be in big trouble.

Or rather, in more trouble. After all the effort of getting the building moved, inch by frustrating inch, down the middle of a normally busy road, it then sat there for a full month while the basement foundation at the new location was finished. It wasn't my fault that we had the permits and the equipment in place to move the building, and then the rains delayed the foundation work. But the council members spoke with smiles through gritted teeth to reporters and angry locals who had to find alternative routes home.

Those smiles quickly faded, however, when I put up the new sign for the café. I chose an old-fashioned display, like the ones outside of 'ye olde' English pubs. You know the kind- everyone could tell it was called the Prancing Pony even if they couldn't read because there was a dancing little horse on the sign. So, as I named the café The *Axe & Stovepipe*, an obvious reference to the sixteenth president, it made sense that I would have a picture of Lincoln holding his famous axe- he really did split rails at one time- and wearing his famous hat. And it seemed perfectly logical that it would be a young version of the president, what with the axe and all.

The fact that the artist happened to think a beefy, shirtless Abe would be the most eye-catching for a store front was an opinion that could not be argued.

The city council chose not to agree.

I looked over at said artist and watched Mica try and capture her thick, long swirling mass of insane curls. Once she ended the most recent battle with her cursed mane of hair, she settled back and watched the moonlight glimmer through her wineglass.

She looked like the Celtic goddess on all those art nouveau postcards- unbelievable hair, skin that would make Snow White turn green with envy and high, Celtic cheekbones with an angular nose. What's funny is that she appreciates none of it- she hates her uncombable hair, she loves to be in the sun but burns after mere minutes, and she's wanted a nose job ever since we'd met as kids.

"Off limits, sweetie." Mica bobbed her glass to Amber, who offered back a quick wiggle of her nose and a short laugh. One couldn't help but notice it sounded like the cackle of a witch. "And how is Liam, Slate? I haven't seen him in a while."

My brother shared one of his brilliant, lopsided smiles- the kind that makes women think they have a chance at getting him to change teams. Then he raised his right hand. "Besides being a bear about his job, he's been designing these, finally. Matching bands. Oh, ladies." He brought the wineglass up to cover his face with a jerk that spilled half.

"Sorry," we chimed, scooting back. When he held his hand out, there was a rush of water as we all moved up to see the ring. The water swelled forward before having to pull back again, leaving a lot of flesh momentarily exposed.

"Sis, seriously. I don't need the image of you naked in a hot tub haunting me through life."

That's probably true. "My apologies, little brother. But you must own to bad timing in showing us your engagement jewelry. I want a closer look- pass it around."

Crystal laughed, sinking down further to hide her most ample figure. I noticed that she too had that wicked-witch cackle working tonight.

"Hold on, Amber." I saw her going for her third drink, which would most likely empty her glass. "A toast- to us!"

"To us." We cheered, but Slate interrupted our chorus of goodwill.

"Wait, wait. That was pathetic, Mist." He stood up with a raised chin as he cleared his throat. Once standing, he frowned. "Well, no. That's just cold." He sat back down in the warm waters, but kept his glass raised. Crystal winked with silent appreciation.

Amber spoke up. "Too late." She held her empty glass out for inspection. "It's time for seconds."

"Not yet for me- I'm more into second breakfasts," Crystal made-way as Mica scootched around, keeping low and covered in the bubbles while refilling glasses from the second bottle.

"And they all go straight to your boobs. That is so unfair." Mica corked the bottle roughly in Crystal's face and I nodded in agreement. It was an envious truth.

Slate cleared his throat. "I raise my glass to you ladies, here. To the mischievous Amber, who somehow wooed a narcissistic book dealer into loaning you something from a private collection."

"Hear, hear," I called and took a sip. The others followed. Slate frowned at me.

"Amber won't be sober enough to make it through my toast if you do that every time." Slate waited for the giggles to reside before resuming what looked to be a speech instead of a toast. "To Mica, who somehow got a security guard to let you all go galivanting through a private residence. I mean, that's talent." Slate seemed genuinely impressed.

He started to ramble on some more about it but Amber cut him off with a derisive snort. "I know how she got him to do it."

I laughed while Crystal and Mica clinked glasses. "He was gorgeous." Crystal added. Mica gave her a wink.

"So you're dating now." Slate made it a statement, his face lighting up at the thought.

"Oh, good grief, no." Mica took a sip as she shook her head. I had to snort myself on that one. Mica wasn't about to be tied down to anyone up in Chicago, not for all the art-supplies on the planet.

Slate *tsked*, disapproval evident. "Mica, you... Never mind. Anyway." He rolled his eyes and continued. "To Crystal, who wrote a brilliant story about your Chicago adventure, now headed for publication in Architecture Digest, or is it Architectural Magazine?" He paused.

Crystal simply nodded. "Something like that, yes." I love her humble nature. She's an excellent freelance writer with one heck of a resume, but she never brags about it. She says a good, midwestern-woman would never do such a thing.

Slate tapped a finger to his glass to show his approval. He applauds good morals at every opportunity. I seriously don't know how we're related. "And to my sister, who started the whole adventure after a trip to the Frank Lloyd Wright museum."

"It was just a hunch."

"How many decades have passed since that grisly murder at Wright's home? Knowing who did it was easy, but you guys, you four, brilliant women from the Springfield cornfields uncovered the why, and that's the hard part."

How nice. I smiled, warmed by his compliment and happy to make my little brother proud of me. I moved the glass back to my lips, only to have him stop me once again. "And," he circled his stemware over the center of the hot tub with the drama of a magician. "You did all of this with zero help from the Chicago community, which is amazing in itself."

"Amen!" We all spoke at once because that was *truth*. No one connected with society was of any help in what was a very societal event. We'd spent a full week way up in Chicago and it would have been much shorter with just a teensy bit of help. But still, we found out why Julian Carlton had killed Wright's mistress, Mamah- *the* great mystery of twentieth-century Chicago.

Slate looked as though he was about to speak again but Crystal shot him a fierce look. "And to us," she said with a touch of menace, lifting her wine to her lips.

"Yes," Slate agreed with a blush. "To our gathering of undesirables, to our galère." We all took a drink between laughs.

"It's generally the same story." Crystal stretched her glass out to Mica for a refill. "Greed."

"Passion," Mica added with a devilish smile which made me grin in agreement.

"Revenge," Amber added. She started to take a drink, but looked at her glass then shook her head and put it on a table behind her. I really like that she knows herself and her limits so well. She might be fourteen years younger than me, but she seems as wise as Crystal at times, who is fifteen years older than Mica. We are certainly a well-rounded group, age wise- twenty-two up to forty-five.

"And this one was all of the above combined, pure and simple. He wanted revenge and money and, in a fit of passion, ended his chances of getting either," I finished. They all nodded. I exhaled, absentmindedly stroking the chain around my neck. It's a bad habit, I know. I do it much too often. I find it soothing, even captivating. It pulls me out of the moment.

"Wait." Oops- hadn't meant to say that out loud. "What were we just talking about?"

"How much wine have you had, Sis?"

I looked at the liquid's deep colors and, with a sigh, nestled back under the suds. "Apparently more than I thought."

We took a few minutes to just enjoy being in a hot tub at the end of winter with a cloudless, star-filled sky overhead. This is my favorite time of the year- cool evenings spent in a bubbling tub of warmth. I close it down completely once June arrives. Hot weather notwithstanding, I don't come out here in the tourist season as that severely raises the risk of drawing attention, even late at night.

I share a courtyard on the west side of the property with the microbrewery Amber's brother owns, and summer nights are long and busy. He'd also converted a historic house falling into disrepair, then moved an industrial piece from up north next to it to serve as the brewery. That had once been a parking lot, so there was no negative impact on the historical value to the city. Plus, it looked really cool.

The image of Amber's brother, Jasper, sprang to my mind. It's pretty impressive. He'd embraced the modern-primitive movement years ago and has a nice, well-developed beard, kept immaculate and trimmed. While he doesn't do that long hair pulled back in a bun thing, he does have piercings running up both ears and sports two full sleeves of tattoos. One side has images continuing past the shirt line and, I admit it, I've let my imagination run away a few time picturing what might be beyond. You can't blame me- he stays in incredible shape by teaching yoga and breathwork down at the VA club by the lake for veterans with PTSD. Amber said yoga really helped him in the months after he left the Marine Corps and twelve years of service when their mother needed him. I appreciated that as I had done the same thing, giving up my college life to return home when my parents died to finish raising Slate until he graduated.

And to get away from Aiden.

The last words fled my mind as I stroked my chain necklace until all thoughts of my former lover faded. I visualized Jasper for just a moment more before he grew hazy as well and my focus shifted again. *Better thoughts elsewhere. Just relax.*

"How's the greenhouse this year, Amber?" Slate had his head resting on the edge of the hot tub, eyes closed. I noticed all the others did as well. She answered without moving.

"It's. So. Warm." She made a sleepy sound as though she was there right now. "It feels wonderful every time I step inside. Everything is growing well this year- I think I've finally got the hang of starting from seeds."

"Well it's about time. What, has it been a full two years since you built it?" Mica smirked, sitting up to take a sip.

"Three, smarty pants. But I'll give you that- I really do have a thing with plants, don't I?" She smiled with happiness. It's hard to be annoyed with a brilliant person so happy in their brilliance. As far as plants are concerned, she's a genius. She'd vended her own stand at the farmers market when she was just fourteen-years-old and began selling unusual, fragrant bouquets. I'd forgotten how incredible flowers can smell- most florist shops have bright flowers with long stems, but no fragrance. Amber focuses more on color and smell than on stem length. She uses antique coffee cups, mason jars and all kinds of interesting things for the shorter stemmed flowers, packing in dozens of items for an incredible and unique display- no two ever looked the same. She's been a staple of the farmers market ever since.

That's actually where we met- I started vending coffee from a converted horse trailer for extra cash at the young market. That had been at least five years before I decided to go for it and open the *Axe & Stovepipe.* Then, one year later, I helped Amber's brother run the city council's obstacle-course to get the *Eighth Circuit Artisan Brewery* opened. Mica had created his sign as well. This Lincoln was fully clothed, however.

He rode a horse in a manly-man way, a bag thrown over his shoulder filled with law books as he went about the countryside on the eighth judicial circuit, passing out justice. It was the town's first microbrewery and three more have opened because of his success. All the others became mom-n-pop centers as shops sprang up around them. It would seem Springfieldians were beer-drinkers all along, but just didn't realize it until Jasper pointed it out.

"Mist, are you coming back to the market this year?" Amber reached behind to grab her wine, swirling it and enjoying the fragrance.

"Amethyst? Are you seriously considering not doing the farmers market? That would be so weird. You've been there for years- that's where we get coffee every Wednesday in the summer. That's where we get those insanely delicious pastries with that almond goop."

"I believe that's *Fantastically Delicious*, not insanely, thank you." Mica said, referring to the French pastry shop that supplied all of my decadent offerings for the café and the farmers market.

I'd been boss-level lucky the year I opened the small café on the first floor. A young and completely broke pastry genius, Mitchel, had just returned from France where he'd spent three years studying their techniques. I had a great kitchen with no idea how to cook, and he needed a place to begin.

It took less than two years for him to open his own shop on the west side of town amidst the new money and developments. But being on Capitol Street, my location was perfect for reaching state employees and visitors.

Mitchel was so grateful I let him spread his wings right from day one that he'd agreed to keep the *Axe & Stovepipe* supplied and no others, outside his own. It gave him a second storefront as the to-go orders in the morning make up half of our business. Coffee and pastries from the *Axe & Stovepipe* and *Fantastically Delicious* fill many legislative offices, state agencies and tourist-focused shops each morning.

Things were going so well, I didn't really need the twice-a-week mornings at the summer farmers market to stay ahead any more. So, every spring, I had to do some soul-searching to decide if it was worth it.

"Slate," I started, not really knowing what my answer would be, but Amber suddenly sat forward.

"Amethyst? How come, in all the years I've known you at the farmers market, and since I started hanging out with this motley crew in the fall, I have never heard that was your name? I thought it was Mist, just Mist."

I laughed. "Well it's not exactly a name that flows off the tongue."

"Amethyst and Slate?" Amber looked between us. "Did your parents have a thing for rocks or something, like mine? Amber and Jasper. Amethyst and Slate."

Slate nodded. "That's it in a nutshell. They were geologists. We spent every summer I can remember doing things that involved looking at soil lines and rocks." He smiled at me. The others might not see it, but I could read the pain behind that smile. Seventeen years later and we still aren't used to being orphans.

Mica leaned over and gave him a hug. Apparently, she'd seen the pain as well. She also managed to do it without anything but her head touching his shoulder knowing Slate would not approve of a shirtless hug. He kissed her forehead once and wiped at his eyes. "At some point, we can talk about them without the pain, right?"

"Oh, I'm sor-"

"Don't." I pointed at Amber. I didn't mean to sound sharp, but she saw there was no bite. "We want to talk about them. Tears may be a part of the conversation, but it is so much harder to never be able to speak about the funniest mom in the world and a man who could sing the birds out of the trees."

Crystal wrung her hair and she sat upright to join the conversation. "He could do that. Literally," she spoke to Amber. "It was amazing to watch. And he also managed to charm the wild crows into hanging out with him."

I reached over and grabbed her hand for a brief moment.

"You knew them well?" Amber took a tiny sip of the cabernet.

"Oh heavens, yes. Before I left Terdman," we all laughed at the name Crystal had given her ex-husband, "I decided to go back to college. My first semester, I had Earth Studies with Delinda, their mom. I was hooked. I took all their classes, special study programs, those summer guided trips," she raised her glass toward Slate. "I was almost done with my masters and had every intention of going for my PhD. We talked about starting tours specifically for homeschooled children, and I was to head that."

"I didn't know that." I relaxed and shifted for comfort, eager to hear something new about mom and dad.

"Umhmm," she nodded, a tear threatening to fall. "But, when we lost them, when that.... selfish jerk driving drunk took them away from us, I took the summer off and did some writing. It just kept going and I walked away from my studies. No regrets. I love that part of my life. I loved every moment spent with Delinda and Jim Butler." She raised her glass high, and everyone did the same.

"You didn't answer my question, Sis," Slate said quietly after a few moments.

"We will, but I won't." Wow. I don't know where that answer came from, but it felt right.

"Ahh," Amber pouted. "Wait, what?" She looked at her glass

and put it back down, this time pushing the table itself away.

I giggled. "The *Axe & Stovepipe* will be back. The horse-trailer with the harlequin design will return, filled with our fabulous fair-trade coffees and *Fantastically Delicious* pastries, and more. But I'll hire someone to man it. I'm simply too busy here, and since Jade won't be helping me this summer, it's lost its appeal."

"Jade!" Amber leaned forward like a shot. "You named your daughter the same way your parents named you- another stone. That's nice." She smiled and relaxed again.

"Why isn't Jade helping you? I know how much you love working with her, and she's great. Some of the kids assisting their folks at the market can't even look you in the eye. That really bugs me, the little brats." Crystal frowned.

"Well not everyone can be as charming as you," I answered as Slate coughed to cover a laugh. "But I'll take the compliment- my girl is wonderful with people. Right now, though, she has that part time job she took on the weekends, she still volunteers with the girl scouts on Thursdays after swim practice and before our dance practice... let's see... debate on Monday and Wednesday, extra swimming on Tuesday and Thursday and, oh yes, soon she'll be with the city's theatre group for the outdoor Muni. It's insane."

"That's insane," Amber echoed.

Strange words coming from Amber, I thought. She has a great business and her own home and greenhouse at twenty-two. That didn't happen without a little insanity in itself.

"I'm so glad she comes to the coffeeshop when Liam and I do in the mornings. I would never see her otherwise." Slate said.

"I enjoy our morning gatherings," Amber said. "Especially Thursdays when your kids stop by, Crystal. I really like them."

"Me too," she added but then froze and looked into her glass. "How many of these have I had?"

Amber kicked water at her. "You're terrible."

"Oh good, then just enough." Crystal giggled heartedly. Soon, Mica joined in. They were connected that way- if one started in on a good belly-buster, the other was swept up in it.

"Is Jade staying here alone while you're in the mountains?" Slate mindlessly slapped at the water foam beneath his chin. "I know she's practically grown and has a busy schedule, but she's only seventeen. She can stay with us if you need."

"No, since it's spring break, she asked for the weekend off from work and is spending the entire time with her friend, Elise, on their farm. Her parents love Jade."

"I hope they'll let her sleep in for a change, even though it's a farm."

"Well, it's the end of April on the north prairies. If they don't have animals or greenhouses, they're just waiting for the fields to warm up enough to plant," Amber added.

"I mentioned how busy she's been when I talked with Elise's folks. Her mom said she would treat her as if visiting a bed and breakfast. Elise and Jade stop by the café every day after school to grab a bite, so they're happy to return the favor and pamper Jade for the week."

"I'm really excited about California, Crystal. You know, I've never been out of the state of Illinois." That drew a round of denials.

"That's just not possible, Amber. St. Louis is only ninety minutes down the road. Surely you've gone on a school trip or something? Don't all the schools visit the city museum down there, you know, where that industrialized building was turned into an enormous adventure park?"

"Nope. Not once. Tomorrow will be my first plane ride and everything. I'm excited." Amber scrunched up her face and arms, wiggling in the water.

"I don't think any of us have been to Northern California, so it should be an adventure," Mica smiled.

"Oh, it will, trust me." Slate studied his glass a long time before taking a sip and swirling it around his mouth.

"I'm going to come over there and smack all the blond out of your hair," Crystal warned.

Slate smiled. "Sorry. The moonlight hit my glass right at

that moment and I couldn't resist. We should schedule these wine tastings around the full moon." He looked at her over the rim, his eyes sparkling with mirth. "And I know you understand that call- a pull to get lost when staring into dark spaces with the full moon guiding you."

"It's almost here, Thursday I believe." Mica looked up at the beautiful orb and closed her eyes, moonbathing. She kept us updated on its phases for our energy work. Then she looked at Slate. "But I'm with Crystal. Why did you say that?"

"I did a reading." Slate looked a bit smug.

Uh-oh. I wasn't sure I liked that look. "A full one, or just in-the-moment?" My brother has an eerily sharp ability when he uses a set of beautiful tarot cards called, *Gaian Tarot*. If he takes the time to meditate beforehand, the deck becomes magic in his hands.

"Oh this was the full monty, Sis. I took a long, salt bath first. Then I drummed for an hour before laying out the table in de-tail- candles, herbs, a few, beautiful stones from mom and dad... all of it."

"You did all of this just to see if our trip goes well? Oh, that's so sweet." Amber practically purred.

"No." Slate laughed. "Hey, I love you guys, but that kind of prep is reserved for my own big questions."

"So? What happened?" I was intrigued.

"Well, it's weird." Slate sat up a little straighter and placed his drink on the edge of the hot tub. He used both hands as he explained. "I had planned on a focused spread about Liam and I adopting," he began.

"Oh Slate," I cried out, surprised. A squall of happy sounds circled the hot tub.

Slate waved his hands. "Nothing decided there. We still haven't set a wedding date. But I wanted to start thinking about my long-term goals. Anyway, after all that prep, I grabbed the cards and started shuffling.

"Usually I close my eyes and keep shuffling while I focus on the four, sacred elements- Earth, Air, Fire and Water. Then I focus on gratitude by listing nine blessings in my life. Finally, I focus on Gaia before laying out my spread in the pattern I chose before taking the cleansing bath."

We nodded in understanding. We did similar rituals as a group and in private. It was one of the things that brought us together, the galère.

"But when I started to shuffle the cards, my hands laid out a pattern before my first deep breath. It was like they weren't even attached to me."

"Whoa," Crystal whispered.

Slate turned his whole body to face her in his excitement. "It was dope. It literally felt like my arms were controlled by an alien. I looked down and saw just a three-card spread, which I usually read as the opportunity, the challenge and the resolution. But I knew at once that was wrong."

"How?" I asked.

Slate just shrugged. "I just knew it. And I realized that this was not about me at all. I drew a card off to the side to help me figure out what this was about, and I drew that card with the four women gathered in a kitchen, mixing herbs. Boom! Instantaneous answer. It was not me, and it was not the number, not the suit- it was purely the image. It was you four."

"Oh my gods," Mica's eyes went wide. "What did they say? What were the cards?"

"Hold on," Slate grinned and playfully pushed her back as she'd scooted close before resuming. "Remember, I knew I couldn't do this in my usual way- not for this spread. So, I took a few deep breaths, wondering how to read these three cards not meant for me. That took some time," he nodded to Amber. "What was it you said at our winter Imbolc gathering when you called to the Center and Spirit? You asked that we all slow down and look at our normal life in new ways, right? Those words came into my head." He tapped his forehead for emphasis.

Amber glowed at his acknowledgement.

"I did that. I took three, breathwork breaths looking at the back of each card. You know what I mean, a focused moment of filling the body with air, and pulling the upper abs in tightly with the exhale- nine second inhale, nine second hold, nine second exhale. And when I finished, I saw it, clear as day." He leaned back, his arms spreading wide as though the cards were right in front of him, bobbing on the foam.

"Each card held the energy of Death."

CHAPTER TWO

"Now that has some power behind it, my friend." Crystal's voice danced over the bubbling waters and we leaned in to hear. It was nice to be in a gathering where the Death card wasn't taken to a literal focus. It can simply mean something ends so that something else may begin. It might be the ending of bad habits just as easily as anything. But it means it's a *major* event and no small thing.

Slate nodded. "Yes, it does. My hands shook; my sister's and this galères' fates are screaming at me? Why me? And, enough so, that questions about taking on the *enormous* role of a parent are pushed to the back? Come on, I was about to schlauchen a cold, purple Twinkie, deep breaths or not." I suppressed a smile- he only swears in other languages.

"How did you read them, even with the energy of the death card?" Mica had lost her glass at some point and patted the water with both hands.

"As soon as I understood that the energy of that card needed to be overlaid first, the rest became clear- it was a past, present and future spread. But this presented a problem- I normally have a question ready and plug it into a spread like that, or at least a very specific event or idea. This seemed... Too unfocused? Too large?" He threw both hands high. "I gave up control at that point and decided to just go in and see what it said.

"Card one, the past, was nine of earth."

"The accumulation of a major event- three cycles of three completed, the lesson is learned, task finished," I said.

Slate's words spilled over themselves as he responded. "Yes, but with the Seeker energy over that, it adds an emphasis to end that, and end that *now*. Don't move forward with what has been before."

"As in no more wine tastings?" Amber's eyebrows shot up.

"Let's not be hasty," Crystal added, taking a sip.

I laughed softly. "I would suggest that it means the way that we have gathered in the past is not the way that we will gather in the future. Nine is positive, so it's saying what was, well, it was wonderful, and is now complete. But what we had... We need to let it go, perhaps?"

Mica pointed to me. "Right. Let it go, let it die. Give up expectations of what this has become." She spread her hands wide to engulf us all. "And," she broke off to look at Slate. "And what?"

"The second card, the present," Slate began as his voice softened. "That card was harder. Where the first card was a minor event, meaning not to take the ending of it being the ending of you all together, the second card was a major event. It was the Star, the epitome of joy."

"Which now has to die?" Amber frowned as she sunk under the foam, staring at everyone at once.

"I think so, but..." I was at a loss for words.

"But not to end." Crystal spoke to herself, her voice barely audible over the sound of the jet sprays. "It seems like it's saying this kind of gathering has come to an end, that we will move forward in a completely different way."

Slate was nodding so hard his body shook the water more than the jets. "Yes! I felt that one like a jolt- you will continue on, but something is going to happen that will change everything."

"Oh, I don't like that," I said leaning back and pinched the bridge of my nose sharply one time. "Sudden endings are not good." The visual I could never get out of my head popped back in- imagining the last moment of my parents' lives.

"It's not the tower, Sis." Slate's voice was soft. "It's not even the hangman. I really don't think it's negative, though I realize that saying 'the death of joy is here' may seem so." He laughed at his own words and I looked up to accept the warm smile he shared with me. "It's not loss, I promise."

"How do you know?" I was trying to breathe away the image.

"Because of the third card, right?" Mica looked at Slate with an expectant lift of her brow.

He nodded once. "Correct. The Third card should not have been in there. It was the card that came as the cover, nothing on it. I don't know how it got mixed in with the deck. This set of tarot doesn't have the intentional blank card, like the original Toth deck."

Amber frowned. "I don't know of a blank card."

"It was only in the earliest set of cards. It meant the possibility of everything." Crystal supplied. "In a way, it was like a "free" card, you can read what you want into it."

"So, with the energy of the death card, what does that mean? We get nothing?"

"Exactly," I said, surprising myself. I felt my eyebrows get lost in my dark blonde hair, they shot up so quickly. I looked at Slate who nodded in encouragement. "It means we don't have a choice. Something big is coming to us, as a group, and we'd better just hang on because we can't control it."

"I don't know if I like that," Mica frowned. There were varying degrees of agreement made as everyone settled back against the tub's edge.

"This is all your fault, you know that," I said with a smirk, looking at Crystal.

"Yeah, I think I have to own this." Crystal kept her eyes straight forward, watching the swirling waters.

Mica made a dismissive sound. "You didn't get us here by yourself, missy."

Amber nodded. "You may have found the catalyst that is taking us gods know where, but we all agreed to get to know each other on our own. We are here," she pointed to the center of the hot tub, "because this is where we choose to be. And we are going there," she pointed to the west, "because we bullied you into letting us join your trip to Shasta Mountain."

"We all want to go see the earth's root chakra ourselves, Crystal." Mica leaned over and nudged her with her shoulder, her voice taking a theatrical turn. "Because the witches will claim all that is to be learned."

Crystal couldn't help but respond in kind. "And all who oppose us will fall to their knees in despair."

"For we shall suffer no fools who defend ignorance," I added just before Amber jumped in.

"And upon the stones of the earth shall our truths be written."

"Not again," Slate whispered, sinking completely under the water until Mica reached over and pulled him up by the hair.

"I was teasing, you know," I said to Crystal. "As soon as you mentioned you wanted to head there and see what this ley line idea is all about, we just about tackled you to the ground to get more information."

"I. Am. So. Jealous." Slate slapped the waters with each word. That broke the tension and I was relieved- I hadn't meant for Crystal to take my words to heart. She can usually tell when I'm teasing. As modern-day witches, people who work with energy, we were always ready to explore the 'possibilities.'

I dreamed that one day we would find a way to make these subtle magicks of modern-day go old school, and, you know, be able to *zap* people or something. But none of it was worth hurting my friend.

As though hearing my thoughts, she reached over and patted my arm. I gave her a snicker in reply. "You just read my mind, didn't you?" She laughed loudly again, which started Mica. Again.

Amber reached back and grabbed the table to drag her glass back in reach. She rolled the long stem between her fingers, but didn't drink. "You can't be jealous, Slate. This is apparently going to get real weird, real quick."

"But it's the Earth's own chakra root. That's like saying it's where the Earth begins, where Earth is, well, Earth."

"Wait…" I began. "Does it shift as well, with this death energy you saw? Instead of it being the place where the root chakra meets the crown chakra, is it instead, I don't know, the place where root energy can't be drawn?"

"Or, is it like the 'root of all evil' instead of the point where good energy begins?" Amber looked at Crystal. "How do ley lines go about acting with death energy?"

Crystal paused, her brows creasing before she answered. "Don't get ahead of yourself. Just because this is one theory of ley lines, it's certainly not found in all the theories. These supposed lines where the Earth's power is accessible is still a topic of heated debate among energy-focused people. After researching a few belief systems on this, I thought this one seemed the most logical and one that was within reach to explore."

All eyes stayed focused on her as she continued. "As far as that death energy coming with us," she took a deep breath before shaking her head. "That's on us, not the mountain. I think we might draw some surprises. Who knows? Many people have been there and swear they felt more aligned afterwards, but that can be true of your own backyard."

"Or in your own, toasty greenhouse," Amber lifted her chin with a touch of smug assuredness. It was true. We'd all found that to be a major part of our personal lives, our own truths. Our magic may not be the things of myths, but it was real. Understanding the energetic realm of existence is possible for everyone. Though, some of us seem to connect with it more naturally than most.

Ley lines. I don't usually go in for things that seem so far out there, though. I mean, really? Earth energy that's accessible on a physical level? Wasn't the true definition of magic to make change in your life, and the world around you, by opening up to some hardcore self-analysis and see what you draw to yourself?

Isn't the point of energy-awareness to be a conduit for this openness, this change? Drumming, dancing, chanting- all these things help the mind release the confines imposed by ego and connect with something greater than self. But could actual lines of power lay across the globe? Is it really possible to tap into these and bring change with touch or directed thought?

Could energy lines heal the sick, nourish the hungry, and heighten psychic abilities?

Like I said, this kind of stuff is usually way off my radar. Crystal said she wanted to research the topic more thoroughly after we'd talked about it in the fall, not too long after Amber had joined our tribal dance class, (and then shortly after, joined in for our tarot and the energy work we do in my basement beneath the café. That one's a bit more private, for sure.)

I forgot all about that conversation until last month when Crystal announced her trip to Mount Shasta to explore the concept of how ley lines lead to the chakra points of the planet. I had never heard this theory, but from the moment she mentioned it, I had to go. It was this burst of intuition screaming *yes*.

I have them from time to time. The last one this strong had been years ago when I decided to talk to the city council about moving the house. No one thought it was worth the time, but the council members grew excited, and the location of the café right across from the historical park with Lincoln's home was helping to bring people in. Everyone loves history, but history with easy access to coffee is always better. The early morning tour buses had recently started letting patrons off outside the *Axe & Stovepipe* as most made a beeline for the shop once they spotted the 'Grab Your Java' sign in our window from across the street anyway.

We even created a private space for the drivers on the second-floor telescope-balcony as a thank you, accessed from the outside by a set of beautiful, spiral staircases, one on each end of the deck. Last week we invited the workers from the park to use it as well- coffee and pastries on us.

If any kind of shop opens up within walking distance of us we'll probably have to stop this little act of kindness so it's not mistaken as a bribe. But not yet. Our city is still small enough not to worry about things like that and there is literally nothing for five blocks in any direction that serves a simple cup of coffee.

Technically, the second floor is off limits as that's where Jade and I live. But the house has a large sitting room and bathroom just inside the balcony that can be completely sealed off from the rest of the house. It's turned out to be a great location for private events. And, it gives the drivers and park volunteers a space to relax and watch the world.

Yes, it had been the right choice to go to the city council. Everyone benefited. And that same overwhelming feeling had struck me when Crystal said she was going to see Shasta. That made me wonder about something.

"Hey all, when Crystal said she was heading west, did any of you get a... a feeling... or something? I got a strong sense of it being right." I sank deeper under the warmth of the bubbles as a cool breeze swept across the rooftop.

"Actually," Mica began, stretching her arms high before seeking more warmth as well. "I had one of my dreams the night before she mentioned it."

"That's dope." Amber whispered to her glass as she continued to twirl it.

"What happened?" Slate asked

Mica shrugged. "It wasn't like that. When I have powerful dreams, it's rarely a series of events. It's more about strong feelings associated with people. I know it sounds vague," she shrugged again. "But I saw Crystal at her computer. She was talking over her shoulder to me as she kept typing. I saw a picture of a mountain on the screen with a single bird flying over, and I leaned in. I knew, I mean, I just *knew* I was supposed to go there. And then the next day Crystal said she was heading to a mountain on the west coast and I asked to tag along."

"I believe your actual words were 'Not without me!'" Crystal laughed.

"The meaning was clear," Mica nodded sincerely before she too began to laugh.

"What about you, Amber?" I was curious about her sudden focus on the glass. It seemed she had some unshared thoughts.

With a sigh she put the cab down again and settled under the waters. "I stubbed my toes, three times." She frowned at me.

Crystal barked a seal sound. "How in the world does that say it's time to go to Mount Shasta?"

"Apparently, I don't get these sudden bursts of intuition, like Mist, or guiding dreams, like Mica, or am driven to research something after scrying, like you. I get bumps and bruises until it sinks it."

"Do tell," I smiled to her before taking a long drink.

"I don't think I would have noticed it- I tend to be a bit clumsy at times." Agreements went up around the tub and she scowled before speaking again. "Not nice. Anyway, three different times while I was in the greenhouse I started to go to a different area, and three times I stubbed my toes if I headed off in any direction other than west. Then I tested it- I decided to grab a trowel on the opposite side of the greenhouse, straight in front of me.

"I moved slow. With focus. On the second step, even though I was being careful, I stumbled on a rock that fell from my painting table, you know, where I paint gnomes on the garden rocks.

"See, it sounds silly. But I turned to the west and made my way without any incident." She rolled her eyes. "That's it. That's all I got- stubbed toes, a cracked rock and a need to head west." She sunk low until the water covered her chin, then made a loud raspberry sound.

"Slate," I began, but was cut off when a man screamed behind me.

"That's Liam!" Slate jumped across the tub in a single step and used Amber's shoulder to bolt himself out before I had the chance to turn back around. The scream had sounded like it was right behind me, but it must have come from below, from the balcony.

Slate was out of sight before we had a chance to put down

our drinks, a clear water trail left behind. Grabbing the long beach towels I kept by the tub, we covered ourselves and raced around the gable to the steps leading down to the attic.

When we reached the balcony, Slate has his hand on Liam's tall shoulder. I watched as Liam ran a hand through his short, black hair as he spoke with clipped words on his phone. "I'm heading over there, Pete. She needs help now! I'm not waiting for you." He shut off the device and slipped it into his pocket. "I have to get over to the park- I just saw a woman being dragged behind the Lincoln home. Stay here- the police are on the way."

"I'm going with you," Slate said, following him down the steps.

"You don't even have shoes on, Slate. Stay here and get dressed."

"I'm not letting you go alone," he answered firmly.

"Here." Amber came through the sitting room holding a handful of clothes and Slate's shoes. He'd taken them off at the hot tub while we had left ours in the attic.

Liam's tall, athletic figure had already disappeared down the spiraling stairs. Slate rushed over to Amber and ruffled through the pile of clothes, grabbing just his shoes and shirt before racing down the stairs. We swarmed around Amber.

"I'll get our shoes." Mica flew out of the room.

I ran to the balcony to look through the telescope stationed there for everyone's use. My fingers stumbled with the controls and I pulled back. "Didn't I lock this in to the south?" I found myself peering right at the Lincoln Home- I thought I'd set the scope to the southern sky so we could catch the moon pairing up with Regulus in the Leo constellation. But it was locked in and facing east toward the historical park.

The Lincoln home is a two-storied Greek-Revival set just one block away. It's visible this high without any help, but the telescope allows a closer look at the architecture and the entire area. I looked through the eyepiece and could see all the details of the Lincoln home, though nothing else. I pulled the view back. Then I swiped the lens slowly over the area. Something at the very edge caught my eye and I looked up to take in the whole park.

It took a moment for my eyes to adjust but then I saw it. "There." One block north of the house, a vehicle was pulling away. "Grab a pen and paper." I waved my hand behind me. "Someone else get on the phone, 9-11."

"I've got a pen." It was Crystal. I looked up from the telescope again, trying to get a better handle on the vehicle's location. Though dark, I could see the two forms of Liam and Slate running toward the house, mostly because of Slate's bright orange swim shorts. Below, I saw Mica move across the empty street.

"I've got a phone," Amber said.

The vehicle was a dark van without lights. "Heading north, wait- now west on Capitol- is a black van. No markings. I'll get a tag number if they get under a strong street light."

It was impossible to keep an accurate eye on the van at a close enough range to read the license plate. Without looking up I asked, "Can anyone see it? Is it nearing a streetlight?"

"No," Crystal replied. "Oh wait, there, I see it. Thank gods for the moonlight. It's heading to seventh street- that should be bright enough. Hold on... The road is blocked with construction vehicles. They're heading back."

"Slate." I jerked up to see where my brother and Liam were, but couldn't find them.

"I think they went behind the house." Amber was standing on her tip-toes to get a better view. From the distance the sound of sirens began to swell. Amber covered one ear with a hand as she moved off to tell the 9-11 operator about the van.

"Get Liam on the phone."

"I don't have mine," Crystal replied. "Can you get the license plate?"

It took me a moment to recapture the van in the telescope view. It was heading the opposite direction now. Before I could zoom in close enough to try and capture the plate number, I saw Liam and Slate explode out of the trees of the park and emerge onto the same street just as the van returned. It swerved toward them in a sudden burst of speed.

"Slate!" I screamed but held tight to the telescope. Behind me I heard Crystal take a sharp breath and Amber yell something into the phone.

Liam jerked to a stop just before Slate pulled him from behind as the van passed, both of them tumbling to the ground. The van slowed but then the police turned onto the same street, ignoring the road blocks and moving around the construction machines. The van put on a burst of speed and moved away.

More than anything, I wanted to rush to Slate and Liam but I stayed with the scope and followed the vehicle as it neared Ninth and Capitol and, at last, modern street lights. When the van entered the middle of the road, it took a sudden turn to the south and I lost sight because of a thick line of trees that border the park.

I ran toward the stairs, pointing to Amber. "The tag starts with LC. Unmarked, black van with LC license plate." I yelled over my shoulder as I raced away, Crystal following close on my heels.

We ran the two blocks through the park to where I had seen them last. As we turned the corner, I saw a second police car stop and officers rush over to Slate, Mica and Liam.

"They're okay." Amber caught up as we slowed our pace, knowing they weren't hurt. We still maintained a soft jog until we met up with them. One of the officers stepped in our direction holding his hand up while the flashlight blinded us.

"Stop right there," he began, but the other officer called to him.

"It's okay Deputy, they're all together- they're the ones who called it in. Glad you're okay, Liam, but no more stupid stunts. Just leave it to us next time."

"Okay, Pete." Liam nodded, rubbing his left shoulder.

I ran to Slate and wrapped him in the tightest, big-sister hug I could manage. "You're okay." I made it a statement and not a question, repeating it several times.

"Yes, I'm good, Sis. A little sore, right there on my rib cage, where you're causing it, now," he squeaked.

I laugh and pulled away to grab Liam in a gentler hug. The police showed great patience as we all made sure our boys were okay, poking and prodding without guilt.

"Okay, ladies, that will do. They're fine." Officer Pete smiled good-naturedly as the deputy pulled out an electronic pad to take notes. "Liam, you were saying you just happened to be looking at the Lincoln home?"

"Hmm-mmm," Liam began, thoughtful, as though not wanting to miss a detail. "Mist has the telescope set up on the top balcony so folks can look over the park, the moon, whatever. I glanced to see where it was set before joining them," he made a motion to include us all. "And I saw a woman, stumbling next to a man, trying to pull away. Then she just collapsed and he started dragging her to the back of the house. I shouted out something and ran over."

"You screamed. Like a girl," I interjected. Liam frowned at me. I really don't know why I said that out loud.

Officer Pete looked away in an effort to keep his composure. "Mulligan, see if anything's been reported about the van." The young man stepped off to use his shoulder-radio just as a third patrol car joined us. As Officer Pete continued to ask questions, Deputy Mulligan led the other officers toward the Lincoln Home. One officer returned to the car and soon followed them, carrying a portable lighting system.

"Ms. Butler?" Apparently, he'd asked me a question but I had been too busy watching the officers set up and begin to survey the area.

"Oh, sorry. What was that?"

"I asked why everyone was at your place. It would have something to do with water, I take it?" He shown his light on Slate's swim trunks.

"Yes, right. We were all in the hot tub when we heard Liam, um, shout out something, and we ran... to, to the balcony. I heard Liam say he saw something and used the telescope to look

the park over. That's how we caught sight of the dark van. And,"
I looked at Slate with a frown, "had the pleasure of seeing these
two almost run over. Did they catch it?"

Officer Pete shook his head. "Not yet, but they're still looking. The partial plate number will help. I'll have more question
for you tomorrow, but for now that's all."

"We'll be out of state tomorrow. We're returning on Wednesday evening." I wondered if we might have to stay.

"All of you?"

"Just the women," Slate answered.

"We're having a 'girls' night out,' but out of state." When
Crystal smiled with sleepy eyes, a slight nod of her head began.
"We're going to the mountains for two days to do some hiking."
I could almost feel her communicating with them through her
smile and calm demeanor- everything's okay, they can leave, it's
all going well, very, very well.

I've seen this before. She never fails.

The officer nodded, slow and smooth in a mirror response.
"Okay, just make sure we have all your phone numbers. We'll
see you when you return. And please, leave by the public streets.
Don't go through the park." With a tap of his electronic pen, he
headed toward a fourth patrol car that had arrived and the officers began to tape off the road.

We moved west, happy to find the construction area had a
designated walking path so we could turn south to my ancient
abode.

"I saw what you did there, Mist." Amber began. "We ran, um,
not down, Officer, not down, but *toooo* the balcony." They all
snickered. "Why are you so worried about the hot tub on the
roof? You followed all codes. It's perfectly legal. You've done
nothing wrong."

I gave her a hard stare. "I still get frowns whenever I run
into three different council members, no matter how happy and
perky I greet them. And you know how much I hate perky. But
that's what I do, I get perky. And nada. That sign Mica made
doesn't give me an ounce of room to wiggle, now."

"I love the sign." Amber practically skipped.

"Quit being so youthful," Crystal snapped at her. Amber giggled and began to skip backwards.

"What a night." Slate rubbed his thighs in the chill air as we neared the cafe.

"I wonder who the poor woman is? I hope she's okay." Amber became somber, falling into step beside Mica.

Liam nodded his head. "I don't know, I couldn't really tell anything about her- average weight, perhaps a little short, medium brown hair. I'm hoping the elephant purse can give them a lead."

"What?" I drew up sharp, bringing everyone to a halt. "Elephant purse?" Then I pointed at the sole car still parked on the street outside the café, looking at Mica.

"Oh, no!" Mica drew her hands to her mouth, and we both turned to head back toward the police. Everyone soon followed, joining our slow run.

"Do you know who it is?" Slate came up next to me.

I nodded, my breath catching in my throat as I caught Crystal's eye on the other side of Slate. "It's my stalker."

CHAPTER THREE

"*Wheee-* first class upgrade." Amber threw her hands in the air and tumbled into the window-seat, staring up at me with an excited face. I looked at her for about three seconds, then turned to Mica waiting behind me in the narrow aisle of the plane. I snatched the ticket out of her hand and plopped into the seat across the aisle.

"Hey." Mica frowned at me.

I pointed at Amber. "Too perky." Then pointed at myself. "Not enough coffee." I leaned back, closed my eyes and held my ticket out to her. She snatched it with a loud snort.

"We would have been in bed two hours earlier if you didn't demand to stay until the police confirmed that Beverly is missing."

Beverly Keys. The woman who, two weeks ago, started showing up at the café every single afternoon at five-fifteen sharp and staying until we closed. I often had to tell her we were closing three times before she'd leave. She never said a word and would just sigh with a helpless sound. I thought perhaps she would say something last night. Well, actually, she did. When I told her we were closing early, as all the flyers on the doors and windows throughout the café showed, she looked up at me and said, "But I still have two hours." I tried to be polite, put on that storefront face I've mastered and explained that the flyers had been up for over a week. She looked around and then showed true surprise as she saw them, apparently for the first time.

She was a tiny woman, probably only three inches over five feet. I don't know where Slate got 'average.' She was also as thin as a reed, even though she ate a full sandwich, a large bowl of soup and at least one pastry every evening. Her hair was super short and curly with a few streaks of grey mixed in with dark brown.

I started referring to her as my stalker on the third night because she stared at me the whole time. Finally, I walked over and asked her if everything was okay. Her response was… strange. She opened her mouth to speak and then closed it. She did that three more times before finally snapping her mouth shut and nodding at me through a grimace. I thought that was the end of it as she'd jumped up and knocked a glass of water over in her rush to get out. But she had showed up the next night and every night since. She didn't stare at me anymore, but she did take furtive glances whenever I walked near.

"Maybe she needed help," I mumbled. "And I was a complete jerk, wasn't I?" I half stood to make room, looking at Crystal as she shuffled by to sit next to the window.

"Well, it isn't like you to give people names, like 'my stalker,' that's true." Why did I ask Crystal? She never holds anything back if you asked for it.

"It fit." Mica handed her bag to the stewardess who put it away. I smiled at that. It was the first upgrade to business class in my life. Then I frowned at how Amber scored on her very first flight. Not fair. "I'm sorry, Crystal, but the way she stared at Mist was more than off-putting, it was downright creepy."

"And now she's missing." Crystal raised her eyebrows, winning the argument and putting me in my place. She suddenly looked eerily like her Nepali grandmother, a no-nonsense woman if ever there was one. It seemed obvious to everyone that Beverly had needed help, and for whatever reason had focused on me, but never managed to speak up.

Amber leaned over her knees to join in the conversation as

Mica took her seat. "It is a good reminder, isn't it? We practice energy work, we tell the universe to make use of us to create a better world, and, well, we need to be prepared for it when strange people pop up- they're probably the ones who need the most help."

I leaned back with a grimace, closing my eyes. I hate it when the youngest one of us shares the wisdom of an old soul. It's annoying.

But true. Since she had joined our energy class last fall, our rituals felt stronger, as though the final piece of an electronic device had been added and now our machine could rev to life. And yes, it was our practice to ask to be of service to our world.

"Why can't we just pick up litter and call it even?" I grumbled.

"You need coffee." Crystal said as she patted my arm.

I opened my eyes and sat upright. "I need coffee. I really do."

"We'll be able to get you something to drink as soon as we're done with the safety announcements." A stewardess appeared out of nowhere at my spoken wish. I could get use to this.

"How do you like it?"

"Um, do you have lattes?"

"Sure."

"A plain, nonfat latte would be heaven, thank you."

"Make mine a mocha," Crystal winked at her.

"Ooh, me too. Extra whipped cream." Amber hugged a pillow that seemed to materialize from thin air. "And thanks," she patted it, looking at the stewardess.

"I'll take a mimosa. What?" Mica looked at our frowns. But then...

A chorus of 'I'll have that instead,' went up and the stewardess laughed as she walked away to help others. "Will do, ladies."

The aircraft closed up and we were on our way just minutes later. Since we'd arrived so late at our transfer in Chicago due to a delay leaving the small, Springfield airport, I still couldn't figure out how we got the upgrade. Perhaps because we were the last four to arrive.

"I love how everyone agrees with my small ideas, like mimosas for breakfast, but when I want to dance naked under the full moon it's all 'No way!' and 'Put down the wine, Mica.'" Mica bent to throw her head down, releasing a tidal wave of auburn curls into the aisle. After she shook it out a for a few moments, running fingers along the edges, she grasped the entire mass and twisted, coming upright and creating a bun with a clip that looked like it was used on Clydesdale horses. She gave her head a light shake. It held together, but barely. She leaned back, immediately bumping the clip against the headrest. "Ugh." She moved the whole pile up, and half fell out. Crystal started laughing as the stewardess stretched to reach her from the empty seat in front of us and hand her a glass.

"That's not true," I said as I accepted my mimosa. "You're the one who suggested we take this god-awful early flight to get the most time in California."

"We arrive only two hours after leaving because of the time changes." Amber drank half of her mimosa in one gulp, then started coughing. Mica rolled her eyes.

"Quit chugging every drink, Amber. Enjoy the bubbles." Amber blushed and took an absurdly tiny sip. We all laughed as she took another four, in quick succession.

"I give up," Mica settled back, battle over. Her hair was piled at the very top of her head.

"And," I continued, "I'm sure we got this upgrade because it's so early. So, to Mica." I raised my glass and the others followed. Amber ditched the tiny sips and finished her drink.

"I'd like to do something for Beverly when we get to our house rental." I added on a softer note.

"I'm thinking you mean more than 'thoughts and prayers,'" Amber suggested.

"Well," Mica began, "our thoughts and meditations can pack a wallop."

Crystal leaned forward. "Let's do it this evening. We can visit the lower trails this afternoon after we settle in and put a meditative walk into it."

I nodded. "Shall we do a chanting walk?"

"Oh, I love those." Amber shook her glass as she leaned forward and the stewardess smiled, taking it and replacing it. "Which one?"

"Let it choose." Mica and I spoke at the same time and we all shared a knowing look. We were often on the same wavelength. Crystal, Mica and I had been like that for ages. It sometimes annoyed the other women in our tribal dance group. When we dance, it's a modern, improvisational style, and the three of us always moved in sharp synchronicity. We'd even *yip* and *zhagareet* at the same time.

When Amber joined our advanced dance class after taking the intro classes elsewhere, she'd fit right into our rhythm in an amazing way. That's why we'd invited her to our private energy class. It's just the four of us, plus Slate. We stay after dance class for an hour's adventure in chanting, ecstatic dance, tarot or scrying. The connection with her in dance class had been fun but it went far beyond that in the energy work.

"I'm presuming," Crystal began, looking at me with raised brows, "that we are going to look for Beverly ourselves when we return home?"

"You know, while we were waiting for the police to reach Beverly's family, I heard them say they found signs of a body being dragged near the Lincoln house, confirming what Liam saw. This could be dangerous."

"But we'll look into this, right?" I nodded to her. The others agreed, solemn faces all around.

"I have a feeling that the change Slate talked about has something to do with this mountain, ey? Crystal, can you tell us a little more about this?" Mica leaned her seat back, and twisted her body to face the aisle, giving Amber plenty of room to lean in, so she propped her pillow on Mica's arm and rested her chin there.

"We've worked our own chakra energy often enough, right?" To answer, the three of us did a rapid, itsy-bitsy spider walk through the center of our bodies and then jazz hand directly over our heads. Crystal closed her eyes and shook her head. "You're killing me. Any. Way." She started again. "The theory is that the Earth, as a living thing, also has a chakra system, each connected to the other through ley lines, or lines of energy. It's kind of saying the chakra points are organs, and the ley lines are the nerves that connect them all, or perhaps the blood lines, arteries. They pulse and move in time, pushing energy all through the planet. And, supposedly, if you know exactly where a ley line is, you can tap into it."

"Haven't some said that the greatest works of humanity are on those lines, like the pyramids in Egypt and South America?" I had read a few things in the past month to prepare.

Crystal nodded. "Humans have been attracted to them on an intuitive level."

"So," Amber began with a skeptic's voice, "exactly what happens when people find them? You said that visitors have reported feeling stronger, more aligned. But we get that kind of result every time we hold a ritual or a do an exercise together. Heck, even when we aren't organized and just go crazy banging on drums, I feel a hundred times more in sync with the universe."

Crystal shrugged. "No one is saying the blind can see, or lost limbs grow back. I really don't know if we'll feel anything, or if we do, if it will be more than what we've tapped into already. I mean, let's be brutally honest here- we already know that we have some pretty crazy moments of focus and connection, Slate included." We all agreed. "And after his reading, I think, if nothing else, this is going to lead us to look into dusty corners we've missed in the past."

She waived her hand and brought the answer to a conclusion. "I really don't know what to expect, if anything at all. I'm going in with an open mind and an open heart. If all we do is commune with Gaia, that's enough for me."

"And how." Amber agreed, stretching her arms overhead as she settled back in her seat. "That's the best- bare feet snuggled into the mud, the birds and animals making a racket, trees whistling in the wind… Who needs more?"

Mica rubbed her head affectionately. "Our little earth goddess, here. The one who talks with plants."

Amber frowned, irritated, then reached up and rubbed Mica's head until her hair escaped from the clasp. "Hey." She tried to catch it before it fell everywhere again but was too late.

"And our little dreamer here, who sees the future when she sets her mind to it."

"Ha," Mica mumbled. "One time out of twenty, I get a glimpse of what I ask. Or I can read someone's emotions." She turned her head upside down and started working on her hair again with a loud groan.

"Why don't you cut your hair short if you don't like it?"

Crystal and I burst into laughter. "Shut up, you two." Mica's grumbling was easily heard, even though she was still bent over the arm of her seat.

I looked at Amber. "She tried that several years ago. It would never, and I mean never, work with her. She had sections poking up all over the place."

"And she walked around with a water bottle all the time to spray it every hour. It only looked good or at least somewhat in control when it was wet."

"Basically, she spent two years looking like a wet poodle." The stewardess walked by just as I spoke and tried to stifle a laugh.

"Yeah? Well, you looked like you'd eaten a basketball when you were pregnant. You held the baby out in front like, like a… basket… ball." She threw her hands up, admitting defeat.

"Pathetic," Amber and Crystal spoke in unison, shaking their heads at Mica. "Picking on a pregnant woman," they said together. We all broke into laughter at that, even Mica.

"Hey, I just realized something," Crystal gently slapped my arm with the back of her hand. "This is the first time you've left the *Axe & Stovepipe* in someone else's care and haven't called every thirty minutes. Good for you, Mist."

"It's killing me, seriously. I'm sitting on my hands so I don't keep checking my phone for a doomsday text from Nic." It had been a year's work on the magical side to get here. I had planted the seeds of letting go of controlling every aspect of the café last February, and every ritual after, I had worked toward that goal. I let Nic take the full wheels for the first time since I'd made him the assistant manager two years ago. He was a quiet guy and had only mumbled 'finally' under his breath before going back to work after I told him about our trip and promised I would not call unless he contacted me.

"Is it your first time away from Jade?" Amber's words were muffled by a deep yawn. I noticed everyone was showing signs of the late night catching up with us.

"Lately, she's the one away from me. She's just so busy. If it wasn't for our dance classes, I'd rarely see her before nine at night."

Mica rested her head on her hand as she looked at me. "She is really loving life, isn't she? She enjoys the swimming competitions and insists on making time to volunteer, and she wants a part time job to earn her own money. You've done a great job making her independent, Mist. She's a real gem."

"And that gem is jade," Amber laughed.

I smiled. "Yes, she is a gem. And I'm glad she's spending a week relaxing at Elise's."

"Yes, relaxing. Right. Knowing Jade, they were horseback riding at dawn, she'll insist on helping to clean out the barn before noon, then they'll go hiking all over the country side."

"I heard her say Elise is going to show her the archery set she uses," Crystal teased.

I groaned. "There is no more room for another passion. She'd better be a bad shot."

"Does she get that from you?" Amber asked. "Or from her dad? I've never known you to mention him."

Mica shushed her as her eyes went wide and she turned to say something I couldn't hear.

"And you never will." I maneuvered my seat to its full length since no one was sitting behind me and closed my eyes.

"And that's the longest conversation we've ever had about he-who-has-never-been-named." I could feel Crystal lean over me as she spoke.

"Oops." Amber said.

"It's not a big deal," I answered, not opening my eyes. "As a matter of fact, it's a zero deal. Nada to discuss."

"Gotcha." Amber's voice was quiet. I didn't want her to feel bad, but that was all we were going to say on this topic. It wasn't long before I heard her and Mica giggle over something shared in whispers, most likely risqué and detailed whispers. I let the tension fall away as the hum of the airplane lulled me to sleep.

THE HOUSE WAS A happy surprise. I stood out front with a cup of hot chai tea while the others finished unpacking. Crystal had rented a cottage, she'd said. But it was more like a hidden mansion. From the front drive, it looked like a lovely, single-story home with wooden shutters framing bay windows on either side of a recessed entrance. A chair with a throw pillow nestled there, the perfect place to read a book or watch the midday light dance across the patio. A strong, stained, wooden porch wrapped around the front to the left side and disappeared around the edge. Tall evergreens hugged the sides of the house, blocking any view of the back, the porch vanishing into the thick pines.

But it was the rear of the house that offered the surprised. The house sat upon a sharp hill and dived down into the backyard. What was visible from the road was actually the third floor, the smallest segment. Two other floors were built right into the hill and stretched wide. The porch that began on the front lawn wound its way to the back, widening at the corner and providing a view of the deep ravine below with the majestic mountain beyond. There was a large paradise of a backyard before the ravine began, fenced to keep kids and pets safely inside.

Driving by, one might think it a cozy, two-bedroom ranch

home. But from the back, with its beautiful wood and stone patio that led to a heated pool, it looked like a resort. A wall of windows covered that entire side of the house, opening the view to every room. All the bedrooms sat on the middle level and offered private balconies.

I slowly walked around the porch, enjoying the way it led into tightly packed trees and then opened up to the majestic view. It felt like a hidden passageway to Eden. Down below I discovered Amber and Mica had ditched their suitcases and were already in the warm pool. Mica's auburn hair trailed behind as she moved smoothly across the water, her athletic shape standing out against the mural of whales painted on the bottom of the pool. I was impressed with the artistry. We're going to have to drag Mica away at the end of our visit. I raised my tea to Amber who nodded from the edge where she hung by her arms, paddling her feet.

Mount Shasta rose behind them. There was still a lot of snow covering the ancient volcano. We had no plans to venture that far up, but now I was regretting that- a close ski slope was just begging for an invasion from our galère. We should have planned for a week, then Slate and Liam could have joined on the weekend with Jade.

I laughed at myself. Just hours ago I was worried about leaving the *Axe & Stovepipe* for three days, and after a few minutes of seeing the mountains I was ready to take a two-week vacation.

Mount Shasta. I mouthed the words, silently honoring the beauty offered. I could see why some believed this to be the place where the root chakra energy met with the crown- where heaven and earth touched. I know this range has nothing on the height of the Himalayas, but still, it holds its own in the 'exalted' category.

I walked the full length of the deck. Instead of continuing to wrap around the house on the other side, though, it separated, wood giving way to flagstone after several feet, and then hard-packed earth as a trail led away from the house. Following it, I soon looked over a large meadow that began on the other side of the ravine, early signs of spring showing in tiny spots of green and colorful flowers still held in tight buds. In another month, this will hold a cacophony of color, I'm sure. An old fashioned, swinging rope-bridge connected the two sides.

"That is just begging to be explored," Crystal said over my shoulder. I turned to find her brown eyes twinkling with excitement. She held out my heavy shawl which I only just realized I wanted. I eagerly handed her my cup and swirled the deep purple and earth-tone wrap around me, the long tassels banging against my knees. "Shall we?" She gestured forward with my cup before handing it back.

"Should we grab them?" I nodded my head back to the house.

"I told them we were taking a sneak peek down the trail." She shook her head. "I can't wait any longer- I need to set foot on these trails." We shared a familiar moment of spiked energy and set off for the swinging bridge.

It was a relief to find it sturdy and well-made. It's one thing to walk across a deep ravine, swinging without support from beneath and trying to walk on tiny wooden boards without looking down. If the ropes holding it up didn't look in good repair, or their anchors, I was ready to find another way to reach the meadow. I took a deep drink, then placed my mug beside the trail before grabbing hold of each side rope behind Crystal.

"Perhaps I'll let you test it out first," I laughed wickedly when a strong wind swept through and set the bridge into a wide, slow swing. She expressed her opinion with a familiar hand gesture but didn't bother to look back at me.

I followed when she was a quarter of the way across, feeling as though the bridge would appreciate it if we spaced out the weight. I have no idea what the bridge needed or wanted, but it just felt like the polite thing to do.

When I was almost halfway across, another gust swept down the ravine, this one strong. I heard Crystal let out a few choice words as she hurried the final steps to the other side. I started to reply when I noticed something move out of the corner of my eye. Looking up the ravine, away from the house, I watched as clouds dropped from the sky without warning and fill the chasm below, rolling toward us like a wave of water.

"What the- oh!" I cut off quickly. As soon as I spoke, the fog seemed to respond to my voice and rushed to the bridge in an abrupt burst, coming from the side, above and below all at once. I could see the ropes at my hands, but not the boards at my feet. "Crystal?" I called. "Are you across?"

There was no answer. The creaking of the bridge grew loud as it swayed without rhythm, buffeted by the strange air currents. The soft sound of wind blowing through the ravine below began to howl as the mist thickened and swirled like a lost storm. I felt as if I floated over the gates of an underworld, held aloft by invisible strings being manned by a bratty god. Ahead of me, a shape took form in the haze and I released the breath I hadn't realized I'd been holding.

"There you are." I spoke with relief to Crystal, waiting for her to come fully into view. But instead of her familiar face reaching through the fog, the shape darkened as its edges shot out like spitting fire, then rolled back into itself. I caught my breath, pushing my foot back along the path. The wooden plank behind me shook, then came lose completely and fell away into the heavy fog below.

"Crystal?" I tried to scream but it came out as a choke. I grabbed my throat with one hand and held to the rope with the other. A panicked sweat engulfed me as I tried to find the next board, but my foot found only air, as though the bridge had simply fallen away behind and left me to float in the middle.

"That's not possible," I whispered. My heart raced as all thoughts locked down in the panicked reality of nowhere to run. Instinct took control and I found myself taking deep, long breaths, calling to all the sacred elements with my emotions as no words formed in my mind. I watched the shadow move forward again.

Mist.

My name echoed, the wind formed itself into a word that

rose from below. I looked down and saw a ghost-like masculine hand stretch out from the haar above the rope, moving toward my hand. I snatched it away and watched the swirling darkness thicken.

"Mist." It was a solid voice now, coming from the solid form of a man, or a creature shaped like a man. I looked up into vivid, plum colored eyes. His face had chisel-sharp cheekbones and a too-long jaw. His hair flew around in dark shades of green, black and blue that tangled with and changed my own. Taller than me by six inches, his muscular frame was evident by the thin linen shirt he wore, a shade of green that reminded me of the canopy that should be around us. It was opened halfway down his chest and I could see the rapid rise and fall of his breath. There was a line of markings starting at his right temple that curled around his cheek toward his nose before diving beneath his jaw line and along the side of his throat, snaking down.

My hand moved forward of its own accord, wanting to trace those familiar lines and symbols but I snatched it away just in time. He reached out like lightning and grabbed my wrist to stop its retreat. With a slow rise, he placed my hand against the side of his face and closed his eyes. "Mist." His voice was a sigh of the winds that spoke for him.

"Aiden." My own voice faltered, barely a whisper.

Jade's father had found me.

CHAPTER FOUR

"You can't be here." Banished memories exploded into life and I stumbled from their weight. I closed my eyes to stave off dizziness as he moved close, too fast for my mortal eyes to follow. His arms wrapped around my waist and drew me near as a soft growl of desire escaped his chest. He dropped my hand and pressed his face into my hair, breathing with the loud, raspy sound of a dying man searching for air. Our bodies melded into a perfect fit as his hands shaped me to him.

My breath would only come in ragged gasps fighting against waves of emotion. *And so many memories*. He moaned low and lifted me. His lips brushed my temple, then my cheek before finding my mouth and crushing me to him.

He cried out in pain as soon as our lips touched, and I pulled away with the need to clear my head. "You, you can't be here. I'm still wearing this." I pushed at him with one hand as the other grasped at the necklace I always wore, the sudden realization of why washing over me as a too-real flood of cached knowledge. It was a simple braid of pure gold with a tree of life made of iron, pewter and amethyst. I held onto it as though it was the lifeline that kept me afloat above the ravine.

He clutched his bent face with both hands for a moment before he nodded and slowly opened his eyes. Shaking with pain, he raised his head to look at me. I could see that his mouth was too red with welts of burned skin. He rubbed his hands together and I looked down, seeing the same affliction. "It was worth it." *You are always worth it, Mist.* His thoughts echoed in the swirling fog around us. I felt his intense love emanating like heat waves, wrapping around me in a cocoon of safety.

"How did you find me?"

He shook his head sadly. "You are no longer visible to me, as you know." His fingers moved toward my necklace, stopping short and waving over it slightly before falling away. "But I was pulled here when you arrived. I could not save your parents, but I can save our child."

I fell back to the edge of the board, wrapping one arm around my stomach as though I was still pregnant and grabbing blindly for the rope with the other. "You wanted nothing to do with her!"

He grabbed my arms over the sleeves. "That is not true, Mist."

"You told me that I could die if I had her, that you would remove her if I wished it."

"And then you left," he whispered. His eyes looked so wounded I thought I would cry.

"What else could I do?"

I felt his anger on the air before he showed it. It had always been like that with him, a creature of the Fae. The elements were entwined so keenly with him that they became an extension of his thoughts and feelings. I saw the maddened fog for what it was- his sorrow and his rage.

"You could have given me a chance. She was not alive yet. Her soul had not found you. I was giving you the choice to not risk yourself." He reached into one of the many pouches attached to his billowing pants and pulled out a ring. "I began making this at the very moment you decided to have her, the moment that she was no longer a mass of cells to you but was promised a chance to become life."

I touched the ring with a hesitant hand, not understanding his meaning. I had intended to keep my child as soon as it had sunk in when he told me I was pregnant just hours after we had been together. Our first, and last time.

The ring was a simple, white band with no ornamentation or jewels. Leaning in, I realized in a flash of insight that it was bone, that it was made of *his* bone.

"Aiden?"

"She is of my flesh, and if you are to keep her safe, you need it, my love, my own." He faded and then materialized behind me in one moment, holding me tight against his chest. Gently he moved my hair and kissed the back of my neck. I felt him shudder, but whether from pleasure or the pain of touching me while I wore the necklace, I couldn't tell. With a sigh, he pulled away.

I suddenly became suspicious. "Why aren't you suggesting that I take off the necklace?" I referred to the way he could force humans to do things they wouldn't normally do. He swore to me that he had never used that power on me, and had presented me with the necklace himself, wrapped in a box with three layers of fabric over it, as a promise that I could banish him forever by simply wearing it. It was the only way he knew to make me believe our feelings for one another were not a glamour that he drowned me in.

He frowned at my words, rising above me before fading into the fog this time. The storm below boiled and cold air crashed over the bridge. I pulled my wrap tighter.

I would never do that, Mist. Not to you. You are my soul. "My love," he whispered, materializing in front of me once more. His eyes were closed as his head formed just an inch from my neck. We stood still in that timeless setting, breathing as one without touch.

After a long time, I moved my hand toward the necklace, wondering if I should remove it. Had it really been a simple matter of misunderstanding? I had panicked and ran, ran all the way back to Springfield from my college home in Farmington Maine. He had never followed me- we had never talked about either of our lives before we met on the Appalachian trail that I practically lived on. It was enough trying to figure out the blizzards of emotions and physical responses he brought out in me, and apparently, I in him, in those months of discovery.

The first meetings were mere ghosts of memories, like a dream had brought us together, one from which I could never quite awaken. There had been much laughter and hours of life suspended as we walked impossible paths bordering mountains, forests and deserts without time passing. When we finally came together, it created Jade in a pure moment of ecstatic joy.

And power. Aiden had been distraught afterwards, and me, at the tender age of eighteen and lacking experience interpreting the mental and emotional workings of men's' minds, much less a fantastical creature of myth, had drawn back, afraid and extremely insecure.

The moment he sensed my insecurity he'd rushed back to me, holding me and talking in that sing-song voice he used to charm the animals of the forest. He laid bare his eternal love for me, but then in moments of confused exclamations, he told me about our child.

"No, leave it on." His voice had gone to that impossible deep rumble that sounded like rocks in a foodmill. I knew those were words he found hard to say. He sighed. "It keeps you hidden from my kind, all of them. And if they knew of you and where you've hidden our child," he paused, looking up at me, questioning.

"Jade." I whispered her name. A strong breezed stroked my face, snatching the word from the air in front of me and echoing it all around us in the thick haze. The fog rolled with a sudden, furious anger. He closed his eyes the moment I said her name and kept them closed.

The mist pulled back like curtains and we found ourselves in the center of a forest clearing, ancient oak trees towering and twining overhead in a seamless canopy that allowed little air. I couldn't tell if it was day or night here, the only light coming from glowing plant life attached to the trees. It was dark and beautiful.

Still, Aiden kept his head bowed. I heard a small baby cry

and turned to see a basket at the base of a tree, tiny hands and feet kicking out. He laughed, a sound that went down into the earth and came up around the basket as the baby sat up, now a toddler with tight, blond curls swinging freely. She looked at us and giggled, then climbed out of the basket and toddled her way to me with arms outstretched.

"Jade!" I gasped. The images of her as a baby are still strong in my mind, and I have a million pictures of her, most of them with Slate playing with her, holding her, showing her things in the yard and our home. But to see a living, breathing version of baby Jade running toward me was more than I could handle. I dropped to my knees, arms outstretched to catch her.

But she changed, growing taller as years were added and she paused. Smiling mischievously, she looked down at the ground, wiggling her fingers. A worm came up to play with her. I remembered this day. Her blonde hair had by then darkened to something between brown and auburn, with only streaks of blonde left. The curls had calmed into soft waves. She wore a sundress I'd made from fabric scraps and she looked like a character from Alice and Wonderland. It was my proudest sewing achievement and fit her personality to the letter. Aiden bent next to me and we watched her make a mess in the dirt, more little bugs coming to play, flowers popping up around her. His chest rumbled with a sound I'd never heard before and I turned to see his face. I saw him fall in love with her in that moment, completely captured.

Jade stood up then, slapping her hands together to clean off the muck and place them on her hips as she looked around, her chin lifted in challenge. She was a pre-teen now, her hair long and pulled back in a ponytail with a bandana in it, no hint of curls any longer. It was sun-bleached and she looked almost too thin and too muscular for a child that age. Her nose was big for her face and her front teeth loomed large, but she was confident and happy. That had been Jade- always running, dancing, climbing trees, playing baseball on the little-league team and never sitting still for meals. She glanced at us, that mischievous smile evident and ran full speed toward the branch of an oak, pulling herself up and climbing fast.

Before I could call out to her, she stopped climbing and dropped to a branch below, landing on her feet and then pitching her body to fall forward. My stomach clutched as I jerked forward in horror. It was a remembered horror- she had done this often at that age. I knew she wouldn't fall, that she would catch herself on the next branch and throw her legs over it in a second to end up hanging upside down and laugh at me.

She did so again. Aiden laughed, a high sound this time, one of delight. I frowned at him. It had been non-stop heart attacks with her at that age as she pushed the boundaries of her physical form. I had constant calls from her coach, the school, the mothers of her friends...

Jade flipped down, the version of herself as she is now, confident, loving, walking toward us with her bright green eyes filled with mystery and humor. Everything had fallen into the right size and shape, and she was beautiful. She had a half-smirk on her face like her uncle and petted Felix, one of her four parrots, as he sat on her shoulder nuzzling her messy hair. Our old mutt, Tucker was at her heels, young and playful again, jumping at Felix and running around her feet without making her trip. I had never figured that out, but somehow they moved as one. My heart tugged at the sight of his happy face and perky ears. I missed him. He'd died this winter. The birds had looked for him and called out his name for weeks. They'd finally accepted that their friend was gone, but I still found Felix sitting in Tucker's bed from time to time.

She has your family smirk. Aiden laughed as his voice sounded around us.

I paused. Something about those words... How would he know it was a family thing?

A feeling of love swept up from the ground and enveloped the image in front of us as it faded, sweeping me up as well. I could almost see the emotion, it was so alive. The creature of light and darkness turned to face me. "I swear, Amethyst," he began. "I only wanted you to have the choice, before her soul arrived, before your body would even know what to do, I wanted you to be aware of the danger. A human surviving such a pregnancy is extremely rare. And it was outlawed by our Lord and Lady centuries ago. You needed to know the risks, and it was all my fault."

I wondered how true that was today, with modern medicine so readily available. Yes, it had been a difficult pregnancy. I was put on bed rest twice. But, the weekly checkups by my doctor and medicine had kept my blood pressure under control. In the end, I spent the last week of my pregnancy in the hospital to be monitored hourly. The last three days, I had to lay on my left side as my blood pressure would rise if I didn't. Fun times. These were the months following my parents' death, and Crystal had moved in with me when I was first put on bedrest, with her small twins. I would never have made it through that time without her, even without the difficulties of my pregnancy.

Something more, though. Something about Slate. Where was he at that time? I frowned. Not all the memories had returned with Aiden. I still felt a shadowed weight of the unknown. But the thoughts turned back to my pregnancy.

They induced my labor and were ready to do an emergency c-section in under three minutes, if required. This wasn't an option hundreds of years ago, and I wondered what Aiden would think if he knew about this. I decided to keep the information on the human side, only.

He looked guilty. I think. I had never seen that before, not from him. "I was too caught up in you," he began but I interrupted.

"Aiden." I stretched his name in warning and he had the decency to look embarrassed. Too often when he was at fault, he would word it in such a way as to make it the other person's fault. I never had the patience for such nonsense.

He laughed again, filling the entire forest. Branches pulled back and the darkness gave way to a soft, filtering light of midday. His eyes shown with warmth as he reached out to cup my face, stopping just short of touching my skin.

I moved my hand to the necklace again. "They can't see me here, can they?" His sharp eyebrows rose. "We are in your homeland, correct? Your lands?"

He shook his head. "No, if we were there, they would sense you immediately. Gods, my own mother would have destroyed the forest before you drew a breath." The trees around us rumbled.

"Then, where are we? And why do they want to destroy me now- I've been to your homeland before." I thought we'd just passed into the land of the Fae again, as we had done in Maine on several occasions. I'd never felt threatened there and wondered if I had been at risk.

How could I have forgotten such things?

"They knew of her existence when she was born- I couldn't hide it. The moment we were together, the magic of life began to form, cells dividing, energy exploding. In the moment you knew you wanted to bring this life forth, the Universe responded and searched for the soul that needed you, and that you need. That is the moment when I was scarred." He smiled at me.

"Scarred?" I was a bit more than annoyed at this choice of words. He wasn't the one who'd just learned he'd be carrying the spawn of an otherworldly creature. If anyone had the right to feel scarred, and scared for that matter, it was me.

"Literally." His smile deepened as he held the ring out again. "From my very bones, my gift to her came forth. For the Fae, it is not only the female who goes through physical changes and feels the pain of labor. My bones began to be...." He paused, looking for the right word. "Scraped? Yes, I think that is it, but it's not quite right. In that moment when she drew her first breath, I brought this forth."

Well, that's just weird. I tried not to think it but I could tell by his hurt expression I had failed. "I'm sorry." I reached forward, not touching him. "That's just a complete unknown in the world of... all animal life on earth." My arms spread wide in a gesture of helplessness.

His hurt expression gave way to one of dislike, and he faded from sight.

"Aiden? Aiden!" I turned around in the forest as it darkened again, a heavy fog rolling through. I found myself back on the bridge and quickly grabbed for the ropes on each side.

He returned in front of me, looking hurt. "I'm sorry." I spoke in a quiet but firm voice. "It's a very strange concept to me. I didn't mean to, to dishonor your... your labor?" The words trailed off to nothing.

"It's called the binding, or a truthing. There can be no doubt of our connection and my duty to watch over her through her life. It is a promise and a protection."

"Oh," I nodded, whispering the word. That really was quite a beautiful concept. I smiled at him and saw the tension leave his body. He stretched out the ring again.

"You must keep this for her until her twenty-fifth birthday. Use it to protect her."

I didn't take the ring. "Why? What happens when she turns twenty-five? And who exactly is trying to harm her? And why? And where-"

He placed his impossibly long fingers over my mouth. I could see a bit of steam escape, but he made no display of pain. He moved his fingers and replaced them with his lips for a deep kiss that left my knees buckling. With a sigh he pulled away and passed his hands in front of his mouth, healing himself. Stepping forward, he drew as close as possible and dropped his head near my neck again. I could feel the waves of desire flow off his entire body, and from his deep groan, he could feel mine as well. There was no bridge, no crazed fog, only an intense awareness of every cell of his body. We stayed there, frozen in a silent dance of pure energy and longing, for an age.

I didn't worry about time passing or the others searching for me. Aiden's very existence played with time like a puppy's chew toy. We'd spend weeks together but when I returned to my little college room, only an hour had passed. If time had move normally, it would have been months before he first kissed me, and a year before we slept together- he had a truly old-fashioned sense of sensibility. But in real time, I met him at the end of May and was pregnant just before the semester ended in early June. I put the necklace on when he freaked me out and returned home as my parents had died the next day. When I told Crystal I was pregnant and that I never wanted to talk about it, she'd accepted it, dropped the topic and did nothing but support me.

I pulled away from Aiden. Had I caused so much unnecessary heartache because I misunderstood him? Had Jade been denied knowing her father because of an over-reaction, because of my stupid short temper? Had Slate and Jade and I worked and budgeted and went without to make ends meet and get Slate through college when everything would have been easier with Aiden to help? What had I done to her life?

He could read me as easily as a set of pictorial instructions from Ikea. "Listen to me, Amethyst." He grabbed my arms and bent low to look me in the eye before releasing me again. "You saved her life. You left before I knew her name. I had no image of her in my head, nothing for the Lord and Lady to use to find you. There was no trace of you in the mountains where we met, and they followed them through to the ends. Without knowing anything about her, they could not follow you beyond."

How strange. I tried to block my thoughts from him, knowing I could if I focused. The fact is, the Fae aren't just magical people. They have a completely different way of looking at things, even little things. They are so connected to the ecosystems and elements that they can't figure out beings who aren't. To them, since we met in the mountains, I must be from the mountains. I must be from those mountains, somewhere along them. The Appalachians run almost the entire east side of the country, thousands of miles. It never even occurred to them that I was from the cornfields.

I had chosen that college so far from home because it had a solid program in Geography and Environmental Planning, but mostly because it had so much outdoor life to offer. Skiing, hiking, boating, yoga on the mountaintops and everything. We have none of that in the flatlands. We have rows and rows of endless corn. And the occasional soybean field. I was outside almost every day I lived in Maine, my student ID discount card in hand and everything within arm's distance. It was an outdoorswoman's paradise.

"But I don't understand, Aiden. Why would they wish her harm? And why are you able to be here with me now if I'm hidden from the Sidhe?"

"My element is ancient fire, sweet Amethyst. This land is what makes me, me." He shrugged, a helpless gesture. "I am unique. All of us, each creature that exists is unique. This is my essence. If you had traveled to any other quarter of the world, yours or mine, I would not have sensed you. Even so, I did not find you on my own. The energy of this earth, here at this site of ancient fire, pulled at me, reminding me that somehow, the soil and power that moved here at one time was what created me."

I was lost. How could a creature from a different realm of existence come into being from a dead volcano on this world?

"And you," he reached for my hands, stopping short and clasping his own together. "You are connected here in a way I did not see before. I found this place because of you!" He threw his hands up, circling. In a blink of an eye he faded to a ghostly image and flew into the canopy, resting on a branch in the shape of a great crow. He screamed his happiness and I laughed freely.

He flew down and returned to his normal form. "Perhaps," his voice became soft. "Perhaps we are safe here, for a moment." He stepped close again, his body an inch from my own; so close I could taste his skin on the air.

"A moment," I whispered, finding it hard to breathe. He smelled like a windstorm rushing through the botanical gardens in the spring, sunshine mixed with earth and spicy flowers. I could think of nothing but the thought of his mouth against mine, his hands running over my body. But I stopped. "If they do sense me, will they know how to find Jade now that you've seen her?"

He drew a sharp intake and stepped back. For a moment he kept his eyes closed, taking slow breaths as though to steady himself. "Leave it on." His words were curt and he didn't open his eyes.

In the next instant he crushed his entire body against mine, his mouth urgent and demanding and I fell into him completely. When he tore himself away, his face was blistering as his eyes steamed. I cried out, covering my mouth in horror. He took several moments to wave his hands across his face, dropping down and calling the fog to swarm up over his entire body before he rose.

"That will have to do," his laugh was weak. While his skin had healed, it was an unhealthy shade of pink which stood out in stark contrast to his colored hair. I wanted so badly to run my hands through those thick, heavy links again, but I made fists at my side to stop the urge. It would likely set his head aflame.

"Thank you for being strong when I was not. The need for you has been hard to ignore these days we've been apart."

"Days?" I laughed. "Jade is seventeen years old. It's been a lifetime. I'm getting old," I said softly.

He smiled and shook his head. "I just saw you two days ago. It was the first time. We made love just an instant before you arrived here. I am still filled with you." He threw his head back with a crazed sound, looking alien in that moment as his face seemed to narrow then return to size. "And I'll go back and meet you again tomorrow, for the very first time. Or maybe we'll dance on the mountaintop under the full moon again. Gods, you are glorious in moonlight. That was the first time I tasted your lips."

I blushed with the memory and he looked directly at my chest. Yeah, that was a crazy night. My mind was getting hazy again, like the last month of college had been. Once we had kissed on the mountaintop, we spend every hour I didn't need to rest making out. He exhausted me, teased me for months and months. I thought I was going to explode if we hadn't finally made love. If I'd known that it would mean I could never see him again, I would have delayed that for years.

I sighed. "Why, Aiden? Why does your Lord and Lady and even your mother want me dead?"

"Because you should not be able to see me so clearly without a glamour. We though all humans who could do so had died hundreds of years ago- they certainly worked to make that true. Because you should not be standing here so strong and beautiful after having my child- it should have killed you," he checked off. "Because I should only be infatuated with you, and not bonded to you for life- I am Sidhe and you are just a human. Because our child will be able to cross worlds without them sensing her, and if you have more, they might be able to as well, even if I am not the father."

He stopped counting and looked up. "Which I am against, by the way."

I held up my hands. "Aiden," I began, "look at me. Really look at me. I'm not the 'beautiful young maiden' you seduced, or, um, who seduced you, from the Appalachian Mountains. I'm older. Time passed for me. Do you truly want me to be alone forever? If we can't be together, do you want me never to know happiness again?" I dropped my hands which had become animated as I spoke. "I rarely think of you- you're like a dream I had almost eighteen years ago. I can't even explain that. And after all this time, you're saying we can never be together?" I shook my head.

"Then quit going into our past, because it's not fair. I can't meet you there. I can only go one direction, and you're telling me that to keep Jade safe, it can never include you again." Tears fell down my face, surprising me- I hadn't felt that burning sensation that precedes them.

Somehow, he managed to go down onto his knees on the boards of the bridge. Gently, without touching my skin, he wrapped his arms around my waist and rested his head against my stomach as he sighed his frustration. "I will find a way, Amethyst." He looked up at me imploring. "I'm sorry it's been so lonely for you. It's hard for me to understand how time moves, but I see you, I see what you are, what you were, what you'll become. I want all of it," he rested his head again. "I want all of you. I will find a way. Give me time-"

I interrupted with a sharp sound. "That's the one thing I can't give you, Aiden. You don't seem to understand the concept." Without touching his skin, I pulled him up. "It's been just me and Jade for so long now, I don't know how or if there can be an 'us,' any more. Well, and there's been Slate of course. He helped to raise Jade."

The storm below suddenly engulfed everything and I grabbed the rope rails tightly. Aiden was lost in the wind as it whipped my hair everywhere.

Slate?! It was a scream from a nightmare, coming from the bottom of the chasm below and beating at me from the sides.

"My brother, you idiot piece of... Knock off this wind right now!" The winds calmed instantly and I found him standing a few feet behind me on the bridge, his head titled down.

"I didn't know you had a brother." He didn't bother looking up.

He lied.

I knew it at once, but the thought faded as I mindlessly grabbed my necklace. "You didn't ask, you spoiled brat." I wrestled with my hair and began to wonder if he had been so immature and quick to anger when I was eighteen. Was I just too immature myself to see it?

He looked at me with a small, sheepish grin that gradually spread. His edges started to shimmer.

I cocked my head to the side. "Are you trying to put a glamour on yourself, or me?"

He threw his head back with a laugh. "That is my Amethyst." He was suddenly right in front of me again, all smiles and eager movements. "I have never met a human female who could sense that. They all just fall right into it, seeing a perfect version of me, all filled with desire and easy to pick as a..."

He broke off when he realized what he'd said.

"Let me get this straight, oh-great-being from another

world." I spoke with a cool tone, but even I knew there was no hope that this would stay calm.

"From ages ago. Ages. Eons before I met you." He was behind me as I blinked, then floating out over the ravine for good measure when I turned to face him. His hands went up in defeat. "No one since you." He was suddenly behind me and holding me close, careful to avoid my skin. "Never, my love."

Then he looked at me as if he had an idea, lifting his long chin up and holding motionless. I had a brief thought that a robin might perch upon it. "I wonder," he mused.

With a pop of displaced air, there were two of him standing on the bridge with chins cocked up, one right behind the other. "What the-" I backed up a bit, blinking. No, they were both still there. Though one did seem a bit... thin? Stretched? I realized when the one in back moved that I could see through him a little. The other version stood frozen.

The faded Aiden smiled in triumph and moved toward me. "I don't know why I didn't try this the moment I saw you. I can only hold this for a short time, though."

"What happened?" I wanted to scream but it came out as a gasp. There were two of him. Two!

He rushed to me and kissed me deeply. It was, strange. I could feel him, but he felt light and weak, as if I could blow and he would be swept away. But the burning sensations must have ceased because his hands were everywhere, pulling, caressing, searching and pressing me against him. His kisses felt like feathers as they rained all over my exposed skin at one time. My knees weakened with the sudden onslaught of desire and somehow, his ghost-like form held me up. I grabbed him pulling him tight to give his form some feeling of real and in those moments, even though I could see him frozen on the bridge, he felt almost whole somehow.

I closed my eyes and we were back in the ancient forest. He pressed me to the ground and I saw dirt fly up to mix with his shadow, adding more weight to his image until he felt normal again.

"I love you," he whispered. Then he showed me.

"TAKE THE RING." He was propped up on his elbow looking down at me as I lay on the forest floor wondering where we were, if not in his world. He titled his head again in that quizzical way and then froze his arm over my stomach. A shadow arm snaked down and began running fingers across my stomach, pushing my shirt out of the way. "Ah, this I can hold a bit longer." I looked down, seeing two arms diverge from his elbow. I wasn't sure how I felt about this, but his feather soft touch across my stomach was nice.

"Why can't I give it to her now?" I ask, turning it over in my hands. A ghost head separated from his real one to kiss me. I felt more hands caressing my body and chose to shut my eyes and not look.

He answered me as he nuzzled my neck, kisses turning to soft bites. With a sigh, he pulled back everything and relaxed on the forest floor, waves of energy rushing to him.

"Where are we?" I pushed up on my elbows looking overhead at the gigantic oak trees.

"We never left the mountain." He took a deep, lung-filling breath, his eyes closed, relaxed. "Give or take few thousand years."

"What?" I sat up, but all I could see was the tight forest canopy. Was there a volcano roaring underneath us?

Yes. And it's wonderful. The answer came from all around. He stretched like a cat and then flopped right back into the exact position as though he'd never moved.

He opened his eyes to look at the tree limbs above us. "Do you know how many are called to their exact spot of creation, the place where their soul was pulled together from the energy of the cosmos, earth and spirit?"

To that I would have to give a big, old-fashioned 'no.' I'd never even thought of it. "How many?"

He moved into a sitting position, started to speak then changed his mind and stood. Once up, he looked around and then absentmindedly created two ghost arms to lift me us as well. I wasn't sure if I could get use to this, but then one of the arms stayed and grabbed my hand. I might have cooed or something.

He shrugged, walking us in a circle and pulling me along. "I've heard of it, we've all heard of it. But no, I've never met anyone who had this chance. I feel incredible. Something has changed in me- it's like there's more to discover about me." His words were soft and he lifted his face, closing his eyes. A shadow self came just a few inches out and pulled me to him, my back to his front. His hands caressed my body as he stood there, lost in thought. "I could stay like this forever. You, this mountain, this is perfect." I started to say the same, but his wondering hands were beginning to change the energy so I stepped forward and he merged back into a solid form. *I want you.* The statement came from everything around us, a strong sense of him emanated from the entire forest.

I realized in that moment that it was him- he was creating a hold on this place and time, spreading himself over all of it. He was growing stronger, becoming a part of the land itself. I closed my eyes and felt his desire sweep over my entire body at once, coming from every direction. Stay with me.

"Will it be like before?" I couldn't stay if any time passed. I wouldn't leave Jade. He knew what I meant. The air behind my ear became solid, a pressure that felt like his lips and teeth bit me, moving down my neck. I could feel his hands, his body, even though he hadn't moved. I sighed and felt him press against me from all sides, too many hands to count as I was enveloped.

"Yes," he said softly. In my mind's eye I could see him clearly, standing in front of a tree trunk that was five times his width. His eyes were closed. His essence spread out over the entire area, rolling up into the canopies and far down into the ground, every strand leading eventually to me as I stood there, wrapped in him from every side.

I nodded weakly, unable to move from the intense sensations. "I'll stay."

CHAPTER FIVE

I was back on the bridge. Crystal rushed forward from the meadow side with some choice words as the haar rolled through and returned to the sea where it belonged. When had I left? Weeks ago?

She paused as the bridge swayed again, but it lasted only a moment. "What the heck was that? Mist?" Her voice was worried as she saw me frozen in place. I nodded once but didn't move.

"Um, yeah." I managed to say. I couldn't stop blinking.

Crystal crossed back to the middle of the bridge and put her hand on my shoulder. "Mist?" Her voice was like a distant whisper.

"Say that again," I coughed the words out. Everything felt so weird.

"What?" She looked confused, but I just nodded.

"Yes. Keep talking. Voice. Helps."

"Helps? Is something wrong? Do we need to go back? Do you need to sit down?" She was pushing me to go back along the bridge toward the path to the house. I nodded again.

It took a few minutes, but we made it across the with no issues. I was embarrassed. But seriously, after being gone so long, plopping back onto the center of a swinging bridge was too much for my equilibrium.

She helped me sit down on a large rock by the trail. I took a few breaths trying to find my center and failed miserably. Then I looked at her and focused. "Okay, um. Yes." This was hard. "Go back. The house. Grab everyone. There's something I have to share with you, something you'll need to see for yourselves to believe." I said the last sentence as one word.

"Mist? What happened on the bridge?"

I just shook my head. "Bring water. Oh, food. No wait, I'll go. I need food." I wanted anything other than nuts and fruits, which is all Aiden had given me in the forest.

"We haven't gone to the grocery store yet. Remember? They jumped in the heated pool? You and I were taking a quick peek of the trails? Then we're supposed to go to the store and-"

I shook my head with more vigor than expected. "No, now. I need real food, now. Let's go. The town. To a restaurant."

Minutes later, I was digging into a stack of shredded chicken nachos, waiting for the others to join me. When we had returned to the house, Crystal headed downstairs to tell them to get dressed and I realized it would take too long. *I was starving.* I yelled something from the patio about starting without them, grabbed the keys and stopped at the first restaurant I found.

We were only a mile away from where the town began and I knew they could walk that distance. It turned out to be the best choice of restaurants in the world because they bring you chips and salsa before they even take your drink order. Brilliant! I love the Mexican people. And my waiter, Carlos brought me bean dip, cheese sauce and guacamole with my iced tea. By the time he was ready to take my order, I had finished half the chips.

"Good gods on Olympus, Mist!" Mica stormed through the door first, followed by a worried looking Crystal. Amber seemed more curious than anything. I could see why Mica was in a fit, though, her wet hair was still wrapped in that hair towel thingy she uses. There was no rushing Mica and wet hair.

"Hi guys!" I called between bites. Carlos was back, bringing my burrito and more chips.

"Ooh, nachos!" Amber grabbed a piece. If the burrito hadn't just arrived, I would have slapped her arm onto the next table.

But it looked yummy, so I slid the half-full plate of nachos over to her as she sat down.

"What happened, Amethyst?" I hated seeing Crystal worried. I tried to smile but since my mouth was filled with a beef brisket burrito covered in verde sauce, I thought better of it. Mica frowned. She's vegan and I realized there wasn't much here for her to eat. I definitely tasted lard in the refried beans.

"Three more teas, please," Mica said to Carlos with an embarrassed smile as she adjusted her hair wrap. "No sugar, thanks," she added when he started to grab the sugar container off the table next to us where I had placed the unneeded item to make room for my nachos. "But a pitcher might save you a few trips." She gave him a brilliant smile and a wink. I tried not laugh, knowing I would choke. Her flirting mechanism overrode her anger response. Then she turned to me as he left. "Talk. Now."

I rolled my eyes and took a long drink. "There," I sighed. "Much better." I looked at their three faces, ranging from annoyed to worried to humored. How to even begin?

"Aiden came in the fog." I dived right in.

They looked at each other with blank faces.

"Is that code for something?" Amber looked at Crystal and Mica. "What does that mean? Did you guys create some secret language before I joined the galère?" They shook their heads.

"First," Crystal began calmly, "Confirm that you are okay. You're not having a stroke or..." She gestured to the food on the table. "A worm infestation of some sort."

"Ew." Mica said, still staring at me.

I nodded, lifting my fork to my mouth slowly so as not to startle them. They seemed rather stressed for just a one-mile hike. I chewed, focusing on each of them one at a time with a smile to make them chill. When I got to Mica, she tilted her head a little, the wrap threatening to fall.

"Wait a minute," she started. "I was sitting across from you last night, between Crystal and Slate."

Last night? My eyebrows knitted together. Oh yeah, the hot tub.

"In the hot tub," she continued. "Mist, I could swear you look thinner. You look like you've lost weight. Since last night." She said sharply, leaning in.

"She does!" Crystal and Amber spoke in unison.

I sat back in my chair, finally feeling like I'd taken the edge off my hunger. Stupid Sidhe, eating barks and twigs. I shook my head. Being in the presence of the Fae left one rather light-headed. Being present with a Fae, well… I stifled a giggle. My head swarmed as the memories started to flee *en masse*. But I was able to pull together full thoughts, instead of just commands from my body like *eat, eat now*. I laughed out loud.

"Um, sweetie," Amber began.

Taking a deep sigh, I jumped right back into it. "Aiden is Jade's father. He's a Sidhe." I swear, after you've spent time with those otherworldly beings, all subtlety flees.

"He's a she? Wha…" Mica looked at the others.

"No, a Sidhe. He's most definitely not a 'she.'" I laughed loudly. Then I noticed their confused looks. "The Fae."

Three bodies pushed back their chairs at once and three mouths dropped open. We are awesome like that. Crystal started to speak but her phone rang. She looked down on the table where she'd set it and lifted a finger as though to punch a button but paused. "It's Slate."

"Slate?" I reached in my back pocket and realized I hadn't grabbed my phone. Oops, or my purse. I had ordered food with no way to pay.

She grabbed the phone and put one hand over her other ear to listen. The mariachi music was playing a bit loud. After a hello, she walked away to the front of the restaurant to better hear.

Mica started to speak but I shook my head. "I can't say anything twice. My brain- muddled as it is. Let's wait for Crystal." I swirled both hands about my head and laughed. I took another deep breath and looked around, realizing for the first time that we weren't alone in the restaurant. "Hmmm… Maybe I shouldn't have spoken yet."

"Uh-huh," Amber agreed. She waved Carlos over and asked for boxes for my food and the bill. She also put in a delivery order that would arrive at the house in thirty minutes.

I sat there, blinking again, trying to get a sense of where I was. No, when, when I was. Am. Sheesh. "How long have I been gone?" I whispered to Mica. It was hard not to giggle at the sound of my voice inside. It was so very strange. Indoors!

"Only a few minutes, hon. We saw the car leave and could see you pull in here. We ran all the way." She broke off with a sharp frown. "Mist, did you, smell anything funny on the bridge? Crystal told us about that strange fog."

I shook my head, then started bobbing my head when Amber spoke, pointing at her with my fork until I realized I wanted what was on my fork. "That wouldn't have made her skinny." She gently grabbed my free wrist, touching her fingers around it as though measuring. "What's this?" She pulled my hand closer, looking at Aiden's ring. Or rather, Jade's ring. Made from Aiden. I giggled again.

"He went into labor." That cracked me up and I barked out a belly laugh. A few of the patrons glanced our way. I covered my mouth with my hands.

"Here." Seriously, why couldn't I link more than two or three words together. But after so much time just sending out feelings, knowing Aiden would capture them... I looked up to see I had thrust my arm out in front of me. Where was I going with this?

"Oh, yeah," I said out loud, smiling at my friends, my beautiful, loving friends who felt like family. I truly love them. "Touch my arm."

"She is stoned out of her gourd." Mica leaned back with a sharp laugh and helped Amber pile food into the containers.

This wasn't right. I wasn't being clear. "Put down all things in your hands, and touch my arm."

They looked at each other before gently reaching out to poke me. Their pokes turned into forceful hand grabs, then the pair of them used both hands and practically dragged me forward onto the table.

"What is this?" Amber spoke too loud, heads turning again.

"Come on, we're getting out of here. Grab the food, Amber." Mica pulled me up and I couldn't stop giggling at the way their voices sounded. Amber signed the check Carlos had brought with the containers, and I was herded outside. We found Crystal on the phone and just saying goodbye to Slate. I called out to him, but she had already ended the call.

"What are you-" she began.

"Feel her." Amber thrust my arm in Crystal's face. I smiled happily.

Crystal touched my lower arm with two fingertips, scowling at Amber. Then her eyebrows shot up as she looked at me and grabbed my arm with two hands. "What on earth? What is this, Mist? Why are you tingling like an electric fence?"

I wiggled a tiny, happy dancestep. "That happened last time as well. It lasted for a few days after we first kissed. I couldn't go to class because I kept shorting out the computers."

"Let's get you back to the house." Crystal and Mica piled me into the back of the car while Amber took the wheel. For some reason, they seemed to think I would fall out of the car, so they sat right on either side of me.

We moved to the top deck in the backyard as soon as we arrived. That turned out to be a good choice as a cool breeze was blowing and helped clear my head.

"I just need a few minutes." Wow, that was better. I think I was finally coming back to earth. I leaned my head back and let the sun warm my face. It had been a while since I'd felt full sunshine. How glorious.

"Jade!" I jerked upright. "Did Slate call about Jade? Is she okay?"

"And she's back." Mica snapped her IPad shut and leaned toward me. It had apparently been more than a moment or two as the food Amber ordered was laid out on the patio table in front of me, covered tight. They were all sitting around the table.

"All is well, Mist." Amber's voice was smooth, soothing.

"Slate wanted to update us on some things about Beverly Keys. But we'll get to that later. You have a lot to share with us, woman." Crystal handed me a bottle of water.

I looked up and could see that the sun was closer to setting than to midday. "We won't be able to get there today. We'll have to go tomorrow morning."

"Get where? What is going on, Amethyst?"

I pointed up the ravine. "There's a path we can take that goes inside the lower mountain. That's where we're meant to go while here. Aiden showed me the entrance." I took a deep drink. "And we're going to need something stronger than tea for now."

"I don't know, it seemed like you were already on something strong." Crystal frowned.

"I wasn't, I promise. And tomorrow you'll have proof. It's going to take a while to get through this tale, but what you need to understand is that when the fog swept over us, I was taken by Aiden to an earlier time, here on this mountain. I don't know how long we were there, but I needed to sleep at least a dozen times. He would have kept me for longer, but I missed Jade and I wanted to go home." I held up one hand to stop them interrupting. "I know, I know. Technically, we just arrived and won't leave for two days. I'll call her this evening and that will get me through two more days. But I've never been away from her for weeks like this."

I sighed, struggling to restart in a better way. "I suppose the story begins on my last month of my first and only year of college. It started when I went walking on the Appalachian trail and met someone from the ancient myths."

We talked for hours. Wine was poured, food containers opened, and questions asked- sometimes barked out in the frustration of trying to accept everything. But by the time the moon rose high in the night sky, we were all on the same page. We separated, each needing space to think things through. Amber and Crystal went on a grocery run. I drank. It was ironic that it was wine that finally helped to lift the lingering haze from my mind.

A great many sighs were heard from my portion of the patio. The best I could figure, I had spent almost two-weeks with Aiden. Running my hands down my arm, I could feel the electrical energy I created in response to him. We debated theories on that and concluded that it was my particular DNA's reaction to the Sidhe. It must be something to do with how I'm able to resist the glamours they use on humans.

But already my time with him began to feel more like a dream than a real event. If I hadn't given birth to Jade nine months after leaving Maine, I probably would have thought it a dream, in time. But I only had to close my eyes to see him, to feel his ghostly arms around me. It was real. We were real.

"I'll wait." I didn't realize I'd said the words out loud, but a wind came and whisk the sound toward the mountain. I sent a smile along with it.

"May I join you- I bring our current life blood." Crystal walked over with a new bottle of cabernet.

"Nectar of the gods," I smiled, raising my glass for her to fill. Then I frowned. "That's almost too literal. I think he is becoming a mountain god, Crystal." She slipped silently into the cushions next to me. "You know all those stories and myths of gods requiring humans to be thrown in the volcano, or river gods who chased maidens?"

Crystal nodded, curling her feet under her hips.

"Aiden said something about old stories of a few Sidhe finding their, oh, I don't know how to describe it... Finding the literal point in this Universe where all that is combines to create each one of them. The energetic point where they were formed.

"He said he feels like there is so much more to learn about himself, here. And I watched him, Crystal. I saw him expanding each hour, becoming more a part of the world we walked in. The trees, the flowers, even the rocks and the dirt answered his commands." I turned to face her as the importance of this point struck me. "He could not do that in Maine. Yes, there seemed to be a strong connection with the natural world, especially with the animals and plants. But it was nothing like on the scale of what I saw here. I really think he's the kind of thing those stories came from." My hand waved on the air.

"And he's Jade's father." Crystal took a large drink. "Our sweet, sweet Jade."

I raised an eyebrow. "Our 'sweet, sweet' Jade has become a trying teenager."

She laughed. "Well, yes, she's certainly not an angel. I've seen her fire, Mist." She smiled proudly, making me laugh. Only we could be happy about raising an anarchist. "And one can't notice when we perform that she's showing a bit more cleavage these days." She wrinkled her nose. "She's not dating, is she?"

I shook my head. "Not that she's shared. And that's what scares me. She's a beautiful, seventeen-year-old, hormone raging young woman." I shook my head. "I can't believe the boys aren't chasing her."

"Well, she is busy as all heck. And I love her swim coach- she instills the fear of the gods into those girls to focus, be strong and not believe the crap boys say that will sideline them with pregnancy." We both fell into laughter. It was true- Coach Myrtle held nothing back in her pep talks. The first time we heard her yelling at them post-practice while we waited in the bleachers, we'd all sat there with our mouths opened. But all the parents agreed that we loved it, especially the dads, and we loved her. She received a basket filled with gift certificates each month from us all, even Crystal and Mica pitched in. And I sent a mocha and pastry to her at school each Monday morning- quad shot flat white, no sugar, *Fantastically Delicious* almond/ blueberry croissant. We love our Coach Myrtle and don't want to lose her to the local state college, which was sniffing around.

"What do you think will happen tomorrow, Mist, under this mountain of your new god?" We hadn't heard Amber walk over. She started dragging a chair to join us. I noticed that she was drinking a soda.

"Come down here, guys," Mica called. We all looked over the rail to see that she had a nice blaze going in the firepit. I can't believe we hadn't smelled that. Eagerly, we all headed down and

Amber grabbed some bags of chips and a six-pack of Pepsi.

"No stalling, Mist." Amber downed her soda and grabbed another one. Seriously, did she never sip? "What do you think will happen tomorrow? What will Aiden do to us?"

"Nothing," I said honestly. "He was drawn here, just like I believe we were." I started to say something but stopped, trying to gather my wild thoughts into some semblance of logic. Memories of our time together were fleeing away at high speed now.

"You know what this is?" Crystal pulled her robe tight and pushed her long white hair over one shoulder as she settled into the lounge chair. The lavender streaks seemed to glow in the firelight. She looked like a mythical goddess of the forests.

Mica tossed her a small blanket from a basket at her side and then one to each of us. I was grateful as it was downright cold. Then she too let her long hair down, nestled down in her chair with a mug of cocoa-mo steaming in her hands- hot chocolate, espresso, Malibu rum and almond cream.

"I seriously have no freakin' idea what this is, Crystal." Mica's voice sounded frustrated.

Crystal laughed. I cringed, feeling a bit guilty. Crystal may have brought us here, but I brought us to a whole new level of bat-crazy weirdness. "Think of all the great epics, those stories that have magical moments when people find something fantastic that was hidden, like a set of runes, or a, a…"

"A book of magic!" Amber interrupted excitedly.

"Yes, exactly. Grimoires or such." Crystal pointed at her. "Those wonderful stories where people find the incredible items of magic or knowledge. You know, clue after clue leads them to a device that changes the scales of whatever battle of good against evil is happening at the moment."

"You think we're going to find a book of shadows in the catacomb of a dead volcano tomorrow?" Mica raised her eyebrows hopefully.

Crystal answered before I could, her voice sharp. "No." Then she took an annoyingly long time to fill her glass, lean back and take a drink. "I think we are about to start the adventure that writes the book in the first place. We aren't the outcast kids who are struggling to find their place in the universe by finding that magical item. We're the unknown sorcerers in the story who brought that magic into form in the first place. *We* will write the grimoires."

"I. Love. You." Mica, Amber and I said it at the same time as we sat back in our chairs. That brought out a round of hoots and snorts.

Mica pushed her feet toward the fire. "Now that is something I can get behind. This loved-crazed Sidhe was a bit worrisome. But if he didn't bring us here," she paused, looking at me.

"Nope." I was firm. "He said it was I who brought him here."

"Well then." She titled her head down and did that hair-shaking thing, throwing her still damp tresses of curls back as she straightened. She looked at me with the evilest of grins. "That's something I can get behind. Let's be the witches of old, the ones who wrote the books, the ones who..."

"Who escaped the witch hunters and didn't freakin' burn!" Amber began a salute and we all followed.

I felt warmth emanate from the chain around my necklace and drew a sharp breath. Everyone looked at me sharply, asking what happened.

"I'm pretty sure that won't be allowed." I held the now glowing necklace out for them to see.

"Oh yeah," Mica leaned back, smiling. "It's on."

Amber laughed freely, reaching forward to feel the warmth of the jewelry and after a moment, we all joined in, cackling like a coven.

"To tomorrow." Crystal raised her glass and we saluted, the galère, united it whatever came next.

CHAPTER SIX

"It's not so bad!" Mica called from the bottom of the ravine. We'd found a little trail made by some animal that took us half way down with relative ease, but the last half had a steeper incline. Mica took a too-loud breath before she exhaled with a shout and began to run and hop like a crazed gazelle. She was at the bottom in moments.

I watched Amber follow suit, but she did a sort of slide thing, hopping from leaf pile to leaf pile which moved her several feet, and landed smoothly next to Mica with an irritating grin of success.

"Why couldn't your mountain god put in a set of freaking stairs, Mist?" Crystal frowned as she passed me, facing the wall of soil and making her way down inch by painfully slow inch. I joined her.

"He's not *my* mountain god," I mumbled. "The truth is, I don't know what he is." Already, details were beyond a clear recall and it felt more and more like a dream with each passing hour. I remembered the overwhelming passion clearly enough, the intense emotional responses on both sides, but conversations and any real understanding of who he is, *what* he is, was getting murky. Again.

"He said there was no glamour, but..." I stopped climbing down and turned to face the bottom of the ravine where Amber and Mica lounged, waiting. I shook my head.

"I really don't think he intentionally cast any spell over me. But there's most definitely an other-worldly schism that forms in the brain after interacting with the Sidhe. You can't play with time and space and have the human mind just accept it all."

"Thus much let me avow- you are not wrong, who deem that my days have been a dream." Crystal pulled up next to me, frowning at the distance we still needed to cover.

I raised my eyebrows. "Poe." She said with understanding, glancing at me, then spread her hands out to take in the view before us. "Is this too, but a dream?" Then she frowned. "Or the beginnings of a really bad horror flick?"

I didn't want to think. I took a breath and jumped, landing in an open spot, and then another, and another. When you focus, time seems to slow, but I was hoping it would slow a bit more as each new landing felt like my knee was trying to jar into my chin. I found myself next to Mica soon enough but jolted and thoroughly battered.

Then we watched Crystal. She took the same focused moment and moved forward but was soon doing more of the sliding thing that Amber had done. On her backside. Cussing up a storm.

"Oh, that's gonna bruise." Amber frowned as the bouncing form of Crystal drew closer. We all gave her space to release any lingering colorful comments. She dusted herself off and joined us a few minutes later.

"This is going to be a disaster." She looked down the path ahead of us. "Why isn't this thing loaded with mountain snowmelt? It should be raging this time of year."

Mica turned to face me and we naturally formed a circle. "She's right, maybe." She held her hand up as I started to interrupt. "We need to be real about this, Mist. Every story of the Fae includes people disappearing, falling into traps that seemed so obvious to others. Is there a possibility that we're not heading into the mountain, but into the realm of the Sidhe? Are we going to find ourselves being used as love slaves to some ridiculous lord of the Fae until we are tossed back here, too old and worn to make it back up there?" She pointed toward the rim.

I looked up in surprise- it looked like a mountain to climb from this view. Anger swelled in my chest but I swallowed it. She had a point. "Look," I began, not knowing where I was going. "I will admit to not being one hundred percent clear on this whole thing. It's already gone to haze. But I trust myself enough to know I'm not being stupid. However," and idea suddenly occurred to me. "Let's presume that I am under a full glamour, that I can't tell day from night right now."

They all nodded in agreement. That made me frown, but I shook it off. "What about your instincts? That may not be your best skills, but each of you has a heightened sense of awareness- you know this."

Amber gave us her smile of an old soul and put her hands in the center. "Grab hold, my friends." Mica and Crystal exchanged a cynical glance, but soon placed their hands in the center. I did as well.

Amber took a cleansing breath (we do that a lot) but didn't close her eyes. "I have felt an incredible connection to this place since we landed. And it has gotten stronger each hour. So much so, I have serious thoughts of moving here, even though it's only been one day. One day!"

Crystal beamed. "Well that says a lot about the lay lines then, doesn't it? Root chakra. You are an Earth-witchy kind of woman. Your connection with the land has always been incredible. And here we are, at the place where that energy is created." I frowned at the familiar words, something Aiden had said.

Amber did her little wiggle dance of agreement. Then she closed her eyes and we followed her example. She began to sing in her surprisingly deep voice. You'd think perky would be soprano. Our voices joined in a four-part harmony of words we created that had no meaning. I realized I missed Slate's tenor toning-sound he added under our voices. As if one cue a bird began to sing, holding one, pure note for long periods. Slate's note. Amber released our hands, smiling. "If that's not an answer, I don't know what is." We all laughed, throwing our heads back in what the creatures of the woods probably viewed as a full-blown coven-cackle.

"Seriously how can it get better? We have moments like that all the time." I looked for the bird who had joined our magical moment.

"Only one way to find out." Amber pointed forward. "That way."

"In another month, this place will be covered in vines and weeds-" Mica began but was cut off by Amber.

"Untamed plants. There are no weeds, here."

Mica rolled her eyes in an obvious way. "Untamed plants, then. My point being, if we had done this any later, this ravine wouldn't be walkable without high boots, bug spray and a machete."

"And it shouldn't be walkable now," Crystal added. "The snow-melt has started."

"Aiden said he would hold the path, remember. I told you. Didn't I?" I turned to look back at the others. Somewhere along the line, I had taken the lead.

They nodded but glanced at each other. "Between bites, yes I think you mentioned it." Amber said.

"And a thousand other things. You rambled quite a bit, Mist." Mica pulled her jacket tight as cool winds swept over us. Her backpack bounced as she lengthened her stride.

"I had to get it all out before it got fuzzy, I think." My heart beat fast at those words for some reason. *What was it?* I shrugged and turned back to face the path, only then noticing we were on an actual path. "Look." I pointed out that we were walking on a trail of crushed pebbles.

"Maybe these just got washed here, down at the bottom." Crystal hummed an agreeing sound at Mica's suggestion but then she reached down to grab a stone that didn't match the others. There were a few scattered on the path that led forward around the sharp bend ahead.

"Amber, can you describe your missing ring?" She turned sharply as she spoke.

"Oh," Amber sighed as her face fell. "Yes, my grandmother's ring she gave me last year. I can't believe I still can't find it. Gorgeous! There are flecks of tiny diamond flakes embedded all around the band. Then there's a circle of amber at the top," she motioned to herself. "Which is why she gave it to me and not a cousin. And in the center of the amber ring is a hard-to-find gem, though it's not too expensive. It's-"

"Kambaba jasper." Crystal stood, holding a piece of dark stone with thick, green swirls. "Found in Madagascar. Some call it 'croc jasper.'" She looked at Amber. "From an energetic point of view, this is a root chakra focusing tool- it directs your personal energies downward and helps to pull in Earth energy. It makes you optimistic about handling the chaos and uncertainty of everyday survival. You know, life."

She looked at us all. "And it shouldn't be here."

In a flash we all searched for one and pocketed them immediately. They stood out against the white/gray pebbles of the path. Mica exclaimed with an athletic jump when she found a particularly large one that had to be dug out.

We found ourselves zhagareeting with it in communal joy when she stood with it in a victorious pose. Mica led the way forward and broke out into a shimmy. I immediately echoed her move without thinking, and the others behind me did the same.

We shimmied and called and danced down the ravine for at least another mile before it changed. We had just turned a particularly sharp corner and the early rising plants and soft dirt gave wave to sudden walls of stone.

"A rock climber's dream," Crystal said as she craned her neck upward. "If they can find it." I looked up to see that the crest had pine trees growing so thick it looked as though the wall of the ravine continued upward, just changing from rock to bark and then to pine needles.

"We're close." Amber raced forward and was lost as the ravine made a second, sharp turn in the opposite direction. We followed just as fast.

"Oh my gods. *Say friend and enter.*" Crystal quoted.

We echoed her amazement, astounded by the large cave entrance that soared dozens of feet overhead. The width had only enough room for one person to enter at a time, though.

"It looks like a birth canal," Amber squinted, turning her head sideways. We all agreed.

"Well," I started. "This was my idea, I'll go first."

"Works for me," they replied in unison.

"Not nice," I mumbled. Their laughter was muted, but it gave me strength as I entered the darkness after a pause. *Be afraid, and do it anyway.* I overhead an old woman say that to her granddaughter at the fair before getting on the Ferris Wheel. It had stuck with me for years.

I let my fingers drag along the walls as I entered. They were smooth and I wondered if water poured through here during the snow melts. Fortunately, someone behind me was thinking and pulled a flashlight from their backpack, placing it in my hand. Before I could find the button to switch it on, I was in a large chamber that went higher than the entrance. The walls and ceilings were covered in glowing worms and strands of mucus hanging like stalactites. They provided numerous soft, blue-green pinpricks of light that moved sluggishly around. I looked up. For a moment it was if I was staring at the stars. I felt dizzy.

It was cold. Winter had settled into these stones months ago and had no desire to leave.

"Whoa," Mica whispered next to me, grabbing my hand. She rested her head against mine for a moment for a quick grab at warmth as Crystal and Amber joined us. We stood there and just took in the beauty. It was hard to wrench myself out of the cocoon, but I was eager to move ahead.

The opposite side of the cavern was just a tall, seamless wall. "A dead end?" That didn't make sense.

"Wait," Mica moved ahead of me. Instead of waving her flashlight across the wall as I had done, she pointed it straight forward. The light was immediately eaten by a deep, narrow opening. It was tighter than the entrance to the cave.

Mica moved her light along the wall in a slow method. Three more entrances revealed themselves.

"One for each of us." My words were barely a whisper, but they echoed nonetheless.

"Wait- Mist." I looked at Amber who had moved back toward the entrance. "Didn't you hear me?"

I didn't know what she meant. She called and I looked at her.

"Step back, Mist." Mica's voice was firm and closer than I'd expected. I looked to find her right next to me. I jerked in surprise. My right shoulder scraped hard against a wall of rock and I gasped as I looked to see one of the deep caverns right in front of me, my body already partially inside.

"What?" I reached for Mica with pure instinct and she grabbed my hand to roughly pull me away. "When did I walk over here? There?" I pointed to the cavern and looked at Crystal for an explanation.

"We called your name three times, Mist." She was worried.

"This isn't right." Amber spoke with a loud voice, yet there was no echo this time.

"What do you mean?"

She held out the stone she'd picked up in the ravine. "If this is supposed to help strengthen our connection to the root chakra energy, and we're standing inside the earth's own root chakra point, then why am I completely unable to ground? I don't feel earth beneath me, I feel a wall of... nothingness."

"That's it- we're out of here." Mica pushed me toward the entrance. And I mean push. She had to. My feet didn't want to move. Don't get me wrong, I wanted to move them. They just... refused.

Between Mica pulling me and Crystal pushing me, I made it back through the entrance, bruised and battered.

Amber took a deep breath and dropped into a squat, her hands digging into the earth. "Okay, we're back."

"Mist, did Aiden show you this entrance, this exact space?"

"I thought so, but," I paused, trying to visualize any part of that time with clarity. "It's faded. We went through many passages…" I shook my head. Had I brought us to the wrong place? "There may be many false entrances."

Crystal had a severe scowl on her face as she looked at me. I didn't take it personally- I knew that look for one of concentration and doubted she even saw me. "Odd that you didn't mention that before, ey?"

Oh, that scowl *was* meant for me. I probably deserved that. With a sigh, I plopped down on the ground and lifted my hands in a helpless gesture. "It's impossible to describe. With each hour, or each breath even, those moments spent with Aiden shift from memories into half-forgotten dreams. I've thought it a thousand times- if I didn't have Jade, I would not believe the Appalachian romance was anything more than a fantasy."

I moved my hand to take in the entire landscape. "And being here, thousands of years ago? That is already so fogged I can barely remember any conversations. Just… just a lot of emotions." I tapped the center of my chest as though I could pull those feelings out and display them. "It's why I never talked about him. I can't."

Only Amber smiled as I spoke. I realized she hadn't heard a word I'd said. She was too busy reveling in the earth energy. Mica and Crystal followed my gaze, and in a moment, we were all calm again.

Amber stood up and looked around, then pointed to the other side of the ravine where an animal trail was clearly visible. It was wide enough for deer to use, or even bears.

And so, we hiked. Amber held her kambaba jasper in front as though it were a divining rod. We all followed suite, happy to let her lead. We walked in silence, the trail meandering side to side for the most part, with only a few, steep inclines to conquer. Between the hiking and the sun, I was more comfortable than I'd thought possible at this time of year, climbing this huge mountain in Northern California.

The air smelled new. Perhaps air is old and stale by the time it settles down on the prairies; I really don't know. But as we walked, taking in the strong scent of evergreens, melting snow and crisp breezes that flew in from all directions I felt as though we walked in the woods as the first humans. Why had we ever left the forests?

Mica knelt in front of me without warning and I almost tumbled over her shoulders. She shot out a long arm and pinned me back, pulling me to the ground as I saw Amber and Crytsal had also done. Amber's eyes were aglow with excitement and Crystal had her lips pursed in a perfect circle.

"What it is?" The others scooted along the ground without a sound until we formed a small circle.

"Look there." Amber stretched her hand up the hill, pointing west.

"I see trees. And rock outcroppings. And new vines. And more trees. Just like-" I gestured in every other direction at once.

I was too busy gesturing to see which one of them flipped my hair over my face. "Look at that bird, right there, Mist." Amber pointed to a deciduous tree that barely seemed to be holding onto a tall rockface on the side of the hill. Its roots stretched over the entire wall of stone, seeking little particles of earth. It was tiny, a sapling by size, but those roots were impressive.

Then I saw the bird. It sat in a larger tree beside the rocks, its leaves barely in the bud stage.

"A swallow?" Big whoop.

Mica flipped my hair into my face. I guess she was the culprit the first time. "One swallow? During spring migrations? Where's the rest of the flock?"

I shrugged. "Maybe it got lost or blown off course?"

Amber shook her head. She lifted her chin toward Mica. "Remember what Mica said in the hot tub? She had that dream?"

Oh yeah! She'd told us about peering over Crystal's shoulder to look at the monitor. She'd seen a mountain with a single bird.

"And look at the bird," Amber continued. "It's remarkable-I've never seen one use the shadows of a tree for camouflage.

If you watch, it will step back and almost disappear in the branches."

"What do you think it means?"

"By itself, probably not much. But look at the bottom of the outcropping. That's a single shelf of-"

"Kambaba jasper," we all finished Crystal's sentence, rising slowing. I couldn't see the swallow any more and didn't know if it fled at our movements or was doing that camouflage thing Amber described.

We moved off the trail and into the still sparse brush. The sharp slope required we climb the dirt more than walk it, but the numerous small bushes made it easy to pull ourselves upward.

Mica reached the single piece of kambaba that sat at the bottom of the rockface first. We watched as she ran her hand over the shelf, clearing off the winter debris. From her pack she pulled the large piece of stone she'd freed back in the ravine. I wasn't sure what she had in mind as she looked at it and then the shelf, but finally she placed the stone on top of the ledge. Switching positions several times, she smiled as she chose one that had it covering most of the visible ledge.

"It fits." Her eyes narrowed as she bent her head with a mischievous grin and stepped back. She was right- the edges lined up in perfect sync.

"Mine next." Amber took her stone out and placed it to the left of Mica's. It nestled against it as though they were fixing a broken vase. That left only a thin, tall piece open in the front.

"That looks like mine." Crystal moved over and set hers in the remaining space.

I rolled my rock around my in pocket a minute before removing it and setting it on top of the three. It took me four tries, but on the final attempt, it slipped into place, completing the shape.

"It's an egg." I don't know what I expected. I don't know that I expected it to look like anything. But for some reason, a prehistoric, pterodactyl egg-shape seemed surprising.

Wind rushed from below, carrying warmth. It lifted the roots away from the rockface and even the little tree itself left the ground. I then saw how the small tree was a strange extension of the larger one on the left side of the rocks, like a running blade of grass that roots itself over and over.

We gasped as the last roots came away and leaned into the larger tree, revealing a set of stone steps leading into the side of the mountain.

I moved forward. The presence of the bird and the strange way our stones fit on the ledge made it unlikely that this was another false entrance. Yet still, I felt responsible somehow and if we were headed into another soul-sucking cavern, I should go first.

I put my hands out to each side, hugging the rock as I stepped down into the darkness. The first thing I noticed was the warmth. Each step down led me away from any last will of winter. But each step down also chased the darkness ahead- the light at the top seemed to have wrapped around my head like a halo or loose shawl and traveled with me.

After a dozen or so steps, I noticed the sound of my feet against the stone began to diminish. A deep, ringing began in my middle ear until it was all I could hear. Shaking my head, I paused on the steps and swallowed hard, trying to reclaim my hearing. When I opened my eyes again, I found that I had reached the bottom of the steps.

A high tunnel made of dirt, root and stone stretched in front of me. I glanced over my shoulder, shadows playing against the wall as the others arrived. Even with the strange light that stayed with me, I walked with my hands on the walls on either side. I sent a small plea to the universe to strengthen Amber against her claustrophobia. Along with it I sent a thousand emotions for the things I couldn't express.

It was happening. Whatever 'it' might be, we had arrived. I pictured Slate at his cards, and wished he was here.

The heat intensified. It felt like a queen's luxury, here. That description seemed... fitting. The heat coated my back like a royal cape, swirling around the ground as we passed. It pulsed against the center of my upper back and made me arch my chest, shoulders up, back and relaxed like a dance pose.

I immediately drew in deeper breaths, as that posture invites. The warmth filled my head and lungs and light, heated air lifted me like a warmed breeze. The balmy air in my lungs seemed to expand out to all my limbs. I had never felt such a connection to the energy of heat, like a sense to be directed as easily as a deep inhale or a quick glance.

The tunnel ended in a rounded space, too small to call a room. The light that walked with me eased itself off my shoulders and stretched to fill the area in a half circle in front of me, leaving the hallway completely darkened.

Some part of the back of mind suggested I glance back to check that the others were okay but I couldn't draw my eyes away from the light.

It lived.

It danced and swarmed over and through itself as it created strings of color stretching from the ceiling to the floor. They sparked and popped like a wet electrical outlet until the light shed its false layer and exploded into its true self- Fire.

The pyre burned with an unknown fuel and the colors of fire and flamed separated again and again until the wall was filled with strands of luminous, devouring elements of every imaginable color.

I couldn't have move away if my life depended on it. I was pulled toward it, hopelessly lost in a brilliance that sought desperately to be known. I plucked at a single string of color, a scarlet bead of fire and I knew it, *I knew it* to be passion. That single, tiny strand from a tapestry of dozens, of hundreds was eager to know me as well.

I stretched one hand out, capturing an azure blue- lonliness- while the other grabbed an aegean green I recognized as the foundation of intention. *No...* It was just one of the strings that made up that foundation. Just one of....

I looked back and forth, desperate to see if I could find the others, to know if I could read this wall of fire, to know if I could understand its very core. I pulled at a coral bead, a bone-colored string, and weaved. The fire didn't burn my hands- it kissed them, grateful that I could connect things in the correct order, that I could weave a true tapestry of Fire's sacred energy.

Even as the idea of intention formed beneath my hands, I released it. Dropping my head with a great exhale, I spread my arms wide and stepped into the wall of flame.

"MIST. MIST? CAN YOU HEAR me? Wake up. Mist!"

I blinked. Steam, or perhaps fog, rolled over me as I looked up into the darkening sky. "It's going to rain," I said to whomever it was who had been shaking me.

"Sit up, sweetie. We need to get moving."

I blinked again as Mica splashed through the tiny stream of water and moved to Crystal's side. She was laying on the ground, too.

"Ugh." I jumped and looked behind me. Amber was in a sitting-up position with her back to me, rubbing her face with both hands.

"Up. Everyone. Crystal's spring thaw has apparently decided to show up."

"It's not mine- oh, forget it." Crystal grumbled as she stood up, shaking her foot as though that would actually get the water out of her shoe.

We were back in the ravine. And Mica was right- tiny streams of water now stretched across it, and they were growing with each passing moment. By the time we all moved to the side of the ravine to begin a desperate climb up, the bottom was more water than not.

"I think whatever was holding it back for us is saying 'time's up- get out.'" I grabbed the base of a large bush and pulled myself up onto an animal trail before offering a hand to the others. We began to climb.

Once more, we meandered back and forth making slow progress upwards. But this time it was a blessing as my thoughts roiled and the need to find a path kept them at bay. By the time we were half way up, the water rushed below and could once again be called a riverbed.

No one spoke. Part of me wanted to apologize. I abandoned them. What must they have thought when I walked forward into a wall of flames?

But oh, the fire... I shivered as goosebumps covered my entire body for a moment.

"Mist?" Crystal offered me a hand this time as she'd reached the top. The last few feet were straight up.

I jumped up and stood next to her as the others stood frozen in a circle. We stared at each other, saying nothing. After several minutes, I looked around and saw a sign showing the way into town. We were only about four miles from the rental home. I pointed to it.

Crystal glanced over, then back to me. "You okay?" Her voice was dull, robotic.

"I'm fine. I just... I was just remembering the flames." I turned to face her fully. "I'm sorry I just left you all-" I stopped suddenly, unsure how to finish what I wasn't even sure I'd wanted to start.

A breeze moved around Crystal. I glance at Mica and Amber and noticed the wind hadn't reached them. "Flames? Oh." Crystal just looked at me. I could see my own confusion echoed in her eyes. Her hair moved across her face and she used both hands to push it away.

I picked up a long strand of my own hair. It fell back into place without a fuss.

Because there was no wind.

"Umm..."

Amber started walking down the road and we silently followed. It seemed we all had a million things to say and not a single word was adequate. After a few dozen steps, Mica, Crystal and I slowed a little, increasing the distance between us and Amber.

"Umm," I repeated, wanting to speak but seemingly unable.

Words were still uncatchable things to me.

"Well, I'd say she's definitely an Earth Witch," Crystal's voice still sounded separated from her emotions. She had words, it seemed, but wasn't connecting to them either, saying things that just seemed like they should be said.

"That would be hard to argue, now." Mica agreed. Her eyes were shaped like large circles, as was her mouth.

"That's just gross. Where's the cute, furry little woodland creatures?" I wrinkled my nose when disgust returned as my first emotion and brought with it the ability to speak again.

Ahead, the ground next to the road where Amber walked… bubbled. Or maybe it was just little quakes. Whatever it was, every step she took seemed to free a dozen worms, beetles or other bugs from the dirt and they'd slither and slime their way after her for a short bit before heading back offroad.

"And I'm pretty sure you get the title, Wind Witch." Mica pushed long strands of lavender hair out of her face as Crystal's hair flew on the unseen winds once more.

Amber turned around. She started to speak, but then broke out into a big smile and dropped into a squat, cooing to the icky things… icking about around her.

I held my hands forward. The tips of my fingers itched. I rubbed my thumbs across them, from pinkies to pointers, like bizarre, full-finger snaps.

I exhaled as the intense itch faded. Of course, the tiny flames burning at the end of each finger should probably have been cause for concern, but I was exhausted; exhausted in a happy way. I'd felt like this two hours after Jade's birth- completely worn out and absolutely content.

Yes, that's it, exactly. I was worn out, down to my very core, and okay with… with everything. There was no room for fear, though I had a feeling this was the effect of shock settling over me, and I would feel different later.

The flames lasted only a few seconds, but I felt relieved. It hadn't just been another event that would fade from my memories within hours.

Fire is mine.

But what does that mean? I don't know.

Yet, I felt relieved. This would be nothing like what happened with Jade's father, the Sidhe. My body vibrated as I moved, seemingly new.

"Is this you?" Amber pointed to the sky then glanced at Mica. We all looked up. The darkening sky was now just dark.

"Oh, I hope so." Mica's voice held so much emotion that I found myself blinking tears away. Such longing!

I watched as Crystal rubbed her eyes and sniffed a couple of times. They had felt it as well.

"Maybe...?" I began, faltering. It was too much right now. I didn't want to talk about it.

"Yeah," Mica answered, understanding my needs in an instance.

"At least a few days." Crystal nodded her agreement.

"At least. I think we'll know when it's time." Amber released a loud breath, obviously relieved. She threw us a half-smile before she moved to the center of the road and took off at a full run.

Knowing there was no rush to understand and discuss what had just happened, it felt like a weight had been lifted from our collective shoulders. With a shared smile that spoke of relief and excitement at once, we accepted her challenge and raced after Amber.

Don't get me wrong. We knew we were different, changed in ways that should cause us all to curl up in the fetal position. But exhaustion has its merits. Pushing our bodies beyond their limits was just what we needed to do. So we did.

CHAPTER SEVEN

"Why. Won't. This. Work- argh!" I slapped my hand down on the armrest of the plane in frustration. Not even a tiny light.

"Well, because if it did, we would be stuck in a plane of fire, Mist." Mica didn't bother to open her eyes. She was stretched out in the aisle seat. We had an empty seat between us- not first class, but always welcomed.

Amber turned and looked at me over the back of her seat, her jewel-tone, silk purple top taking a second longer to settle into place. She and Crystal sat in front of us and had the same luck with seating. "It makes sense. You were standing right on the volcano in the earth's own root chakra point of power. I mean, wow! I bet it will take all of us some practice to get in synch with our gifts. We have powers- Eeee!" She scrunched up her arms and flipped back into her seat. Mica laughed, again, without opening her eyes.

Yeah, it was pretty cool, heading home with a new set of tools with which to play. Heading home as old-school witches.

Real. Witches.

No one spoke on the walk back to the house after our trip to Gaia's Cavern, as we called it. We each went our own way for the rest of the trip. As soon as Mica sat down on the plane, she'd closed her eyes. I was eager to hear everyone's story, but we were giving each other the space needed.

"Okay." Mica sat upright in a sudden move. I frowned at her, wondering if mind-reading was one of her new gifts.

"Anyone else ready to talk?" Crystal and Amber turned in their seats.

"I am, but not here." Amber took a loud, long drink from her water bottle. Ever since we'd returned, we'd all been struggling to feel hydrated.

"Yeah," Crystal and I agreed.

"But I would like to talk about something," I began, giving the two in front of us a chance to get comfy.

"When I was, um, eating everything in sight, Slate called. Somehow, we never got around to talking about it after you confirmed Jade was okay. You said it was about Beverly?"

"Oh, yeah. Man, that feels like a lifetime ago. He confirmed a couple of things after talking with the police, which apparently they like to do after you already know the facts." She made a face. "One, Beverly did not show up to work. She lives in a guest home her sister owns, and she did not return Sunday and is considered missing because of the car being left at the café, and the elephant purse that Liam saw. It helps that Liam has some weight in the community." She took a long drink of her iced tea.

"Two, the Lincoln home is now considered a scene of a crime and officially off limits for a few days. I think until tomorrow, actually. Since it's a historically significant site, they can't keep it locked up long. "Third, Slate learned that Beverly works for Lauren Ryan's office. She's head of the state's historical homes."

"Oh wow, and she's dragged away near a historical house. That can't be a coincidence."

"Perhaps," Crystal shrugged. "It could just be a good location for whatever reason this happened. She was sitting just across the park's street at the *Axe & Stovepipe*, after all."

"Is that all?" I asked Crystal. Before she could answer, Mica jumped in.

"Nope. I've got some info." She leaned up to press the button for the flight attendant. I was glad to see it- we could all use another round of something wet. Even though I'd just finished my third bottle of water, I couldn't seem to get rid of my dry mouth.

We waited for the flight attendant to bring us more drinks. I changed to orange juice hoping a sweeter drink might help.

"Okay, shoot." Amber sipped an iced tea through a straw and sat comfortably on her knees to face us. Crystal had her knees up on the empty seat in a half twist position.

Mica opened her mouth to speak but then closed it. Her brows knitted close as she tried again. "I know we want to wait to talk about our, um, experiences, but let me just state that one aspect for me is definitely a stronger dream connection.

"It's changed. What I had has been strengthened..." She trailed off looking confused and overwhelmed. Then she charged in with a determined lift of her chin. "Last night as I was fading off, I began to think about the events of the night before we left. Why did all that happen just as we're heading off in search of a source for energetic mojo for the first time? You know I don't believe in coincidences that strange."

We all made sounds of agreements. It did seem a bit much.

"I kept coming back to Beverly, stalking Mist." She held her hand up as Crystal started to speak. "I know you don't like that word, but it's the truth. She followed her everywhere with her eyes, she wouldn't leave until asked to, she was there every single evening. But, only after-"

"After we were in the paper!" Crystal slapped her headrest.

"Oh, that's true! That article came out and had a picture of us in front of the cafe." Amber's eyes were wide. "And the reporter seemed fixated on Mist."

"What?" I scowled at her.

"You didn't read the article, did you?" Mica gave me a half-sneer.

"I didn't need to read it. We lived it."

"But you hung it up in the café, right where people place their orders."

"I'm a business woman- I'm not going to pass up free publicity."

"Well, it's true." Amber took another long drink. "The journalist focused in on you quite a bit more than warranted."

I frowned. "Sorry?" This didn't seem like something for which I should be shouldering blame.

"My point," Mica continued, "is that you were shown as having done a lot to solve a mystery. She shows up the same evening that story broke, and she fixated on you. You mentioned it seemed like she wanted to say something every time you told her it was closing time, she wanted to talk, right?"

"True." I twirled the straw between my fingers for a moment. Then I sat my glass down on the table stand and ran my hands across my pleated salwars pants, finding the silky folds comforting. Finally, I just shook my head with a sign. "I can't think of a hint as to what she wanted. But it would seem to be pretty damn serious."

"It's money," Mica whispered. She leaned in, throwing the ends of her mustard colored wrap across her right shoulder.

"As I was saying, I was thinking of her just before I fell to sleep. I pictured her sitting on the patio facing the park, as she was on Sunday. I don't know when my wondering thoughts became a dream, though, as it seemed to be the same. But I dreamed of her. She kept getting up to go talk to you, Mist, but every time she did, a wall of fog or smoke got between you two and she couldn't see you. She tried to blow the smoke away but it would reach in and cling to her throat, and she walked away, defeated. I felt as if this was her umpteenth attempt. Just one more failure. Then she was sitting back on the patio again for a long time. She just sat there, waiting for the fog to leave her, and then a man put a hand on her shoulder. She looked up and there was real fear in her eyes."

"Poor thing." Crystal drew her jacket tight and reached up to turn off the air flow positioned on her seat.

Mica nodded. "You know how my dreams are often just emotions, right? Well, I had major details this time, but still the emotions. She was really frustrated, and with herself!" She punched Crystal's headrest in emphasis.

"But then the scene changed. She was sitting at a desk working on a computer, a small office with a door leading to a larger office. Money starting to fall all around her from the sky. Instead of trying to grab some, like you'd think anyone would, she jolted away from each bill, shrinking down to the floor as she tried to keep from touching it. She pulled herself into a protective fetal position, her hair and clothes getting messy and her face became drawn and exhausted. The scene changed again.

"This part was really weird. It was dark, and she was struggling to reach up to a table and grab a pastry. It looked like one of the tables at your place, Mist. The ones you made from those reclaimed pieces of fence from New Salem where Lincoln ran his general store."

"Hold on a second." I grabbed my purse and hurriedly looked for the pen and small notebook I kept in it. With quick fingers, I drew something and showed it to Mica. "Did it look like this?" I showed her a picture of a pastry trying to disguise itself as a hamburger.

"Yes!" Mica hit the paper. Then she pointed at me, her eyes going wide. "You sell those in the café, don't you?"

I nodded. "It's a tarte tropezienne. She gets that every single time she's there."

Mica closed her eyes and raised both hands as though calling to her vision. "The emotion changed." She took long minutes to relive the dream. "Sisters, that woman needs us. She's starving!"

"Oh no." Amber's eyes glistened.

"The money fell around her at work," I said after a few moments. I whispered the words, actually. The others had sat back in their seats and didn't hear me. I didn't feel the need to repeat it- all I had was a hunch that we needed to check on her work. Maybe she'd left a clue at the desk Mica had seen in her dream.

"Idiot!" I jumped, looking across the aisle of the plane. The woman across from Mica yelled at the flight attendant as she tried to help clean up a drink laying across her table.

"I'm sorry ma'am," the attendant said calmly. "I wasn't prepared for your son to kick the table." Mica reached across and offered the attendant some of her extra napkins. She took them with a quick smile as the passenger continued to complain, but less loudly now and I could see that she was... she was embarrassed?

"Oh my gods!" I grabbed Mica and pulled her half into my seat.

"Oh! Um, okay." Mica looked up at me from my lap. "Doing okay, sweetie?" The lady across the aisle looked at us with surprise. I guess this looked like a romantic moment. I just smiled at her and pretended to stroke Mica's face.

"Please stop that," she said. I looked down and realized it was more like little slaps than gentle strokes.

"Sorry." I pulled her up and dragged her into the seat next to me, leaning in to whisper.

"That woman is embarrassed she barked at the flight attendant."

"Yeah, she should be. Why the histrionics?"

"No! You don't get it!" I screamed whispered and Amber and Crystal turned in their seats.

"What's up?" Amber gave us her wizened smile, head cocked to the side with a half-smirk on her lips. "You just discovered something, Mist. Out with it."

The others looked at me, questions written all over their faces. "She turned a pinkish orange color. Maybe hints of red, I don't know. It was squeamish?"

They all whispered, "Who?" I nodded across the aisle, begging the Universe that they wouldn't look over at the same time. The Universe ignored me.

Crystal frowned with a tilted head. "No, no pinks, no orange, no hints of squeams." She smiled at me. "And what was in your O.J., my friend?"

I looked again, and the color had vanished. I shook my head. "I swear, it was like she was glowing for a moment there.

She had a sudden burst of color change."

"Oh, I think I know what's happening here. Oh wow, Mist." Mica leaned in with a big smile as she said my name loudly. She gave me a quick kiss on the head.

"Yes," Amber agreed. "Mazel tov, my friend." She raised her glass.

I was getting pretty annoyed by their happy faces. "If someone doesn't share this great moment of insight, I'm going to start knocking heads together."

"Auras, Mist. You are learning to see energetic auras." Mica leaned back to close her eyes.

"The energetic ley lines will increase psychic awareness," Crystal quoted, though I don't know from what source.

Auras. "Wait!" I leaned forward, everyone jerking back to face me. "I know absolutely nothing about these. I mean abso-positive-lutely nothing." They all leaned back with soft laughs. "Guys? Seriously? Come on."

Mica patted my hand soothingly as she closed her eyes again. "Quit whining, Amethyst."

Sometimes my friends are very annoying.

WE PILED INTO the *Axe & Stovepipe* late that afternoon. We were eager to discuss everything- how to help Beverly, what our personal experiences had been, plus how we were to honor the gifts and the responsibilities they brought.

And was it all true? Had we really just been reshaped into the witches of old?

As we reached the entrance, Amber was in the lead and she drew up short without warning. We watched her run her hands over the intricately carved set of front doors. They are stunning, I will admit. It had taken me months to build them using pieces of salvaged wood, some of them quite exotic with smaller pieces I had saved from plane renovations up at the airport. It really is all about who you know, and I knew an aviation mechanic from our high school days.

I doubt I would have tried to save the old house and reinvent it as a café if I hadn't grown up in my dad's workshop. When he wasn't out hunting rocks and talking soil lines with mom, he was scraping, sanding, pounding out some needed item for our lodge-styled home. I could run the plane, the jigsaw, the belt sander and the router by the time I was twelve. So could Slate. When I needed to sell the house we grew up in to buy the *Axe and Stovepipe*, he moved in there with Liam, and I think it was so he could save the workshop. They had expanded it and rebuilt the main room to soar with enormous tree trunks as supports. It was beyond beautiful.

Amber turned to us with a smile. "There's something about these doors. I'm not sure what it is, but they are talking to me." We moved into my café, pulling her in as well.

"I should definitely get away more often." I smiled at the others. When you're in the same rooms, day in, day out, it can get mechanical. Taking just a few days away made me appreciate the beauty of the place. The restored floors and walls, the unique tables and the gorgeous counter where customers ordered before grabbing a seat and waiting for their food and drinks to be delivered.

And it was packed. Usually we have a crazy morning as coffee and pastries are our thing. Then we have a nice flow of coffee drinkers throughout the day, with the online pre-order, curbside delivery option we added really taking off. If we wanted a drive-thru, I'd have to remove a porch or the courtyard and I didn't want to lose any of that. The curbside choice seemed to be working and we had a designated crew from six am to noon just for it. I wasn't sure why it was so crowded after five.

Then my eyes bugged as Nic, our short-order cook... Oops, no. My assistant manager, walked out from the kitchens. He had super short hair, closer to being bald than not. He stood at least two inches beyond six feet, maybe more, and his work at the local Y had given him a rock-solid body. He wore a diamond earring in each ear. They were tiny but stood out against his cocoa colored skin. He was dressed simply in a light blue checkered linen shirt with the *Axe & Stovepipe* apron covering most of it, and simple brown trousers. His Asian eyes twinkled with delight as he marched quickly toward us, wiping his hands on a towel.

After I was crushed within an inch of my life, I stood back and exclaimed, "You're gorgeous!" I said it a little loud, apparently, as most of the room busted up with laughter.

"Why do you think it's so busy in here?" He smiled playfully bringing another round of laughter as he played to the crowd. I'd never seen him like this. I grabbed his towel and whacked him with it a few times.

"Not that, jerk face." It was true, he was an extremely handsome man, but I knew him when he was a scary homeless guy with wild hair and zero muscle mass. He was like a second brother to me, and the feeling was mutual.

I pushed him with little grace, backwards and into the kitchen. The others followed, confused. Once back there, I had to keep pushing him as there were several workers scurrying about to fill orders. Wait, I'm not sure I hired all these people. I looked over my shoulder at them even as I pushed him out the back door.

I pointed to them. "Um, in a minute." Then I circled him, smiling wide. "I cannot believe how beautiful you are!"

"You mean handsome. And ruggedly so." He had a soft accent that he didn't understand himself.   "Mist, what are you doing?" Crystal laughed. "You've known Nic for years- are you just now seeing what a gorgeous specimen of masculine magnificence he is?"

I shook my head, unable to lose the smile. "You're forest green, with deep, deep purple swirling throughout, alive with energy. There's a turquoise edge in places, that keeps changing to a beautiful brown. It's just, wow." I sank back a bit, still awed at the colors dancing around him.

"Oh Mist, that's beautiful." Amber's eyes filled and she moved forward to give Nic a hug. "I love purple and greens!" She patted his arm when he frowned in confusion.

"What did you guys experiment with in California? I knew I should have sent Slate with you. No, wait. Liam. Liam would have kept you in line." We all giggled.

"She can see auras now, Nic." Mica drew her long curls over her shoulder and lifted her eyebrows while she waited for his response. "We think."

I looked at Mica's stance. I knew that stance. I knew what it meant when she held her hair that way. "Mica," I said warningly.

She seemed to catch herself. "Oh, yes of course. She looked from me up into Nic's warm brown eyes. "Sorry about that. Sometimes your, what was it, rugged handsomeness catches me off guard."

They both raised their hands up in surrender. "I swear to the gods of old to not play with the affections of any friends or family of Mist's."

Amber grabbed her knees as she laughed. "I have never heard that. Did you make Cole say that as well?"

"No, but he needs to." Nic pointed his finger at Amber. "You keep away from that wild one, here me?"

Amber nodded with a laugh. "I swear to the gods of old that I am too smart to buy into any of his lines. And until the time that his wild oats are sown, I promise to stay out of his line of attack."

"Brilliant." Crystal smiled with approval.

Nic looked at me with a serious expression. "Aura? And I'm all greens and, and other stuff?"

"Mostly shades of moving green, yes." I smiled. "I've only seen a few so far, but you're the first one that has colors moving. It's really stunning, Nic. You have a heart of gold."

He reached over and pulled me into another hug. They were incredibly rare from Nic, but two in one day? "You helped me find that heart again, sister." I returned the squeeze fully.

He let go and pointed to the second floor. "Why don't you guys relax on the upstairs balcony and I'll bring you some dinner."

"That's a wonderful idea. They don't feed you on the planes anymore. I think it's ridiculous how 'streamlined' service is now." Crystal stretched up to give Nic a quick kiss- she was one of the few allowed to do so. But Nic knew she had taken Slate and I under wing after our parents died, and then, nine months later, Jade. She was family.

"You guys head up and I'll grab some drinks." I headed for the kitchen.

"Wine," they called in unison. Nic laughed loudly as he disappeared into the café. I headed for the basement to find some wine.

We'd barely had time to get comfy when a waiter came up the stairs carrying a tray. As he set out small plates for each of us, and then presented a gorgeous bruschetta on a wooden board in the center, I looked at him sharply. "What is this, and who are you?"

He stood up, laughing. 'Mr. Berhane said you might ask that. My name is Jake. I'm studying culinary hospitality at UIS. Mr. Berhane came by a few weeks ago looking for extra help while he tries out the new line of vegan dishes this week. I'm really interested in learning how this will be accepted, especially here in a small city where the horseshoe is considered gourmet food."

He smiled as we all snorted. It's true- Springfield's claim to culinary fame was to take a toasted piece of Texas toast, put a huge hamburger on it (or sliced turkey, ham, Italian sausage) then load so many fries on top that it threatened to spill over the plate. The whole shebang was then covered with cheese sauce. Each restaurant who offered these had their own, secret recipe, heavily guarded. There are competitions devoted entirely to the horseshoe. And never dare get between two chefs arguing if the cheese goes *under* the fries instead of *over* them.

"Weeks ago?" I raised one eyebrow, looking at him with more intensity that I probably should have.

"Hmmhmm," he nodded, unaware of my change in attitude.

The others looked down and busily started piling shares of

the bruschetta onto plates.

"This started Monday, right?"

"Hmmhmm," he said again.

"And how has it been?"

"Packed every night, Ms. Berhane. I mean Butler! Sorry about that." He laughed as he walked away.

"Hmmhmmm," I said softly. "Weeks ago, ey?"

"Oh my gods, what is in this?" Amber lifted half of her piece of bread above her eyes, poking gently at tiny pieces of something layered on the bottom. The other half was hungrily being consumed. "Is that an olive tapenade under there?"

"Where did he get tomatoes like this before the farmers market? You can't get this kind of flavor from a greenhouse tomato." Crystal reached for a second piece, her first already gone.

"This is vegan? This can't be vegan. Isn't that a parmesan cheese on top? Oh my god, I want six more of these." Mica reached for her second piece and I decided I'd better get in there while I could.

All my anger dissolved at the first taste. "Okay, Nic is a god," I said calmly. But I shook my head sadly. "We aren't really set up for a full-scale dinner service. We're a tiny step up from a coffee shop, selling simple sandwiches and soups and a few made to order items. I'm going to lose Nic, aren't I?" I flicked the top off my bruschetta. Stupid tapenade."

The waiter returned then, bringing corn chowder. I perked up. You can't really make a decent corn chowder without bacon. Perhaps this would all just fail.

"You're hoping this stinks, aren't you?" Amber's eyes were bright as she took a sip straight from the small bowl, looking at me over the top. She closed her eyes. "Sorry."

"Dangit!"

"Is, is something wrong, Ms. Ber... Ms. Butler?"

"Just tell Mr. Berhane to get his butt up here," I growled.

"Well it's pretty busy, oh, yes, of course." I turned fully to face him, my eyes shooting daggers. He took the hint.

"It will be just like with the pastry chef. I find these hopeless cases, I give them every opportunity, and what do they do?"

"They soar." Said Crystal as she finished her soup.

"Right. Soar. Right out the door. Crap on a cracker."

"It'd better not taste like crap on a cracker." Nic's deep voice preceded him up the stairs. I stood up and waited for him to cross the balcony.

"Dangit, Nic. I leave for three days and you, you up and get yourself all ready to open a restaurant. When were you going to tell me?"

For the second time that evening he threw his hands up and backed away. "I'll be back when you're able to talk without steam coming out. You have a hundred patrons below that I need to make happy."

I stomped my foot. "Well of course you do because you're awesome! And I'm being an idiot, I know!" I yelled the final words. My so-called friends were laughing with tears streaming down their faces. "Oh just bring it over." I waved in an exaggerated manner to Jake, who was frozen on the other set of stairs.

As one, Crystal, Mica and Amber grabbed their purses. "He'll need a big tip." I ignored them.

Two courses later, consisting of outstanding nachos made with black beans and homemade chips (with a vegan cheese I couldn't accept as not coming from a cow) plus handmade coconut milk ice cream with strange little pistachio cookies I want in my burial chamber, I had calmed down.

Jake cleared the table and the ladies each gave him five dollars. Nic came up a few minutes after, dragging a nearby chair over to join us.

"Better now?"

I sighed, wanting to say oh, so much more. But I am grateful to have friends who don't let me get away with much. "Yes."

"Good. Now, let's get down to business." He held up a hand to the others. "You can stay. You should stay. She'll want to talk it over with you afterwards anyway, probably run around under the moon or something, so this will save time.

"Now, we both know I can't afford to open a restaurant. Even if every happy customer in here these last three nights- and there have been many- were bankers, none of them would give me a penny. Before helping you at the farmers market, I have no record of income for my entire life. And we all know why." He lifted both hands off the table briefly and then dropped them back down. That's a story for another time, but yeah, we all knew it.

"So, I wanted to use this time to try out something and see how it would work. There are a lot of people at the farmers market concerned with how animals are raised, and most of them really limit their meat purchases to just the small, local farms."

This was true. People are more aware of animal treatment these days, and most folks who attend the farmers market each week want to support the small farmers instead of corporate farms and enormous animal sheds where the creatures never see the light of day. The number of small farms had increased as a direct result of our large farmers market, which literally drew thousands of people each weekend.

"I figured if it worked, great. If not, I could work off any losses if needed. And I did it now because you so rarely give me a chance to do much, even though I'm supposed to be your assistant."

I narrowed my eyes and frowned at him. He was right. "Yeah, yeah. I know." I had been trying, though. For a full year, it had been my focus.

"You are trying, though." He smiled at me. It seems everyone can read my mind. "But there's nothing here that can't be learned by one of our staff members. What I'd like to do is this," he leaned in. "Let's turn the attic into a kitchen, with the purpose of catering, and offering a vegan menu here on just the weekends. We can add a dumb waiter and back stairs would easily fit. When you took me on a tour of the house after the move, I couldn't get the image of that huge, unused space out of my mind."

He pulled a notebook out of his back pocket and handed it

to me. "Just look this over. It's all the numbers, the goals. And here," he reached for his shirt pocket and handed me a folded piece of paper. "It's the numbers from just the last two nights." I got a rare, full smile as he stood up. "I think you'll be happy with them, if nothing else." He headed for the stairs. "We have a line out the door now. I think we should get some of those outdoor heaters so we can use the patio on nights like this where it's cool, but there's no wind. Bigger than the one you use here on the balcony. Think it over." He waved to us all and vanished down the stairs.

"Well," I said leaning back.

"That was something," Crystal always encourages what she calls 'wise risks.' She says it's the American Dream in action.

"It's a great idea. His recipes are ridiculous." Amber was using her fingers to get every drop out of the ice cream bowl.

Jake came up the stairs. "Boss said it's cocoa-mo time." He smiled.

I frowned. "We don't have a liquor license."

Jake laughed. "Actually, they're from next door and no money changed hands."

"Ah, my big brother." Amber smiled as she took a mug.

"To Jasper!" We all raised a mug to the owner of the *Eighth Circuit Brewery*.

"He knows I'm back, safe and sound. I'll run over there before heading home to see how he did with the greenhouse."

"Okay then," Mica drummed her fingers on the tabletop. "Let's get started. What shall it be first? Share what happened in Gaia's Cavern, or plan on how to find Beverly Keys? I know she's alive- that dream wouldn't have come if there was no hope."

We all agreed.

"I'm actually feeling less of myself since leaving Mount Shasta," Amber began. She pulled her crochet shawl tightly over her shoulders and adjusted the heater that sat behind her, sending it up another level. I hadn't realized how cold I was getting until she gave us the extra warmth.

"I was, ugh. How to say it? I was connected, plugged in.

Gucci. Since leaving, I feel drained. I would love a few days to just let it all settle in. I want to sit in my greenhouse and my meditation room and walk the winter labyrinth those Dominican Nuns have out at their eco farm, you know? I need to let it, oh what is it, percolate? Mix in, deeply. Like gunk in my toes needs to rush up to my head-”

"Okay, we get the idea." I wrinkled my nose at her. Crystal whacked her with her napkin, closed her eyes and shook her head. "Let's give ourselves time to let it all sink in, and also a little time to explore. I just discovered this aura crap is real; Mica has reached boss-level dreams- what are you guys going to come up with over the next few days?" That brought smiles all around.

"All right then," Mica gave the table a decided knock. "That gets shelved why we work on self-discovery. How about we gather on the next full moon to share in sacred circle? Tomorrow is this month's full moon- that gives us four weeks to let toe gunk rise." Crystal took a drink of her cocoa-mo and whacked Mica with her napkin without missing a beat.

"Can we get a mountain symbol tattoo together?" The idea just struck me. "I'd like to mark it, mark the event."

Crystal nodded slowly. "Mark ourselves as belonging to Gaia's Cavern, honoring her."

Everyone agreed that we'd do it on the new moon in a few weeks. There were true artists in town who did tattoos. One even had regular showings in small galleries in Chicago and St. Louis of his paintings.

"Okay then, Beverly." I placed my hands on the table in front of me. "I think tomorrow, when the park isn't busy, I'll go over there and see if I can learn anything from them. Maybe they've overhead things from the police that weren't shared with Slate."

"Don't you give them free coffee?"

"Yeah, so they owe me." I laughed. "And we need to get into her office." Then we grew quiet, wondering what else we could do.

"I suggest," Crystal began slowly, "that since we're supposed to be next door tomorrow night for Jasper's brewery event, we each spend time tomorrow trying to hone our new skills on how they can help this woman. I mean, the police are working on this right now. We have zero leads. I think we're going to need a little witchy help to figure out the next step."

"I have to meet with the city about a mural on the old savings and loan bank building. That's going to take up most of my day, but I will definitely fit this in."

Amber agreed. "I have to catch up on three days of greenhouse neglect, but I'll focus on Beverly as well."

"And I have a deadline tomorrow. It shouldn't take more than a few hours if I start early. I'll try and join you, Mist, if I get done in time."

"And I have homework, it seems." I held up the notebook with a smile. "Seriously, I love his idea and I have to wonder if it's time to move out and convert the entire second floor to seating. I've loved living here, but it seems to be outgrowing a space for dual purpose.

"But you'll leave the hot tub, right? I love the view. And classes in the basement?" Mica leaned forward at the last question.

"It's a great location. But I think we need to be prepared for that to become storage, if needed. If we expand to catering and a full dinner, I don't see it staying to just the weekends."

"I'm glad it's a vegan menu he's creating." Amber smiled. "Jasper's brewery is all about the deep-fried goodies- there should be no competition."

"And it's a simple thing to leave the café and go to his outdoor patio for a drink after dinner. It might bring in a whole new group of people if he creates a place for them."

Amber nodded. "Do you mind if I mention it."

I held up the notebook. "I haven't even opened this, ladies. Can we not plan the third expansion quite yet?"

"Okay, but it's good to know all the possibilities. We need to keep eyes open for a place to dance."

"I think you need a studio that has space for your art, and for your dance classes, Mica. I'm trying to move out of my brick and mortar and into a home, and you need to move out of your home and into a brick and mortar."

"Oooh." She wiggled her fingers in front of her face, shaking her head. "How many artists go under when they open a shop outside of their home? No, it's a nice thought, but there's a reason you don't see art shops everywhere- it's a great idea that gives people the warm fuzzies, but actually supporting it is another thing altogether."

"What about those wine and painting parties that pop up everywhere as a gal's night out event?" Crystal had taken us to three different ones.

Mica shook her head. "Not steady enough in a place this size unless I had the perfect, and I mean perfect location- cheap and visible."

"Yoga." I don't know where that came from, but once I said it, I liked the sound of it. "We only have two studios, and they're pretty nichey. One of them only does hot yoga."

"And may I add an 'Ew!' to that." Crystal laughed. "Hot and smelly is what it should be called."   Mica tilted her head. "I do know a few great instructors who have large followings. And if we could hold dance classes there, art events, and I had a separate little nook with the right light and natural views…" She laughed. "And a partridge in a pear tree. But who knows. I can stay open to the idea and see what percolates. I think something has to change."

"Well now that we've solved all the issues of the world, I need to leave and say high to Jasper next door before heading home." Amber stood and looked at us warmly.

We rose and shared secretive smiles that spoke all the words in the world without a sound.

CHAPTER EIGHT

"Wow! That's gorgeous." Crystal extended a jeweled arm in my direction, one that I grabbed and pulled close. She was wearing a tribal bracelet on her upper arm made of some kind of brandished metal, dark and molted. The entire exposed side was covered in thick button-like things with three large stones and fake emeralds. "Where did you find it?" I looked up at her.

"Imad." I groaned and released her arm. When she shopped with him, she found the most outstanding deals and I didn't want to hear that she paid fifteen dollars for something that costs eighty at the dance festivals.

She cackled wickedly, saying it all. Then she walked through the main room of the café into the second seating area, moving to the windows. "The place is empty."

"Finally." I stood up and joined her. "It's been packed all morning. As soon as nice weather starts, even if it's just one day out often, they arrive." I raised my hands, wiggling my fingers as though tourists come up from the ground like worms.

"Ha! I bet it made for a crazed first-day back."

I frowned at her and shook my head. "It's amazing. I was gone three days and Nic reorganized the new curbside thing so that it works five times as well. Plus, he changed the way the counter is set up and we are seeing better impulse buys already."

"He needs a raise." She took a drink of the new, organic vegan mocha. It was good, but I preferred my non-fat latte. However, with the prices of organic, free-range milk getting higher and the price of almond, coconut and soy getting lower, I was willing to supplement from time to time.

"Yeah, I'm trying to figure out how to budget the costs of renovations, needing to move out and support a completely separate household, and then give him a good share of the profits from the new expansion."

"Ugh. Money."

"Yep. However," I lifted my mocha in her direction. "I'm choosing not to carry that worry around. Or at least I'm choosing to not do so and partially succeeding. He's got some great ideas. We have a secured location. I think it will work."

"So, is he dating yet?"

"Nope. He's keeping to his oath, as far as I know. He's staying dry and celibate for ten years since the day he started working for me at the coffee cart. It's been seven years so far. He is determined to set life straight and make sure he comes at it from a strong place."

"I'm glad he's decided to seek counseling at the state vet's clinic. Lord knows we fought hard enough to get that provided by the state."

I agreed. We had marched and protested and called and written everyone who had any authority at the state level. Well, us, along with about thirty thousand other members of the state who wanted our veterans to receive, for free, the counseling they need. "I didn't know he told you about that. Good. Maybe that means it's working and he can shed all the crap his mom laid on him."

She shook her head. "Why some women choose to have kids when they don't want them is beyond me."

I had to agree. "Shall we go? Jake has the kitchen under control. He's working here three days a week now. I think Nic has picked him to handle his duties as he works on the expansion and catering ideas." Then I laughed. "But I think Tammy would have something to say." I leaned out of her view so she could see what I had seen reflecting in the window- Tammy was giving Jake a lecture on how to correctly reset the tables after a customer left.

"She's been here a long time. I like her."

"Me too." I replied. "But nothing has been said and I'm not going to preemptively stop a problem I'm not sure exists. Shall we?" I gestured to the enclosed patio door. We paused, looking at the table where Beverly had sat on Sunday. How did she get from here over to the park? We walked out and headed to the Lincoln Home historical park across the street.

The visitor's office is smaller than you'd think. But people don't want to stay inside and walk around looking at Lincoln stuff when they can go into his old house and walk around looking at Lincoln stuff. Plus his neighbor's homes, the streets, the gardens. It was a preserved neighborhood, basically. This was the place that made a rail-splitting shop owner into a lawyer and then into a president. Even though he was born in another state, he called Springfield home and it was the only place he'd ever owned a home of his own.

The lobby was empty of tourists and the two employees were refilling brochures. I knew one of them from the café, Emma. She has a larger than life sense of humor with a laugh that filled the café every time she visited. I really like her- warm and friendly and, as I looked at her, I could see a slight pink around her edges. It was beautiful against her dark skin and hair. And it was peaceful. I hadn't seen anyone's in the café all morning, even when I tried. Perhaps it worked best when there was just one person. I tried not to stare but failed. Pink isn't one of my colors, but they way it danced about her warm skin was breathtaking. I couldn't tear my eyes away. She noticed.

She visited the café with two other workers from the park only once a week. When she saw me, she smiled and approached. "Are you delivering now?"

"Um... I don't think so." I waved my hands in a definite 'no' and she laughed.

"I bet you're here to check on the recent events, aren't you?

Fay said it was people from the café who saw everything and called it in."

"Fay?" I didn't recall meeting someone with that name at the café.

"Uhum, yes." Emma headed back to the display she'd been working on after a quick glass at the other woman, standing behind the counter and frowning in our direction. "Our new director here." She nodded her head to the other woman.

Fay was a thin woman with an athletic frame, like someone who did weight-lifting or yoga regularly. Her blond hair was piled into a tight bun that pulled at her temples. She wore a tailored pin-stripe pantsuit that I adored, though it seemed a bit more formal than the park needed.

"Is she trying to lift up the prestige of the sixteenth president?" Crystal whispered to me. I. Swear. To. The. Gods. Can everyone read my thoughts?

"I haven't seen her at the *Axe & Stovepipe.*" I replied to Emma.

"And you won't. She thinks it's one step away from a bribe. And she thinks that step is about as wide as her eyebrows."

I glanced back at Fay. She was sporting a thick set that was all the range with the teens these days. "I'm sorry to hear that. It just grew as a thank you, not the other way around. I guess anyone not there from the beginning might see it that way. I'll talk to her before we leave."

"I'm not sure that's a good idea, but I suppose it can't hurt anything. Just, well, Mist, please keep the woo-woo on the down low, okay?" Emma winked at me. We had run into each other at the local metaphysics store more than once.

"I hear and understand." I laughed as Crystal tucked her telling necklace into her shirt.

"Emma," Crystal started. "You were right when you said we wanted to see about the event. The last we heard, there were no leads. Has that changed?"

"Sorry, hon. None that I've heard. If Liam hadn't seen that unique purse, and you ran back to tell the police to whom it belonged, they wouldn't have any leads at all, from what I hear."

I nodded to Emma with a smile. She seemed to have a solid grasp of things and knew more details than I thought were public knowledge. We thanked her and walked to the counter to introduce ourselves.

As we drew near, a distinct, light green color surrounded Fay. When she looked up from the brochures, however, it tinged with an ugly yellow. I must have shown I was startled as her eyebrows shot up in a questioning manner.

"Sorry, I didn't mean to scowl," she said smoothly and stuck out her hand for me to shake. "I'm Fay. You must be Mist Butler. I've heard about you at the city council meetings."

"Oh?" I shook her hand with a smile. "Something good, I hope."

"Some of it," she said shortly and returned to her work. "Is there anything I can do for you? If you're hear to invite me to coffee and pastries, I'll have to say no thank you."

"I understand." I smiled, trying not to let my annoyance show. "It really is an odd set up. It started when one of your tours was not having a smooth start to the day- the Lincoln house was limited in availability because of a filming, the rain had messed up the gardens, and I think, of all things, the bathrooms were closed because those rains caused a pipe break on this side of the street."

Fay paused to look up at me. "How did that equate to pastry and coffees?"

I looked at Crystal with a laugh. "It does seem strange from the after side, doesn't it?" I gave Fay my most winning smile, the one that brought the city council to my side, the one filled with ooey-gooey mojo. "In desperation, they brought the entire tour over there to use our restrooms. We just happened to have a guitarist playing, who has one heck of a wicked sense of humor. He could tell they were all upset as they waited in line, and he played some, well, humorous songs that soon had them laughing.

"The bus driver was also with the tour company, and he

was so relieved that he wanted to buy the park workers some food and tea to say thanks. But he didn't have any cash. So, I sent him and the park people up to the balcony while our musician soothed the tourists' weary souls. Your crew was pretty frazzled after dealing with the Chicago attitudes for hours.

"Then, after everything had settled down, the driver returned with the park volunteers that evening to say thanks. We had a packed house with locals and when they started talking shop, the next thing I knew they were giving a full-out lecture on the park, my café, the city, and my patrons loved it! So, your park people and the tour company were thanking me, and I was thanking them, and, somehow...." I spread my hands in a helpless fashion.

"Somehow it just grew into a thank you thing." Crystal laughed. "It was really nice having them get the locals excited about the history that we take for granted here."

"That is so very true- no one appreciates all the work that happens right under their noses to keep the history alive." Fay was passionate as she spoke, her green aura spiking in places. "Well, that's not such a bad thing, then, is it. I must admit, it seemed like a bribe," she raised an eyebrow as though challenging me. But Crystal and I just laughed it off.

"Perhaps I'll visit your café. I've heard that you're now offering vegan items, is that true?"

"Um, yes, just started this week. Here," I reached into my bag and pulled out a coupon for a coffee. "My resident genius has created a vegan mocha that is unbelievable. Give it a try."

"Thanks," she said simply, snatching the card as though I might change my mind.

"Oh, it is scrumptious," Crystal began. "You know who loves it, Liam." She turned to Fay as though adding her into the conversation just occurred to her. "You might know of him, at least now, perhaps. Liam Lindsey. He's the spokesperson with the state EPA? He's the one who saw..."

"Yes, I know, I know. It's really... remarkable that he happened to look through the telescope at exactly the right moment."

I gently stepped on Crystal's toe. Fay's aura had taken on a sickly shade. We were on to something.

Crystal nodded, not changing her expression at all. "Indeed, remarkable. I wonder," she lifted a finger to her chin and I struggled not to knock it away. Talk about cliché. She saved the moment by scratching her chin briefly and relaxing her hand again. "I wonder if he saw everything, though. You know when something startles you, you draw back, right? Then he'd have had to look through the scope again."

I pressed harder on her toe as I watch the sickly green intensify in size. She needed to keep it up. "Like, oh I don't know, was someone else with them?" she said casually. I let off the pressure on her toe as the aura faded some. "Or did she perhaps drop anything?" I pressed harder, wanting more information because that had caused a real response.

"Or since Liam noticed her purse, was it perhaps because something fell out of it, uh, ahem." I squished that little toe! Bingo- something she had is missing! Crystal coughed, covering, what I now realized to be, a squelch of pain. I moved my foot away from hers.

Then I went ahead and moved casually about two feet down the counter, looking at the brochures, out of reach of her feet.

"I'm sure I don't know anything about that. The police have been through here at least five times. I can't imagine they would have overlooked anything at this point. They just let us open the park again this morning. So, you can imagine, I have a lot to do."

"It was good to meet you, Fay." We laughed at the strange coincidence of Crystal and I saying the same words at the same time. Imagine.

We didn't need a bat over the head to see we were being dismissed. I gave Crystal plenty of lead space. When she stalled at the door, holding it open, I opened my purse, looking for anything that I could pass off as needing. Anything. Come on!

"Ready, Mist?" Oh, that was Crystal's innocent voice. I really am in trouble.

"Sure, sure." I patted my bag once, waved to Emma and headed out. "Please don't hurt me," I whispered as I passed through the doorway while she held the door open.

"Oh no, not here. Not now."

Great.

As we walked in the parking lot, I saw in the reflection of a tinted car window that Fay was looking at us through the window. "Geesh, she's watching. We'll need to go back to the café."

"And I need to get back to work. We can't go looking for whatever fell out of her purse now anyway." We watched a tour bus pull in.

"I'll see you tonight at the Eighth Circuit?"

Crystal turned and gave me a wicked smile. "Oh, you'll know I'm there."

Great.

"SO LET ME GET this straight?" Amber stopped piling the soil into a pot and looked up at me. I mean, really looked up. She's so short. Her hair had half escaped from her little gardening hat, and the pretty flowered apron she wore was covered in dirt and mud. She had a good amount on her face as well. All in all, Amber was a wreck. Plus, she looked exhausted.

But glowing. She was in her element, for sure.

"You stomped on Crystals toes as a subtle gesture?"

"No, I didn't stomp, just, you know, squished things a little. Whatever, it worked. Fay freaked out, aura-wise. She knows something. She knows something was dropped. We need to get over there and check it out. But they have cameras all over the place, now. I'm surprised they never needed them before."

"Wait." Amber started slinging dirt again. "I know I've seen cameras there."

"Dummies. Up 'til now, that seemed to be enough. However, I'm curious how the funding for a camera system was paid for but not the use of it. I can't imagine a committee said to install cameras but not to turn them on. That makes no sense. These days, they can record electronically, no need for film. Even if it's not monitored, what could be the difference in price? It doesn't make sense."

"Huh." Amber shrugged and kept slinging. She was really a messy little earth witch. "Help me move this." She grabbed the other side of a giant container that I was pretty sure was designed to be moved with a crane. She did that annoying 'here, no here, no let's move it back to here' thing until I realized she was playing with me and I walked away from the pot sharing a few choice words.

"Seriously, how do we look around without being seen?" I leaned against her work table.

Amber walked over and started absentmindedly stacking empty pots and organizing the table. "The first thing that comes to mind is that we take the tour." She reached out and grabbed a small mortar and pestle, rubbing it down with her apron. I nodded in agreement. That made sense. "I mean, they give them every day. Two of us could go take the tour and see if we can find anything." She looked behind as she spoke, pinching off a few leaves from about four different plants and throwing them into the stone pot.

As she grabbed the pestle and began to grind the leaves, she looked up at the ceiling, lost in thought. "I've been thinking about Beverly all day, how she's lost, alone and suffering, if we go by Mica's dream."

"And we do," I added.

"Uhum," she said absently. She applied great pressure as she ground. I wondered what kind of leaves she was using. "I agree. We are meant to find her, Mist. I feel like that visit to the mountain was so key in how we do things now, though. We aren't searching blind." She stopped grinding and smiled at me, a slight lift to the left side of her lip. "When witches seek, we always find. We do not grope through darkness, blind."

Cute. Before I could say that, though, the bowl she was grinding in fell over. Then the powder that was all that was left of the leaves fell out.

And kept falling. It fell over itself again and again, stretching out to form a short straight line. Then that line inched its way to the edge of the table and leaped off.

"Don't lose sight of it!" Amber yelled at me as she raced around the table.

"No, no I don't think I'll look at anything else right now." I snarked. I couldn't help it. What did she think- I would go get a cup of tea and check back later on the magically moving line of herb dust?

It inched its way across the floor of the greenhouse, which was mostly rock. When we were almost to the end of room, it started climbing a bag of potting soil. Once at the top, it kept going up until only the very bottom granules were touching the bag. With all the theatrics of high diver, it threw itself off the edge and behind the bag, complete with a triple twist.

Amber smiled at me. I frowned. I mean really? Theatrical herb dust? She bent down as she pulled the bag away and then let out a scream. I jumped forward, but she was already standing again, her hand cradling something that made her smile, and then cry.

"My grandmother's ring!"

"Oh my gods, Amber!" I ran over and grabbed her hand to see. There it was, the jasper with amber and a band covered with diamond flakes. "I can't believe this. How did you do that?" I was laughing now. This was crazy.

She had tears streaming down her face. "I don't know, it just, well you were there." She slapped my shoulder, then put the ring on the middle finger of her left hand, holding it up high to admire it.

I slapped her back. "You have to go on the tour tomorrow! You'll find it if something fell out of Beverly's purse. Maybe?" I didn't know how this worked.

She shrugged. "I think it's worth the try. Heck, we can even try to just find Beverly herself."

"Yeah that would be better, wouldn't it?"

"Let's try and repeat it." Amber rushed back to the table. But then she just stood there. Eventually she shook her head. "Nope. I have no idea what to mix for that. Nothing is calling me. I think it's too big of a stretch for me now. Perhaps one day?" She trailed off with a small smile.

I reached out to grab her hands. "Then one day, we will get to freak out with joy again. That was brilliant, Amber. And if you can repeat it tomorrow and find what Beverly dropped, that would be amazing. If not," I put my hands up for a second. "No problem. We will find the way to do this. All of us together."

She threw herself forward and gave me a big hug. Truly, I'm not a hugger, but this certainly deserved more than a hearty handshake.

WE GATHERED THAT evening at the *Eighth Circuit Brewery* for Jasper's patio opening he held each spring. It was a bit nippy, but he had some large heaters spaced about and Nic was right- it made all the difference in the world. Wooden beams stretched overhead, soon to be covered by twining vines once the growing season was in full swing. French-styled metal chairs and tables were scattered about, and beautiful hanging baskets from Amber's greenhouse were everywhere. I knew these would be taken inside at night as frost would kill them.

There's a fire shelf built into one wall with cerulean blue and white tile frame, and the in-ground fire pit at the top of the patio had sand piled high all around it.

Mica was seated at a large table, two men standing beside it, each holding the house glasses filled with something cold from the tap. She had her hair piled up but a lot of loose tendrils flowing down across her shoulders or framing her face. The peacock shawl she had around her shoulders caught the firelight with tiny rings of reflective beads.

I watched Amber and Jasper join them, Jasper slapping one of the men on his back and pointing back to the long bar. The two men raised their glasses to someone I couldn't see and, after saying something to Mica that made her laugh, disappeared inside. Amber shook her head, laughing and joined Mica.

She wore a long wrap with green swirls that reached the ground and her short hair sported a scarf. Her hooped earrings were visible even from the café, where I was standing as I put away my phone. I was probably bugging Jade with all my calls, but I was eager to see her again. However, I wasn't going to end her vacation at Elise's house, so I just called. A lot.

I watched Crystal join them. She wore a deep turquoise colored pantsuit in an Indian style, which she loved to do to celebrate her Nepali heritage. The silk top draped long, falling to mid-thigh. Strapped around her waist was a shawl identical to what Mica had around her shoulders. I watched them laugh. We all had that shawl.

Such beautiful, sparkly friends, I thought as I joined them. I was the plain Jane tonight. White linen shirt (yes, the café shirt,) and black slacks. And dark green flats. It's not that I dislike heels. It's closer to a deep, burning hatred that rises from the pits of my blackened soul kind of feeling. I despise them. I won't wear them, period.

I walked through my courtyard, mentally placing a few heaters about and liking what I saw. But as I walked through the bocce-ball court that Jasper and I shared, I frowned. While it was something that sounded like a cool thing, the truth was, it was used only an average of ten days out of the year. I counted. It was one of those things you think adds a great deal of ambience, but then it turns out to be more of a beautiful image than a useful item.

Jasper met me when I reached his patio. He wore some kind of jewelry in his beard. This is new. I thought it made him look too much like a pirate.

"It's gotta go, don't you think?"

"Huh?" I blinked at him, with zero grace I might add. I've had just about enough of people reading my thoughts.

He nodded toward the court. "The court is barely used. I bet there were less than two dozen days that people played last year."

"Ten." I nodded in agreement as we walked to the table. "But what would we do with the space?" I enjoyed having a mutual space for both of our businesses. In the end, we could cut it right down the center on the legal line, I suppose. His patio could be extended easily. And judging by the crowd size, he could use the space.

"Amber has a few ideas. I'll let her explain, but I think you'll like them." He smiled at me warmly. "And welcome home, Mist. It's good to see you back."

I watched him walk away, probably taking more of a look than was warranted. I mean, a man should be able to walk to his job without being ogled every time. But as I saw the female patrons enjoying the view, I knew that was rare. Humans.

"Really?" Amber gave me one of her rare frowns. It was so out of place that I let a laugh escape. That was not well received.

"Sorry." I held up a hand. "You're right. That was lacking all class, demeaning to his dignity, and mine, an un-asked-for, depraved-"

"Enough." She was in full scowl mode now. An unexpected finger gesture soon followed. I frowned, stroking my necklace as my thoughts grew hazy. *What had we'd been talking about?*

"Amber," Mica raised her glass. "I've never seen this side of you. Welcome, snarky-Amber."

"Welcome," we all chimed. I didn't raise a glass. My hands were empty. I looked down at them with a scowl.

"Here you go," Jasper said leaning in from behind, his lips close to my ear as he placed a beer glass in my hand. I shivered, and it wasn't from the cold.

"That's the best kind of magic." I smiled at the galère and even Amber had to join in.

Jasper was gone before I could turn around and thank him.

"Seriously?" Amber seemed genuinely hurt as I sat down. "You were just with Aiden."

I cringed at the sound of his name. It had never been spoken by us, not in such a public place. I sighed loudly. "That's not a word we can say, guys. Not ever. Words carry on the wind. I can't have that word carried to the wrong ears."

They all looked surprised. "But you're absolutely right, Amber. My only defense is that any time with, him, soon feels like a dream from long ago. I know it was just yesterday that we left California. I know it. I keep telling myself that just two days ago, I was holding him. But, *geesh*. It's so far from me now.

"If I had to place that moment in my life, just by clarity and memory, I would say it happened at least a decade ago."

"But didn't you say Ai... Um, you said he was almost human there, right?" I appreciated Crystal's catch of words.

I nodded. "I know. I guess it doesn't matter. Anything to do with the Sidhe, in whatever form, messes with the brain's ability to handle time shifts." I lifted my hands in a helpless gesture. "I don't know how to digest any of this."

"Well not like that!" Mica, sitting to my right, forcefully grabbed my elbow and yanked it down. "Hey- oh look at that." I smiled despite the bad timing. A tiny light glowed in the area above my palm. It went out as soon as I spoke. But it had been there. Wow!

"It seems things are manifesting quickly." Amber grinned as she held out her ring and explained what happened to the others. "Which brings me to this." She reached behind her seat to a tote bag I hadn't seen.

"For each of you," she said with a wicked grin.

"Oh. Amber." Crystal turned over the hand-crafted book she'd received. On the front was the impossible task of dried flowers and herbs arranged to look like air blowing through words.

I looked down at my own. The handmade cover was made of thick paperboard and felt like canvas. The binding was an intricate series of knots that added weight and substance. It was large, the length and width even. The design she'd created for my cover was a forest on fire, but instead of killing everything in sight, the fire released the seeds from the pods, and new growth was visible everywhere. I opened it to find beautiful, linen-like paper, just screaming for words to be added.

"Archival paper, they will last for ages." Amber brought her own out then and showed us how to store the pen inside. She had already written a few pages, added some decorate swirls to the edge that I admired.

"I don't know what to say. Amber, these are incredible works of art." Mica, our resident artist, turned her book and looked at it from every angle. She let out a long, appreciative whistle.

"I know, right!" Amber leaned forward, eager. "I can't make stuff like this!"

"Hogwash," I said. "Your bouquets are works of art."

She waved her hand, dismissing my words. "Yes, yes. But I have never, and I mean, never been able to make pictures of any sort. Do you know why I paint those crazy pictures on rocks?" She thumbed to Mica. "Because she made me some color by number templates. I couldn't draw on a rock freehanded if my life depended on it."

"I love your frogs. They are so evil," I leaned over to tell Mica. She gave me a quick, double eyebrow lift.

"But these," Amber continued, "commanded my attention as soon as I got home last night. I have not slept. Okay, maybe a few hours. But not enough to count. These things... I don't know... demanded I make them. And yes," she leaned back. "They are awesome. But they told me why they needed to exists as I made them."

No one said anything. We all took a few sips of our drinks and just let it sit in, looking at her with some skepticism. She grinned with a naughty energy. This was going to be good.

"Ladies of the galère, how many stories have you read where people find a hidden, magical treasure that saves the world? A scroll with the formula for a magical elixir, a mighty sword that will only respond to the bravest, most noble of knights?"

"A ring of power."

"An amulet."

"A book of shadows."

We almost shouted, causing people to look. Amber touched the side of her nose with her ring finger. "Exactly. But, my friends. We are not the ones to find these magical items." With a bit of smugness in her smile, she leaned back and spread her arms to include us all. "Behold, the old witches."

"I think you mean 'witches of old,' Amber."

"Whatever," she answered, clasping her hands on the table top. She relaxed some, as though a weight had lifted. Then she yawned deeply. "Like Crystal said, we aren't the ones who find the books filled with all the answer."

"We're the ones to learn the truths in the first place." I blew out a breath.

"And that means, we'll have to figure out the hard questions to ask before that." Crystal gave us a short nod and took a hefty drink of the amber ale.

"Since we're giving out gifts," Mica began, reaching behind her seat for another tote bag I had not seen. I looked under the table quickly to see if I was missing anything else.

Mica gave me a brief, quizzical look before facing Crystal. "I made this for you, but I sent it off with a friend who was visiting a kiln specialist. I wanted it fired by someone with more expertise than me. It arrived this morning." She leaned back and smiled. "Coincidentally."

"Oh, Mica." We were all breathless. It was a black cauldron the size of small mixing bowl or large cereal bowl. Crystal held it easily in both hands and I could tell it had some weight. It had an art nouveaux style with a bronze, three-legged bottom. Just below the smooth lip, a band of intricately woven leaves ran around in fully. Crystal lifted the handle, which looked like a wrought-iron half ring, and let it gently fall to the other side so she could see an image on the belly. It was a female cloud, blowing a strong wind forward.

"You can actually drink out of," Mica spoke softly. "Amber contributed some of the minerals. I thought you might use it for scrying as well."

Crystal looked up with a big smile, her eyes bright with unshed tears. With a title of her chin, she dumped her glass of artisan beer into the cauldron. Since her glass was almost empty, it didn't go far so she grabbed mine and added some as well. Then she did the same with the offered glasses by Mica and Amber.

She lifted it high, then brought it down, tilting it to take a drink. "What the... Who is that?" Crystal froze with the cauldron tilted toward her face. She moved her head to the side, as though to offer a view to someone behind her. I noticed then that it was to let in more light.

Moonlight.

Crystal jumped up, knocking the table slightly and moved away from the overhead beams, standing right on the edge of the patio. We followed quickly. She placed it gently on the wooden rail, careful not to spill anything. She leaned forward and moved to the side, allowing the moonlight to fall fully on the liquid.

"I see a woman. I don't know her, but she's looking for someone."

"Let me grab my book and I'll try to draw her," Mica started to run back but Amber grabbed her arm. "No! You can't use it yet. Grab a napkin or something."

"I have a small sketchbook in my purse." Mica nodded once and went to get it.

Crystal didn't move, her hands gripping the rail tightly enough for the veins to pop. She whispered, speaking to the cauldron. I swore I saw the liquid swirl in response to her voice. Then she started speaking clearly again.

"She's looking for someone she loves. Her heart is breaking.

She's climbing the stairs, walking in the forest, calling from the top of a, a castle? Everywhere she goes, she wrings her hands and looks and looks."

Mica came back just as she began to describe her. In just a few moments, they both stopped at the same time. Crystal stood up straight.

"Well okay. That was, that was, wow. Just wow." She turned to look at us, her eyes wide and she leaned against the rail taking deep breaths.

"Is this her?" Mica held up the picture she had drawn.

Crystal raised an eyebrow in surprise. "That's pretty close. Nose is more pointed, jaw is bit more square and cheekbones aren't as pronounced." She nodded to each change Mica made.

"How did you do that?" Amber looked over Mica's shoulder.

"I interned in college with an illustrator who was also a police sketch artist on the UNLV campus." She smiled. "Pretty dang good training on how to remember interesting people I see to draw later."   "Do you need to sit down, Crystal?" I cupper her elbow. She looked at me, her eyes abnormally large.

"I need a drink."

Amber lifted up the cauldron.

"That'll do," she said, and drank it down in one smooth gulp. All of it. Wow.

We made our way back to the table just as Slate and Liam came out, carrying appetizers. "We're here." Slate lifted the platter high overhead, waving with his other hand. Liam, his hands tucked in his suit pockets, strode behind, nonchalantly. "What, no drinks for us?"

We must have looked a bit dazed as they both drew back slightly. Then Slate set the platter down as Liam waved over a waiter and ordered a full round. "Okay, galère, what's up? Did something happen at the mountain?"

"No. I mean yes," I stood and gave them both a quick hug and then they found chairs to drag over. I shook my head. "Too much."

As Liam sat down, he casually picked up the drawing in

front of Mica. "How do you know Bonnie?"

We all looked at each other. "Bonnie?"

"Hmm," he nodded as he bit into an over-sized, deep-fried mushroom dipped in a spicy red sauce. His eyes went a little wide as the spice hit and he looked around for the waiter. I handed him my glass and he took it eagerly. "Whew, thanks, Sis." I smiled deeply. Even though he and Slate hadn't married yet, he accepted me as his sister-in-law already and began calling me 'sis' the day they got engaged. With my beer in hand, he eagerly finished his mushroom. "Gawds, these are delicious." I laughed. Sometimes his southern drawl showed up when he was truly relaxed.

He pointed one finger at the picture. "Bonnie Keys. That's Beverly Keys' sister. I ran into her at the station when I dropped in to talk with Pete."

"Sonofa-" Crystal slapped the table, hard. "Yes!"

Liam raised an eyebrow. Slate seemed nonplussed by her response and started digging into the mushrooms.

"Apparently, we need to see her." Mica smiled warmly at Liam.

"And soon- tomorrow." Amber grabbed her book and put it back in her backpack, then started collecting the others. "I'll put these back for safe-keeping while we smack beer and sauce-laden tables all over the place." She gave Crystal a smirk.

Crystal frowned. "Good idea. Sorry."

I looked at the guys. "Amber made us some beautiful books, our new grimoires; then she ground some herbs and magically found her lost ring by following the inching herb dust; Mica made Crystal a scrying cauldron and Crystal saw a vision of Bonnie, right over there." I pointed to the patio rail. "We found a sacred cavern in the mountain and were blessed by Gaia and, oh yeah, I saw Jade's father. He gave me a bone ring. Yep. That sums it up." I took my beer back and dove into a mushroom.

Now it was Liam and Slate's turn to look dazed.

"Sonofa-" Slate repeated Crystal's words, and her table slap. "I knew I should have gone to mount Shasta. I knew it!"

"You have a pretty strong gift already, remember?" Mica ran her fingers through Slate's hair with one hand, then patted in back into place, squeezing his ear with gentle affection.

"Several," Liam said with an evil smile.

"Liam!" I slapped his arm, laughing as I did so. It was so rare for Liam to say anything risqué that it made everyone laugh.

"Yes, true. But I didn't get a grimoire." Slate looked at Amber pointedly. She bit her lip and looked away. "Can you tell us about those?"

"You said we can't write in them yet. Why?" I was suddenly eager to start writing down everything while it was still fresh.

Amber opened her mouth to speak, then frowned and shook her head. "Can we make that a part of the 'later' discussion?" She leaned across the table to gently touch Slate's hand once. "We're giving ourselves a few days to digest what happened in the mountain."

"In," Liam said quietly. "You all keep saying 'in,' not 'on.'"

"Yep." Crystal answered. "In."

Amber continued. "I had quite an adventure in getting these made. I don't think we're supposed to use them for general ideas and musings- we need to keep a separate book for that. What goes into these has to be... earned."

She looked at Slate again. "Join us. We're going to talk about everything. I actually do have a book for you, but it's not done. I don't know why. I started it in the same frenzy and theirs, but then it just, it stalled. I'm waiting for something, but not sure what it might be."

Slate got up from his chair and walked around the table, gave Amber a quick kiss on top of her head and returned to his seat. Everything was good.

Right then the waiter returned with our drinks and two different appetizer trays. "On the house," he said with a smile. I'd smile too- when you bring free food and drinks to people, you get a great tip.   When he left, Amber talked about the grimoires. "The paper needs to last. The pens included are the best kind of ink to use. You know, the oldest surviving books were from the Etruscan era."

"Wow." That was impressive. "How could papyrus last that long?"

She shook her head. "They used flattened sheets of gold."

"That could get expensive." Liam took a fried oyster from a tray and passed it around. I just handed it on when it was my turn- no bottom-feeders for me.

"But you wrote in yours," I reminded her. "How did you know it was time?"

Amber sighed deeply. "There's a cost." Then she reached up and removed the scarf around her head. It had been positioned to partially cover her forehead. As she removed it, a long bandage was revealed, running across her entire forehead.

"Oh, what happened?" Mica jumped up, knocking the table hard this time. Somehow, very little spilled.

"I'm okay. Ten stitches. Scar should be minimal, if any. They made them super tiny. I'm okay. Sit down, sit down." Since she was so much younger than the rest of us, it wasn't easy to corral five worried bodies back to their seats.

"Are you saying we have to make a blood offering to use the grimoires?" Mica pulled her shawl close, then freed her hair to cover her shoulders. I really hated her sometimes. If I freed my hair after pinning it up, I looked like I had just crawled out of bed.

"Hopefully not." Amber wrapped her shawl around her head again with Crystal's help. Then she frowned. "It wasn't the blood, it was the stubbornness I had to give up."

Slate snorted. "You are the least stubborn of any of us. These guys are going to have to sacrifice fingers, and my sister's going to need to lose a whole limb."

"True," I frowned.

Amber held up her hands. "I think the first lesson is to improve listening skills." She took a small sip of her drink. We all looked sufficiently chastised and waited patiently.

"You may have noticed, I sometimes can be a bit clumsy." I wasn't the only one biting my lip on that. "And I never really thought about it, but the whole thing is about me not paying attention to things that I'm not focused on." She shared the details about finding her grandmother's ring with Liam and Slate. They acted like they wanted to speak but held it back.

"It's probably easy to accept that my grandmother's ring isn't the only thing I've lost. After Mist left, I discovered that the ring could help me create the right herb mix to find the right item." She looked at her ring for a long moment. "I don't know what it meant to my grandmother, but it certainly is a tool. I tested it a half-dozen times." She turned it out to face us. "With this, I found everything I could think to find.

"But crap, I kept tripping over my own feet, I knocked things off tables, and I pulled the greenhouse water system out of the ground at the entrance. Then I took out my book and started to write out the herb mixes that worked. Somehow, I hit the wall with the table at just the amount of force and the right angle to knock my decorative scythe down off the wall and right onto my face!" She pointed to her forehead.

"Too much. Even I'm not that clumsy. So, while getting my stitches, I did some soul searching about my consistent clumsiness." She sighed. "It's not just that I don't pay attention to my immediate surroundings while I'm working on a project, I don't pay attention to anything outside of my life. I'm disconnected from the world. I don't get involved with others, I don't help out, volunteer, you know, do unto others and all that jazz."

"Oh honey, no." Mica reached forward across the table. "You're just twenty-two. You're asking too much of yourself."

"Good grief," I began. "You have your own home. How many people your age can say that?"

"Exactly." Amber sighed. "How many people my age are so into their own thing that they can buy a home while still a teenager, like I did three years ago? They're usually just finishing college, heading to the Peace Corps and crap."

"You're being way too hard on yourself." Liam shook his head.

"No, you all are being way too easy on me. And that's what

these books require. We have to take some serious time to look at ourselves. I have been so wrapped up in making my flower business a success since I was, what, fourteen? Do you know I have never volunteered for anything? I have never donated clothes for a clothing drive."

"Amber," I started.

"No. She's right." Crystal reached forward to pile some fish onto her plate. "Sorry, sweetie. But I agree. At twenty-two, you should have done some volunteer work for others by now. You should be more aware of what's going on in your community."

Amber nodded sadly. "Yeah, I've been too involved in my own interests." Tears were threatening to spill from her eyes. "I don't know how I deserved anything in the mountain. I mean, I've always thought myself special, you know- talent to grow things, to understand the needs of my plants." She sighed loudly. "But I've never used it to help my neighbors grow their plants, heal their sick trees, volunteer at the city parks or the state parks for that matter. I mean, even if I wanted to totally ignore humans and all the crap we cause ourselves, I never offered my skill to help the natural world. I just sat up there on my green throne and thought 'How worthy am I?'" She rubbed the side of her nose as she dropped her head down.

"Once I, hmm, accepted this about myself, I was able to see the swirls on the sides of the pages. I didn't design them, I just grabbed the pen and traced. Then the words and the herb recipes fell into place. So that's that." She let out a long sigh. "I suck."

After a few moments of shared silence, Liam spoke up. "You have met me, right?" He waved his hands. "Hello, Amber Greene. My name is Liam Lindsey and I'm with the Illinois state E! P! A!" He reached across the table to shake her hand as we all released the tension.

"I'm happy to inform you that we are re-instating the River Watch, Forest Watch and Prairie Watch volunteer programs. We need citizen scientists to take one weekend of training, and then collect data throughout the year, ten days max."

"It's being reinstated? How wonderful! Amber, I did the forest and river watch when it was running a few years ago. The training is really interesting and the work, while hot and messy, is fun."

"Hot and messy? I'm in!" Mica reached for the mushrooms.

"Mica," Slate began, but Liam put a hand on his shoulder.

"Let Mica be Mica. Lord knows we get enough grief just being ourselves."

"Let us a raise a glass," I began with a thump to the table. "To thine own self, be ever true." I spoke louder than intended.

The hoorahs echoed as other patrons raised a glass as well. Any excuse for a toast would do in Springfield these days.

I looked out as the moonlight danced in the road. A line of Uber cars awaited all who needed them- something Jasper made sure happened with up-front tips. As my throat tightened and my eyes burned a little, I raised a silent glass to Jasper, to the drivers, and to my parents. I caught Slate's eye and with a tiny nod, he did the same.

CHAPTER NINE

"How did it go with the city on the bank mural project?" Mica waited for me on the front porch. I spoke to her through one of the opened windows as I finished helping the crew clean up. What an insane morning. Fridays. People like to start the weekend with a treat, even if they still have a day left of the work week. Well, some do. The politicians often take Fridays off and head back to their homes in Chicago and around the state.

Mica leaned down so she could look at me through the screen as I wiped a table. "I'm going to make you a new sign." The she stood up straight and paced the porch.

I finished a few more chores and ran upstairs to change out of my work clothes. I didn't want to meet Bonnie smelling like pastries and coffee. I put on a light sweater with nice jeans and grabbed my mother's wrap I often wore. When I joined Mica on the porch, she had her hair thrown over one shoulder and was gently stroking it. I looked around, expecting to see a good-looking man, but there was no one. I shrugged to myself- I guess she does it without thinki… Oops, no. A man was getting out of his Tesla across the street. Lobbyist. However, the scowl on Mica's face as she looked up at my sign made me think she hadn't seen him.

"Must be some sort of internal sensor," I mumbled.

"Hmm? What was that, Mist?" She smiled and joined me.

I shook my head with a laugh. "Nothing. What's wrong with my sign?"

"Pbththt." She threw her head back as she dropped her hair. "They must have said a hundred times, in not-so subtle ways, that it needed to be 'family friendly.' Look at him! I see riskier pictures on gym billboards. Those women have enough skin showing that they should be wearing tassels." She put her hands on her hips. "Nope. I love him." She turned to me sharply, pointing at her shirtless Lincoln image. "He stays put."

I raised my hands in defeat. "I never planned on taking him down, even if you wanted to make a new one. I love him. And to tell you the truth, I get a million compliments on this sign from the tourists. We should put in on some mugs and shirts, Mica. The city is just wrong- it's not a negative."

"Would you mind telling them that?"

"No," I replied, heading to my car in the back. "I need to get renovations approved to expand to the second floor. I can't afford to lose one council member."

"You've decided to expand, then?"

"I meant if I renovate. If. I haven't even looked at the notebook from Nic. I really need to give it some attention this weekend." I stopped in the courtyard for a second to look at the blooms coming up. "You know, I should have mentioned to Amber that she has done something for others- look at these gorgeous bulbs coming up. She planted them in the fall and wouldn't let me do more than cover the costs. Most came from thinning her own beds. This is going to be phenomenal in a few weeks. People were taking their orders out here this morning and I know it's because of these new blooms. I can't wait until the urns out front bloom again- she worked magic on them, for sure."

"I'd let it be. She has a heart of gold, but she believes she should do more. I say we let her lose on the world." She did a quick twirl, enjoying the warm spring day. Six in a row. What a treat! I couldn't remember having this many nice days in early spring, much less all together.

Liam had given us Bonnie's address last night after a quick call to his friend on the force. He'd simply told them we wanted to offer the family our support. Bonnie lived in one of those areas it was hard to describe. The houses were almost one hundred years old. Some had beautifully maintained homes and manicured lawns, then you'd turn the corner to the same style of homes but in bad shape. One more turn and it was well kempt homes that were a bit newer, then another turn to homes that were one step away from being abandoned.

The address took us to a maple lined street with modest homes where everyone took obvious pride in their front yards. Lilacs were coming into bloom and a variety of bulbs were displayed in every yard. The homes here were set a bit further back and partially hidden by large trees, except for Bonnie's. Her house was a two-story Tudor set close to the front with a wrap-around porch and beautifully ornate flower stands that I wanted to steal and put in the courtyard.

The driveway was wide, and we could see a guest cottage at the back of the property, tucked away behind large hydrangeas and small, flowering dogwoods. The placement of the two buildings provided plenty of yard space and the cottage looked to be the same age and style as the main house.

We parked on the street and walked up to the beautiful porch to find a cement bowl on a table close to the rails. It was filled with water and had pink flower petals floating around in it. What a neat idea- if you're going to provide a bird bath, go all the way.

"All that needs is a tiny gopher statue at the edge, setting up a nail station." Mica flicked the water as we rang the doorbell.

"Hello." A short woman with gray hair answered the door. I could see the family resemblance immediately. "Oh, I know you!" She opened the screen door wide to invite us in. As soon as I was in the entrance, she threw herself into my arms.

I looked at Mica over her head. '*What do I do?*' I mouthed the words.

'*Hug her. Hug her! Mist!*'

'*Fine.*' I gently held the strange little woman and let her get it out. I could feel her tears soak my shirt, and my heart opened at that- she was really grieving. I suddenly felt like the Grinch when he was being mean to that adorable, little puppy.

"We'd like to ask you a few questions, if you're up to it." Mica said softly after the hug had gone on for a while.

"Oh, of course. I'm so sorry. It's just, I haven't had much hope this week. She's been gone since Sunday and the police don't have a single lead. If you hadn't taken them to her car, we wouldn't know anything."

She invited us to sit down on a soft flowered sofa. The room looked like a formal sitting room and was appropriately decorated for that goal. Lots of sitting spaces.

We declined her offer of coffee and I decided to jump right into it. "Bonnie, do you know why Beverly started coming to the café, and why she came every night?"

"I told the police, but they didn't seem to believe it." She grabbed some tissue. "It seems clear to me. She wanted to talk to you about something she wanted you to figure out. She saw the article in the paper. It was pretty impressive the way you found all those hidden details, and after more than one-hundred years at that. And since she's only focused on work and our gardens, well, there's no mystery about the bird baths so it must be work related, right?" It took her a moment to catch her breath, having said it all at once. "Oh shoot, and she volunteers at the senior citizen. I should have told them that, perhaps."

"Oh my," Mica said soothingly. She had her hair over her shoulder again, stroking it. Well I'll be damned. It seemed to be calming Bonnie down as she watched. Huh. I looked at Mica, frowning, and mouthed the word '*freak.*' She just smiled wider.

"Do you know what this mystery might be?"

"I haven't a clue. She wouldn't say anything except that it was important to her. She's, oh I don't want to speak badly of her. She has a heart of gold. But she is not good with people outside of work. I've visited her there, you know, heading to lunch and such. She spoke so forcefully to her subordinates and was just wonderful with her boss, Lauren Reynolds. Very professional. But outside of work," she wiped her face again as tears fell. "She's painfully shy. She can't even speak to the mailman. It's a real problem. That's why she lives in the cottage- she can't handle dealing with a landlord, or even a real-estate agent. I don't know how she's able to work, but I don't press. She puts on a different personality and makes it work. She does it."

"Yet she volunteers with the elderly?"

Bonnie nodded. "Only because our mother worked there and she practically grew up in that center. I don't think a week of her life since the age of ten has gone by without her being there, and I mean that literally."

"Bonnie, would you mind if we took a look at her cottage? We might be able to see something the police missed."

She looked at us skeptically.

"You know," I said leaning in with a soft voice in a secretive manner. "The way we found some of those clues in Chicago was inside the house, even though the police had been over it thoroughly and it had been renovated."

That seemed to work. She led us to the cottage along a well-worn path behind the house and unlocked the door.

The place was warm and comfortable. It seemed Beverly had a thing for flowers inside the house as well as there were planters overflowing in every corner.

"This is lovely." Mica smiled with real appreciation. She liked a balanced room and the colors were soothing, but not mundane. Mica walked around the large room which was a combination living/dining/cooking space. There were two doors at the back, one for a bedroom and bathroom, I presumed. Mica glanced at me, shaking her head. She found nothing out of the ordinary.

"What a beautiful bay window seat." I had wandered into the kitchen area that had a small table with only one chair. The other side was a well-cushioned window seat that could hold three people.   "That was Bev's perch where she would spy on the birds." Bonnie smiled. Then a look of horror crossed her face. "Oh my god, I said '*was.*'" She made a gulping sound and ran from the house.

"Poor thing," I said softly, watching her leave. "Oh hey, Mica. Come here." When I looked up to watch Bonnie leave, my eyes rested on the three-month calendar hanging on the fridge. I moved closer, flipping the calendar back a month, then another.

Mica walked over and looked at it before finally shrugging. "What is it? I don't see anything."

"Look here." I pointed to the first day of the month. In very neat penmanship, Beverly had written 'Jason Hurley.' "And here," I turned to the previous month. Again, on the first of the month she'd written a name. 'Paul Shims.' February had three names on the first day- 'Marta Wend, Teri Muir, Sydney Lief.'

Mica already had her notebook out and wrote down the names and dates. "I'm not sure I see the importance of these, oh wait." She pointed her pen at me as her eyes went wide.

"Exactly," I smiled. "For someone who can't talk in public, she has a busy social calendar. We have to presume these are either people from work or people at the senior citizen."

"And that's more than we had before." Mica punched my arm as she cackled. She glanced at her watch. "Amber and Crystal should be taking the tour at the Lincoln home right about now. When are we meeting them at the café?"

"One o'clock. I can't wait to hear how Amber's spell worked."

"We've got extra time. Senior citizen center? And I have the perfect reason- it's right next to the old bank. When I was looking at the space, I wondered if they'd let me have some tendrils extending to their building. Now we can find out." She did that head-toss-pile-everything-up-high-with-a-couple-of-hair-sticks thing.

I turned to the door, covering my laugh with a cough. She could keep trying, but those things never held her hair up for more than a few minutes. She still carried them in her purse, determined to find a way. She said it was a geometry problem and she just needed to find the right angles. I ran my hands through my rather thin, just below the shoulders-length hair. Blond and brown layered locks wasn't anything impressive, but at least it wasn't such a pain to manipulate. I envied Mica's hair for its beauty, but not for its upkeep.

Come to think of it, I have the most mundane look of any in the galère'. Crystal has long straight white hair with beautiful streaks of lavender, Mica's hair is right out of a scene in Avalon, and Amber sports a spunky look with her short, red, bouncy locks that dance when she laughs. My hair just kind of hangs there. Like hair.

It didn't take long to get to the center in the old part of the downtown area. The building has a large space in front reserved for buses and several covered benches as well. The small parking lot on the side of the building, which marked the end of the block, reserved more than half of the spaces for handicap parking. We ended up parking in the back- a small alley with allotted parking spaces running parallel with the building. I was glad it was a clean alley- those seem to be vanishing these days as the town grew.

We saw Beverly the moment we entered the center. A large poster was hanging over the receptionist's table and showed a photo of Beverly reading to a small group of elderly women. Several of the women were knitting or crocheting. Some just looked off into space as though mesmerized by the story she read. Beverly looked more relaxed than I'd ever seen at the café. Below, it read MISSING, begged for people to report any information they may have and then listed the police contact information.

Mica moved to the receptionist desk but I headed to a large lounge to the right. There were small versions of the same poster taped to the walls and support posts. I stopped to look at one more closely.

"It's a real shame, isn't it?" A tall, elderly woman paused next to me, looking at the flyer. She had beautiful posture and was dressed in a simple, but elegant white pantsuit. Her gray hair was cut short and curled around her face. "Did you know her?"

"A little. She came into my coffeeshop in the evenings." I smiled.

"Beverly? Huh, that's surprising. I'm Ellen. I've known her since I started volunteering here decades ago. I do hope they find her." She offered her hand in greeting.

"Me too. We were the ones who notified the police, and our friends." I gestured to Mica.

"Oh, that coffeeshop! The one with the sign." She nodded. "Yes, I read about that in paper. I also ready about what you did up in Chicago. Are you assisting the police?" She looked hopeful.

I shook my head. "Not in any official capacity. But we are trying to see if we can uncover anything that might help. Would you mind answering a few things for me?"

Ellen was more than ready to help and gave me a quick tour of the center, explaining how Beverly read to the patrons who had vision problems. "It started as an exploration of the classics, but somewhere along the way, it shifted to those steamy historical romances." Ellen laughed with a twinkle in her eye. "I can see why she chose your café."

I grimaced. Perhaps I did need a new sign. "You said you've been here for decades, Ellen. Do you recall anyone named Jason Hurley, or Paul Shims?"

"No, those names don't ring a bell. I have a great memory and make a point to get to know everyone who comes here." She tapped her forehead twice. "Dancing keeps the brain sharp, keep that in mind. I taught ballroom dancing for years and I'm still sharp as a tack."

That explained her great posture as well. I asked her about the other names and if she could think of any other places that Beverly liked to frequent.

"There are none. But then again, I didn't know she visited your café regularly, so perhaps Bev has a few secrets still." She smiled sadly. "I hope I have the chance to ask her."

"Me too." I placed a gentle hand on her shoulder and she tapped it several times, looking away and losing herself in thoughts of Beverly.

Mica and I met at the door a few minutes later. I told her about sharp-minded Ellen and she reported the receptionist didn't recognize the names as well. Then I told her that we were all taking ballroom dancing when we hit fifty.

"No need. I know all about the connection between mental sharpness and dancing. It's improvisational dance that's key, like ballroom dancing, and our own American Tribal Style classes, to a lesser degree. Picture a couple dancing in the ballroom- each movement is decided and communicated, or responded to, in a breath. Press the waist to tell your partner to step back and Bam! New neural pathway created. That kind of dance is just a constant flow of making instantaneous decisions- improv. So, it's just a constant flow of making new pathways in the brain."

"Well that makes sense. I think my brain hurt the first time I had to take the lead and decide all those cues on the spot."

Mica laughed as we got into the car and headed back to the café. "Exactly. Improv dancing is pure brain energy."

"Well then you're going to live to be three hundred, the way you change patterns and movements on us constantly. Dancing with you in the lead is exhausting."

"See how much I love you guys?" She laughed. "Welcome to the torture chamber that's good for your mind." I frowned at her, to which she replied, "Now that you've seen the benefits on Ellen, I'll see what I can do to kick things up a notch."

With a groan, I pulled back into the garage behind my home and café. I never knew which to call it. Yes, it was home, but mostly it was the café. Maybe moving to a place with a real yard and without a brewery next door was the right thing to do. I was enjoying living right in town and walking to places. Jade was close to just about everything she needed. But it also had its downsides. We were barely through the café doors before Amber grabbed my hands and pulled me upstairs to the private home. I glanced over my shoulder and saw Crystal pushing Mica.

"I wanted to grab a drink," I started, but Crystal interrupted me by yelling to the kitchen over her shoulder.

"Can you bring up four iced teas, please?"

"And a bite," Mica said.

"Plus some grilled veggie rolls? Thanks." Nic whacked her on the tush with his dishtowel, and I wasn't sure if Crystal's 'thanks' was for the food or the smack.

"I take it things went well?" As soon as we were in the sitting room next to the balcony, Amber started jumping up and down with her hands clasped liked a three-year-old. I realized that she had something held in her hands.

"Chill out, sweetie," Mica laughed.

"Oh no." Crystal pointed a finger at her, long strands of white and lavender flying around as she turned. "No, no, no! We need to shout it from the rooftop. I'm ready to stand on the top gable and squeal away with her." Crystal started laughing at her own words and tumbled into one of the wingchairs lining two walls. She looked more exhausted than ready to climb.

"Yes, it worked." Amber pulled a chair to one of the wooden tables in the middle of the room. I didn't keep the tables set unless an event was scheduled. She placed a small, common orange/brown notebook in the center of the table, the kind found in every office supply store.

"Oh, oh," Mica pulled a chair up and picked it up.

"The spell worked?" I really didn't need to ask, but I wanted to hear her story.

"Yes, and you know what's really interesting about it this time? Rosemary." She spoke with a finality, as though that said it all. Crystal nodded emphatically and giggled like a school girl. I was beginning to wonder if they had smoked some of this 'rosemary.'

"I'm going to need a bit more." I opened the patio door as Tammy brought us up a tray of glasses filled with ice and a pitcher of tea. She'd also grabbed an assortment of pastries left from the breakfast rush. I absolutely loved a woman who agreed that dessert should come first.

"Tammy," I exclaimed, looking at the tray as she started to leave. I held up a green twig. "What's this?"

She shrugged. "They're planted right next to the patio stairs and I pinched a long stem to add to the tray." She shrugged again. "It just seemed the thing to do and it smells wonderful." She sniffed her fingertips. "I hate to wash my hands," she said with a laugh and left.

I turned to face Amber, holding the stem up for her to see. "You were saying?"

Crystal started laughing so hard she cried. Mica just shook her head as she smiled and returned to the notebook.

"Rosemary? Oh, I wonder if Tammy should be brought into the galère'?"

I hadn't thought about that before. We did seem to work well together. Maybe there was more to it. "But what is it about rosemary, Amber?" I filled the glasses as she continued.

"Every time I practiced the finding spell at home, I knew exactly what it was I wanted to find. The herbs changed, depending on my connection to that item- that's key. What did the item mean to me, how did it make me feel? Nostalgic? Something to do with money issues? Something that was a gift from someone I loved, or disliked?"

I wasn't sure I understood, but I nodded for her to continue. "But for this event, I didn't know what it was. How do you find something that A- you didn't lose, and B- you can't describe?"

"Then I touched some rosemary and it felt, oh what, extremely familiar, yes. Familiar. I cook with it all the time, I brush the bushes every time I pass to release the scent, I use it in the closet and drawer pouches with lavender." She sat back to drink her tea as though that explained everything.

"To balance out a complete unknown, she needed to have something completely her own." Crystal dragged her chair to the table.

"Oh, I see. And how poetic." I smirked at Crystal. "How were you able to release the herbs outside the house? Didn't the tour guides keep you close."

Crystal began. "That was the strange thing. When we arrived, I saw Emma first and asked about the tours. She said that they are ridiculously understaffed right now, and Fay would be giving the late morning tour herself, by herself. They should have had three new people join in February."

I glanced at Mica just as she looked up at me.

"At first," Crystal continued, "I wondered if we should go back and try another day, but we really don't have time to spare, do we." She made it a statement. "So, I walked over to Fay, buttered her up by saying her remark about how we locals don't participate in the historical gems we have here had really gotten to me, yadda yadda." She took a drink, nodding to the patio door at the same time.

I opened it so Tammy could bring in our Mediterranean sandwiches. They were grilled veggies with fresh herbs and local cheeses on hoagie rolls, which meant they were kind of smushed when grilled. Nic and I had created the recipe together the first year we opened and it was still our biggest seller- Portabella mushrooms, roasted red peppers pre-marinated in a garlic, basil and black pepper sauce, sautéed onions, eggplant and zucchini. Yum.

Between bites, Crystal continued. "Anyway, Fay took it hook, line, and stinger."

"Sinker," I corrected. "Have you ever fished?"

She looked thoughtful a moment. "Actually, I don't think I have. Hmm, isn't that strange? After all the field trips I've taken with your folks, you would think we would have ended the day fishing at least once." She shrugged. "Okay then, sinker. Fay corralled about thirty people together and we headed out."

"Thirty?" Mica looked up. "That seems a bit on the heavy side for those tours through small hallways and viewing spots that are five feet wide."

Amber nodded vigorously and tried to speak but gave up and waved at Crystal as she had taken too big a bite. It was hard to take tiny bites of a thick sandwich.

Crystal dunked a piece of her hoagie into the cream cheese

of her pastry. I frowned and she caught it. "The bread taste like basil bread because of that sauce on the peppers. It's heavenly with the cream."

Of course, we all had to try it.

"I'm not putting that on the menu," I said as I rubbed my tongue with my napkin. She ignored me.

"I've been on that tour in years past, and this was a mess. While she could lead us all through the streets and gardens with no issue, when we got to the house, she would take ten people in, thoroughly lecture those outside to touch nothing, then lead the ten through the house and out the other side, lecture them over there, and collect ten more."

"It was stupid," Amber said through her food. At least I think that's what she said. "And perfect." She swallowed and then took a deep drink.

"That meant people were milling around outside, and since we knew where Beverly Keys had been dragged, it really wasn't difficult to wait for the area to be clear before I poured out the herbs. They made a beeline along the ground, under the edge of a brick that was partially broken at the base of the house. The color of the notebook is the same as the bricks. It must have fallen and apparently bounced, as it was up above and behind the broken piece. No police would have ever seen that. I had to feel around for it."

She looked at Mica sternly. "And I didn't like that. I know the kind of things that lurk behind broken bricks and crawl around the dark places."

"It was worth it," Mica replied, lifting the book to me. "Mist, look here." She pointed near the bottom of the page and read out loud:

2/1- 3 people; 3/1- 1 person; 4/1- 1 person

"And we know that three people were supposed to be hired-"
"In February." Crystal finished her sentence with a hard thump to the table.

"What's on the rest of the page?" I leaned over Mica's shoulder.

"To me, this looks like a notebook she kept next to the phone. While talking, she must have made notes of conversations. She has a date and name above new entries, and then a topic line and comments made. But this page starts out the same, and then interrupts with this entry."

"Does it have a name before the entry?" Amber refilled everyone's glasses, adding two packages of raw sugar to her own.

I watched Mica run her finger across the top of the page and then down. It had the same system. Her finger stopped at the one just above the dates:

4/10 10:38 A.M. Marta Wend
-Checking on new start date- it's been two months
      -Start date has been changed four times (?)
      -Has other job offer and must know a definite date
TD*unaware of new hirings- need to check

"Marta Wend," Mica and I shouted as looked at each other.

Quickly, we shared what we'd discovered with Crystal and Amber.

Amber tapped the table. "Beverly discovered something odd on the tenth, the paper breaks the story about us on the twelfth, and she started coming in to the café, when?"

"Yeah, it was right about then." I nodded.

"Is this enough to take to the police?" Mica put the notebook on the table.

Amber started waving her hands excitedly. "But wait, wait! There's more to our story. It wasn't just my magic in use today." She grinned at Crystal.

Crystal was silent a moment, obviously trying to decide how much to share. "My gifts are in air, specifically in communication. That makes sense- I'm a writer, right? Scrying is a form of communication. "She got up and paced.

"Crystal," Amber said after a few moments. "Just say it. It was so Gucci."

Crystal laughed quietly. "It would appear, that I can put a

suggestion into some people's mind- a gentle nudge to share their thoughts on things. I can, um, make people communicate, a little?" She shrugged. "Something like that."

"Exactly like that." Amber jumped up. "When every group had finally gone through the Lincoln house and we all gathered on the road, Crystal here whispered to me that she wished someone else in the group would bring up Beverly. And Bam! A woman, who couldn't possibly have overhead us, asked Fay about it. And you were looking right at her, weren't you?"

Crystal agreed. "Yes, I had spoken out loud more to myself than to Amber, really, and was kind of lost in thought, looking at this lady with the brightest red hair I've ever seen. And then she asked." She shrugged again. "So, of course, I had to try it a few more times."

"More like a few dozen times. She focused on every single person on the tour."

"We really weren't learning anything new, and I didn't have specific questions, so I started nudging people to ask about things they really wanted to know about Springfield. I was thinking the tour itself, but I wasn't specific and folks started asking Fay all kinds of questions."

"The weird thing is, Fay got completely flustered with one lady's question." Amber jumped in. "She asked if Fay knew anything about the recent rumors flying around that the Dana Thomas House is haunted. We perked right up at that- it's a Frank Lloyd Wright design and recent matters...." She trailed off, her hand stretching forward then falling away. "She went on to say that they had taken the ghost tour down by the Old State Capitol, and the company was trying to decide if they wanted to add the Dana Thomas House into the tour. They said at least half-a-dozen people have heard strange sounds coming from there."

"And it's closed for a renovation right now, isn't it?" It seemed the paper had mentioned something about the springs under the floor of the two-story ballroom needing repairs, and they decided to close the entire house.

"Yes, just at the start of this month." Amber confirmed.

"And Fay's face became flushed." Crystal's hand rose to her face as she excitedly described the events. "She tried to change the topic but I urged more comments. People said things like 'no one has seen any workers there,' and 'banging noises have been heard in the dead of night.' With every comment, she seemed more flustered and actually yelled for everyone's attention and then changed to the topic of the kitchen gardens."

"It was really weird." Amber nodded.

"We waited out the rest of the tour and then came straight here. I don't know if Fay's involved with anything about Beverly, but there's definitely something worrying her about the Dana Thomas House."

"Did you try and get her to say anything about it?" Mica asked.

"No," Crystal shook her head. "The opportunity seemed over. I didn't want to jar the conversation- it would have seemed out of place."

"I agree," Amber added. "What she did felt like a natural conversation of the people gathering. Nothing was out of place. It was brilliant work."

"I suppose we need to be careful about that sort of thing." I resisted the urge to see if I could start a fire in my hands.

"So, what do we do now, galère'?" Mica collected empty plates and tidied the table. "We have a few possibilities."

"I think Crystal and I should visit Beverly's office. She can see if an opportunity arises to ask about those names, and I can read Lauren Reynold's aura to see if she's hiding something." At least, I hoped I could.

"Why don't Amber and I go back to Beverly's home." Mica pushed her chair back to the wall and everyone followed her lead to do the same. "We were so eager to check those names, Mist, that we didn't check her bedroom. I wonder if she kept a notebook there? Either way, I'd really like to buy one of your hanging baskets, Amber and give it to Bonnie. She's really suffering and we were empty handed when we visited today."

"You're right," agreed. "We don't want to take food as though someone died, but I think a basket to brighten the patio would be appreciated. They love flowers."

"I appreciate the offer of payment, Mica, but this one's on me. Let's head over to the greenhouse and pick out something special."

"No," I said, much more sharply than I had intended. My eyes widened in surprise at my own words. "No, you need to go there first. I... I don't know why, but you should go straight there." I felt so helpless trying to figure out why that was true, but I knew it was. I shrugged. "It's a hunch. Maybe, um, maybe you can ask her to go with you to the greenhouse and pick out her own basket? I don't know. But I feel strongly that you should head over there right now. Now. Go." I felt a little dizzy with this hunch, unlike the few before. It was a hundred times stronger, insistent.

"Then we're off." Mica grabbed her wrap and put some money on the tray for Tammy. We all did the same and I placed it on the patio, knowing she would be by to pick it up before long.

THE STATE'S HISTORICAL preservation offices were north of town in a converted bridge, of all things. It was architecturally interesting- a glass tunnel of rooms built directly over a large running river. Technically the space belonged to the Illinois Department of Natural Resources, but the preservation groups had space in it as well about midway across the bridge.

Crystal had to get to work as soon as we entered as the receptionist showed zero inclinations to let us through to Lauren Ryan's office. "I'm sorry ladies, but I can't. I'm just a temp and have only been here one week, but I'm quite certain Ms. Ryan will not see anyone without an appointment."

"I think we had an appointment, Cheryl, right?" Crystal leaned in close after glancing at the employee badge the receptionist wore. "Something that was scheduled before you started here. I'm sure," she stressed the words and looked intently at the young woman, "that we are right on time."

Cheryl put a hand to her brow, frowning. "Of, of course Ms. Thapa, Ms. Butler. I'm sorry I didn't see it. I'm sure, I'm sure it was here just a minute ago." She scrolled through a few pages on her computer screen, shaking her head. "Where did I just see your names?" She was mumbling to herself, then she sighed and looked at us with a smile. "I'll go announce you if you'll just wait a moment."

As she walked away, Crystal and I did a little high five. We could hear voices in the other room, one of them rising with anger a bit, but then Cheryl came out with a sheepish grin and motioned us forward.   She suddenly gripped the edge of the door and brought her hand to her temple. "Ooh," she said quietly, then looked at us with a small laugh. "Wow. Sudden headache. I've never had one hit like that before." She smiled and walked to her chair. As we watched, she grabbed the back of it and rubbed her temples with the other hand.

Crystal looked at me with a frown and started to move back, but we were at the door and Lauren Ryan was greeting us. I shook my head at Crystal, once, and moved forward with an outstretched hand. We would check on Cheryl before we left.

"It's good to finally meet you, Ms. Ryan."

"Please, it's Lauren. Though, have we met? You look very familiar?"

"Oh, I'm glad you recognize us," I smiled, turning to Crystal briefly. "It was probably in the paper. We solved the mystery of why the murder took place at Frank Lloyd Wright's lake-home in Chicago." She knotted her brows briefly and I noticed a dull color flare around her entire body. It was gone in an instant.

I glanced at Crystal who gave me an emphatic 'no way' motion with her hand. I pinched my fingers together as though to say 'just a tiny bit' and she reluctantly nodded. I knew I'd have to guide the conversation in the right place first, though.

"That's why we made the appointment with your office a few weeks ago-to follow up on some details about his work here in Springfield." Yep, we were on to something. A light blue aura came into full focus. She was on edge. Okay, Lloyd's work in Springfield. What's going on?

"But first, we are so sorry to learn that it was your assistant who is missing." I sat down and watched her light blue aura spike to dark for a quick moment. Interesting. "I'm not sure if you know, but it was from my coffeeshop that Liam Lindsey saw it happen." Oh wow. Blue to orange. I hadn't seen that yet. "We'd love to help in any way we can, you know." I watched Crystal give her a strong look with a slight tug of chin.

"Well if she wasn't so nosy, like you," Lauren said without a pause. Then she sat back and blinked rapidly. "I mean, I mean... Oh, I'm so sorry I said that. I'm just upset about Beverly, please forgive me." She quickly straightened a few things on her desk.

Crystal must have just given a simple nudge to say what was on her mind, I deduced. Nothing forced or against what she might want to do, like she had done to Cheryl.

"Of course, of course." I said sympathetically, waving it off with my best shopkeeper smile.

"Lauren," Crystal began gently as she placed a hand on the desk. "We won't keep you today, what with all the chaos and we're sure you're worried." I saw her aura glow a very happy, pastel blue at those words. "We just want you to know," Crystal continued, her voice slowing down, "that if anything is worrying you, hanging on your shoulders, we would love to be of help if we can."

Lauren immediately held up one finger to us. "Just a moment if you please- I must have something checked." She turned her chair to face a side table with a phone system and pushed a button. "Cheryl, I need you to confirm that the workers are not starting back on work with the orphanage before Wednesday, right away." She turned back to us before Cheryl had a chance to reply, rising.

While she was distracted, I tried to get one more thought in. "Or if there's any mistake we can help remedy...?"

"That is very kind of you. But unless you can go back in time and change email accounts, I can't think of a thing." She frowned and blinked several times. "Yes, it would help if we could reschedule this conversation about the work of Frank Lloyd Wright in this area another time. I appreciate it."

"Of course. We hope there's some good new before the weekend is over." I saw Chrystal tilt her head. "Oh, there will definitely be news before then." Lauren whispered to herself, but I heard it.

Turning back as though a thought had just occurred to me, I raised a finger. "The orphanage you just mentioned wouldn't by any chance be the one Eva Monroe started, would it? The Lincoln Colored Home? I'm glad to hear it's finally getting the attention it deserves."

Lauren sat back down and I saw her aura turn completely white, blanched of any decency. It was so unnatural that I shivered. Her reply was cold and short. "Yes, we've finally been able to purchase it." She turned to her computer. We were dismissed.

As we walked out, Cheryl waved softly to us as she picked up the phone. Her face looked exhausted and she kept one hand to her head. Just as we reached the door, we heard her talking to Lauren through the phone and listened intently from the other side.

"I'm sorry, Ms. Ryan. I really do have to leave. No, I'm not prone to migraines, this is the first time I've ever-. No of course- I'm sorry you feel that way. Thank you for everything. Yes, I'll make sure to gather all my things."

Crystal had tears streaming down her face as we left the bridge building.

"It was as much my idea as yours, Crystal. I'm so sorry." She was inconsolable. "Let's go by Bonnie's and see if the girls are still there, okay. We'll figure this out. We'll find a way to help Cheryl, I promise." I had no idea what we could do to help Cheryl find another job, but I was definitely going to try.

She didn't say a word as we headed south. I tried to get her mind off of the issue as there was nothing we could do at that moment. "Did you hear how Lauren described the inquiry?"

"What do you mean?" Crystal's voice was weak with stressed. I had to fight back tears. "She didn't ask when they were starting the work again, or if they were starting back by Wednesday for sure. She wanted to know-"

"That they weren't starting before Wednesday." Chrystal nodded thoughtfully. I let out a deep breath, glad I could shift the gears in her mind for a while. "Yes, that is odd. After what I did to Cheryl, ah gods." She put her face in her hands a moment. "Oh man, Mist. I hurt that woman. I mean, she was in real pain. And I made her lose her job."

"What was different about what you did with Cheryl and with the people at the park?" I tried to get her thoughts off of the pain she'd caused. We would deal with that for sure, but Beverly needed help now, I rationalized, knowing it was weak. *Harm ye none...*

Crystal looked out the window for a few moments, then took a deep breath. "I think, aaah, that's a good question." She released a long sigh, shifting to look at me. "I just nudged them to share thoughts. I didn't try to change their thoughts, or their desires. With Cheryl, I didn't even give that a try. I didn't try to suggest that maybe she had missed something."

She nodded her head with energy. "That's it! I didn't even try to make her a part of it. I forced a completely new reality on her. I tried to supplant my extremely foreign desire onto a system of handling visitors that she already had in place."

It was one long word to me, but I managed to catch her meaning. "That means," I started, but she took it back immediately.

"That means I never ever ever ever try and force my thoughts and desires onto anyone ever again, anywhere no matter what. I can nudge them to share their thoughts, or consider something, but not ever tell them to do something they don't want to do. Ever. Again."

Tears streamed down her face, but I think they were cleansing. She was nodding to herself.

"And how many people come to the coffee shop that work

in an office, Crystal?" I had an idea forming if needed. "We can hold a job fair at the *Axe & Stovepipe* if needed. Today is Friday, but we'll have her working again asap. I promise. We won't let her slip through the cracks."

Crystal grabbed a tissue from the glove compartment and cleared her sinuses in a very unlady-like way. I smiled in approval. "Well that should make-"

"Oh gods on Olympus!" Crystal leaned forward and unclipped her seatbelt, ready to leap out as soon as I slowed. We had just turned onto Bonnie's street and saw Mica standing near the road, wrapped in a blanket next to a fire engine and talking to a police officer. Fire fighters were moving back and forth between the street and the cottage.

"Where's Amber?" I parked several houses away and raced after Crystal who hadn't waited for me to come to a complete stop.

Bonnie came out of the main house with water bottles in both hands, Amber trailing after her and holding more. "Thank the gods," I released a breath as I reached Mica and, ignoring the officer, wrapped her in a bear hug.

"We're okay," she said, pulling away after a moment. I wiped a bit of soot off her nose. Her hair and clothing were soaking wet. Amber arrived and I noticed she was clean and dry.

"What happened?" Crystal had just freed Amber from a quick embrace and took one of the waters, handing it to Mica.

Amber pointed to the cottage. "We, um," she started, then glanced back at the officer. Fortunately, she didn't seem to notice Amber's hesitation to speak in front of her and kept writing on an Ipad. From my angle, I could see she was using the Crime-Pad app that had been on the news repeatedly because of a local case- the defendant's attorney claimed it was something that could have been hacked. The judge didn't agree. So, it seemed, the officers are free to keep using it.

"Is that all you need, officer? I'd like to go change now, if so." Mica twisted her hair and we watched a waterfall escape.

The officer tapped her shoulder com and mumbled letters

and numbers in it. I have no idea what she said. But shortly, she gave Mica and Amber the all-clear and we started to move toward my car to talk.

Before we could take a step, Bonnie threw her arms around Amber. She's certainly a hugging kind of woman. "Thank you so much! If you hadn't grabbed that hose, we might have lost the whole cottage, and all of Beverly's things." She took a shuddered breath.

Amber held her hands. "It's no problem. I don't think you'll have any loses, except for the sofa. And fortunately, the water from the garden hose was only on a moment - I bet the house will dry out in just a few days."

Bonnie hugged Mica, then. "And thank you for beating out the fire with your shawl. I'll be glad to replace it."

"Oh, no worries. I have others. Please don't give it another thought. I'm just glad we dropped by when we did." Mica patted her shoulder and took off the blanket, placing it on the fire truck near other supplies.

We said goodbye and walked to my car.

"You're sure you're both okay?" I couldn't help noticing that Mica's sweater didn't look like it had been beating out a fire.

"We're fine, just soaked and freezing. It's a nice day and all, but not when you're soaking wet in April. I'm going to head home and change. Amber, will you catch them up?" Mica started walking to her car across parked on the street across from Bonnie's home.

"Are you sure? It's your magical story, not mine."

"I believe we're all meeting once more at Jasper's patio party tonight, right? I'll fill in any missing details. I really want to get into dry panties." She waved and started to sling out her wrap to put on, then thought better of it and tucked it under her arm as she headed off.

"Wait!" Mica called. She jerked to a stop in the middle of the street, jogged back over to us and handed Amber a key. "And I believe you have a little magic story to tell as well." She touched her temple in farewell and jogged off again.

We headed to my car, Amber climbing into the back. "Let's head to my house, it's just a few miles away from here." Amber rubbed her arms. "I want to put on something warmer. Mica's water works really chilled me."

"She was crying?" While it wasn't unheard of, it was a rare thing to witness.

I looked at Amber in the rearview mirror and she gave me a brilliant smile. "That crazy witch pulled water out of the air!" She drummed her hands on the back of Crystal's seat.

Crystal and I looked at each other in shock. "I thought Bonnie said you used the garden hose?"

"Yeah, I grabbed it to cover what she'd done and sprayed some on the floor." She leaned back with loud sigh, holding her hand up. "Let's wait until we're at my house. I need some hot tea. When I say she chilled me, I'm talking bone-chilling here. I literally ache inside."

Crystal and I shared a meaningful look. We needed to get a handle on this discovery stuff before someone got truly hurt.

We reached her house on the west edge of town a few minutes later. Amber had chosen a great location when she bought it three years ago. The houses here were older with mature trees and sat on one, two or three acres of land. A large farm had been down the street from her when she bought it, but it was currently being transformed into tight little plots of starter-castles. I just couldn't understand the design- huge, two-story homes built with a cookie cutter and close enough to pass the grey-poupon out the window and set in your neighbor's home. If I paid that much for a mini-mansion, I would expect an actual yard on each side. But, it meant Amber's property value had increased over night.

The house itself was, well, unique? I'm trying to be nice. It looked like someone had inherited a bunch of salvaged barn wood and made a home out of it. The roof was seven, separate slabs, all tilted outward at a sharp angle with a white covering of some kind of rock material. It set sideways on the lot so that the garage faced the road with a dirt and grass path instead of a driveway.

There's a large space in front of the house opened up for grass, and then trees run thickly all the way to the property line on each side. You couldn't see the greenhouse from the front, but that's where she had put all her energy. The other end of the house was the kitchen and had a door leading out to the back yard. It immediately changed into an enormous, half-covered patio with large sheds lining one side. There were also three, large walk-in coolers in line with the sheds that she'd purchased from a used restaurant supply store in Peoria.

Beyond that was a wide gravel path leading to the greenhouse. No trees were near that area, and she had put in a permanent foundation to hold it firm during the tornado season. Or seasons. In the last few years, we'd started getting them regularly in the fall as well as the spring.

When we pulled off the road and into the driveway, a red Ford pickup sat there and two men were measuring the front side of the house.

"Oh, for heaven's sake, what now?" Amber grumbled as she got out of the car. "Dad, Tony. What are you doing?" Amber walked over and gave her father and brother a hug. They were just as petite as she and the family resemblance was strong. We said our hellos and received more than a few curious glances from the men. We'd only met them a few times, and they didn't know what to make of us still. They felt Amber had moved out too early and since she started dancing with us, they acted as if she was a lost soul at times. I was insulted but tried to keep my irksomeness to myself.

"Martin is buying siding for a big project and said we could get some at a great discount. We can get this house updated at a bargain." He smiled with pride, as though it had never occurred to Amber to try and make the house look a little less weird.

"Dad." Amber's voice was strong. She actually put her hands on her iddy biddy hips and stared the slightly taller man down. "I already told you- this house is coming down in just two years. I don't want to put anything into it because it's all coming down."

"Well, Sis, I don't think you realize how expensive building a home can get. There are building permits-"

"Two-twenty-five at the county office on third street." Amber interrupted.

"You'll have to get an architect, or a set of building plans."

"Mark from Treadeau's Architectural Homes in Champaign-Urbana. He's already measured the property and worked out a general design. We meet to finalize said design this summer."

"Does he have a builder in mind? You know, they can charge you an arm and a leg. Why not just redesign this place, a little at a time, without taking such a risk? What if the economy tanks again?"

Amber closed her eyes and took a breath. I hate to say it, but I was kind of enjoying this. It was really rare to see this side of her.

"Dad, you and Tony go home. I have guests. We'll talk about this another time, but I want you to consider this as you drive home. One- I bought my own home, successfully, without a co-sign, at the age of nineteen, with half of it paid upfront. Two- I have a contract with ten state offices to provide their indoor plants. The state contracts are hard to undo, and those offices aren't going anywhere. That's as recession-proof as it gets."

She grabbed each man by the arm and marched them to the truck. "And three- when I build the new home, it will have a full, poured foundation basement. I won't have to run to the neighbor's during the tornado seasons. Isn't that a better home, instead of trying to make a silk purse from this insane sow's ear?" She laughed to ease the tension.

We waved goodbye and moved to the front door to give them privacy. We could hear them talk a bit longer, and then laughter all around. That was a relief- it's never a good day when you end it at odds with family.

When she came around the house into view, her smile was fading. She looked tired and wrapped her arms around herself. "Greenhouse," she said softly and nodding us in that direction.

We went around the house to the end and walked silently into the large space.

"So warm." Amber paused as she crossed the threshold and closed her eyes a moment. Crystal and I shared a worried look.

With determination, Amber walked over to one of three work stations and grabbed a coffee mug from the table. She went around the greenhouse, taking snips of different plants and putting them right into the cup. She walked out of the greenhouse on the other side for a moment before returning and shutting the door hard with a loud bang.

That made her acknowledge us for the first time. "Sorry- it sticks."

"Can we help?" Crystal walked forward but Amber just shook her head, her eyebrows creased. She took a bottle of water from the dorm fridge next to her table and poured it into the cup. The she put it in the microwave.

I took off my wrap as she did so and placed it over her shoulders. She immediately grabbed it close and looked at me with a weak grin. When it was ready, she took her mug and wrapped her hands around it, putting her face over it.

"Oh be careful, that's got to be hot." She nodded at me.

"I'm not drinking it. It would kill me."

I looked at Crystal with a something more than a little concern.

"Um," Crytal began.

Then Amber lifted the cup and breathed deeply. I watched as the steam wrapped around her face, like a caress. It ran through her hair, lifting the soft curls, then down her throat and into her shirt. She breathed again and the steam grew. Her shirt lifted away from her body as steam wrapped around her and my wrap fell from her shoulders.

We just stood there, watching, rooted. The steam rolled through the sleeves of her shirt and flowed over her jeans, inside and out. After a few more breaths, we could only see her hands holding the mug. Then she stepped through the mist toward us, her normal smile returned.

Crystal reached out gently and took the cup from her. Without a word, she looked around, then nodded as she reached for a trowel on the table. "I'll just bury this out back."

Amber yawned deeply and stretched. "Good idea, yes- that might kill the grass, though. Thanks." She sounded sleepy.

"I'm going to get this one tucked in," I said to Crystal as she left the greenhouse.

"Good idea," Crystal agreed.

"Oh, that sounds wonderful. I could use a nawaep." Her words ended on a yawn and I gently led her into the house. Just like the coolers, it had an electronic pad to unlock the door and we all had it memorized.

I steered her to her large, four-poster bed and covered her with a throw from the sitting chair nearby. She was asleep in moments and I joined Crystal in the living room.

"What the hell was that?" Crystal was washing her hands with about a cup of soap in the kitchen sink.

I had nothing. I raised my shoulders helplessly. "Good heavens, we have got to get a handle on these, these growth moments."

"You know in some of the witch stories they had bindings put on them when they were babies, supposedly to protect them. That always pissed me off, but now I'm thinking it's a good idea. How are we supposed to learn without blowing each other up?"

We moved to the living room after deciding we should hang around a while to make sure she was okay. Every fifteen minutes, we went in to basically watch her breathe. There's no nursing manual for how to check on magic gone amiss.

"I think we should call Mica." I agreed and Crystal took the phone outside so she wouldn't wake Amber. I looked at my phone. We were supposed to meet Slate and Liam right after work for an early dinner at the *Eighth Circuit* in a final show of support for the spring opening. It was already three in the afternoon.

I texted him: *I need you to draw one card for me before we meet tonight, please.*

He didn't reply right away so I got a drink of water just as Crystal walked back in. I told her what I had asked him just as he texted back: *Sure. One card draw needs to be very specific. What do you want me to ask? Are you sure just one?*

I showed the text to Crystal. Good question. She took the phone from me and typed:

Yes. Focus on one thing.
~How do we learn without killing anyone~

CHAPTER TEN

"She's got a lead." Cole put his phone away and smiled in that gorgeous-enough-to-be-all-the-Greek-gods-combined way that leave women weak in the knees. He held his glass of the *Eighth Circuit* 'beer of the week' precariously and more than once it threatened to spill over. That would be a shame as his tailored suit had to be worth more than my car. The man just couldn't stand still. He moved with a constant source of hidden energy, maintaining an eye out for any new people entering the bar inside while pacing around our table.

The galère was gathering. Slate's business partner was telling us about the lawyer he'd hire, a woman of course, as he searched for his birth parents. Last summer he had taken a DNA test and discovered that he wasn't Hispanic at all, as his adopted parents had been told. He was one hundred percent Native American. But the test couldn't pinpoint to which tribe he belonged, so he hired a lawyer.

Being a lawyer himself, one might think he would save some money and tackle that in his spare time. But one would be wrong- he has no spare time. Cole put every ounce of his energy into making the business he and Slate had started two years ago a success. They provided research services to law offices and state agencies. Cole, with his smile of the gods, was mostly focused on gathering clients. It didn't hurt any that he registered for the 'Cornfed Hulk' contest at the state fair each year- it was a bizarre trial by whatever whacky obstacle course of errors the creators could come up, as long as it had a corn theme. You had to be in great shape to climb the kernels of a one-hundred-foot cob and monkey climb across a butter swamp. The course from last year was almost a quarter mile long and this year's course threatened to be even longer.

Men.

"That's wonderful," Amber offered. He made his way around the table to her side quickly, but then pulled back a few feet. She sat close to one of the seven-foot-tall heaters on the patio. They really did change everything. The temperature had taken a quick, nasty dive but the triangular heaters that shot flames through glass tubes were not only beautiful; they made the courtyard comfortable, even when winter decided to say hello again.

We had tried to get a room indoors, but Amber insisted that she was feeling fine and completely recovered, though she had chosen to sit close to a heater. She wanted to support her brother's patio opening weekend and having a large table filled outside had drawn others to join us, which was the point.

The patio was packed. As were the indoor areas- all three bars and tasting rooms had standing room only available. We hadn't seen Jasper since we'd first arrived.

I watched as Cole gave Amber a rather suggestive smile. "Want to go chat about it somewhere quiet?"

Amber laughed. "It doesn't get any better than this- great food, wonderful people and outdoors on a cold spring night? What could top that?"

Cole lifted his glass to her. "Can't blame a fella." As he drank, his eyes scanned the bar. With a smirk, he set his glass down between Slate and Liam. "I think I see the future Mrs. Thompson over there." He smacked Slate on the back. "Don't wait up."

Mica gave a loud laugh and raised her glass to his departing figure. "I admire his determination." Slate just leaned his head down into his hands.

"He needs to get done with this wild-oats period. He seems to have a thing for female lawyers- we need all lawyers in the area to like us, not despise us because he left before breakfast." He looked up at Amber. "Tell me, what makes you impervious to his over-flowing charm? Is it your herb amulets? Can I buy a few dozen of those?"

Amber smiled through a yawn and stretched for a long moment. I saw Mica from the corner of my eyes. She frowned with concern and drop her gaze to her glass. That was a look of painful guilt I had seen on two of my closest friends today. I really hated it. Amber patted Slate's hand. "It's a phase I see every day at my age. It just seems to be hanging on tightly to Cole. Don't worry about me- I'm the gardener and can recognize oat-sewing when I see it. I will say though," she held up her glass conspiratorially, "that once he's through with this phase, I think I might marry him."

"Well hoozah then, my friend." Liam laughed. "We'll get you dentures as a wedding gift, because that's how long you'll need to wait."

We all giggled and then Crystal yawned loudly and dropped her head on Mica's shoulder.

"What is with you guys tonight?" Liam shook his head and stood up. "Come on, galère'. You have done your duty to Jasper, Amber. Up, up, everyone up. You're all going to walk over to Mist's home, do a little magical circle making and then talk. Slate's been a worried-winnie since your text, Mist, and you all appear exhausted enough to fall asleep in your beers."

"I don't want to leave you alone, Li." Slate got up reluctantly.

Liam just pushed him toward the café. "I have the next forty years with you- I won't begrudge you an evening here and there. I'll send food up in one hour so you can get the fru-fru stuff out of the way and should be settled in to talk. And Mist," he came over and put my wrap around my shoulders as I stood. "Just grab some extra blankets and let everyone crash at your house. I know none of you have had a second beer, but you're all already exhausted. Do I need to grab some extra pillows or any-thing from home?"

I briefly grabbed his arm. What a great guy. "No, I've got plenty. Plus air mattresses."

"Good idea." Crystal gave him a quick kiss on the cheek.

"No arguments from me." Amber rose and Mica threw her heavy, crochet shawl around them both. They took the lead, arms linked.

We moved my living room furniture to the edges, except for the coffee table- it was a sort of five-sided piece dad made when we were little. He'd taken a large piece of maple and roughly cut a lopsided rectangle, then took one end and nipped off the edges. No side was sharp, or smooth for that matter. Hard to describe- I just called it the coffee table. It had a side for mom and dad, Slate and me, and our dog. Underneath were a number of drawers but they didn't reach the floor as it was open underneath.

I know, complicated. Just picture a large piece of wood the size of a door floating across the ocean for a few years that gets banged up on some large rocks near an island and then makes its way to the beach. The castaways love it.

I grabbed the air mattresses while Crystal raided the linen closet. Mica and Amber crushed some kiwis and strawberries and put them in a picture with ice water and a screened top. Slate grabbed some candles, sage and my broom-corn broom and set about clearing the space of any negative mojo. At some point Amber started singing under her breath and we soon all joined in with a simple, familiar and comforting chant.

Gods, that felt good. I could feel tension leave that I had been carrying since I crossed the swinging bridge. *You're home.* It was my own thoughts, but a wiser, higher-elevated version of me. I closed my eyes as we gathered around the coffee table on our knees or sitting on pillows. We stayed like that a long time- the room filling with the scent of burning sage, the sounds of our deep breaths rising and falling in unison.

Finally, Slate started shuffling cards. I almost stopped his hands to hold the peaceful moment a bit longer. "I did not draw before we met tonight. I want each of you to shuffle the cards. While you're shuffling, focus on why you asked me such a..." He shook his head. "Such a downright scary thought. Be honest."

He handed the deck to Crystal. She shuffled a long time. Her voice broke several times as she spoke. "I hurt a woman. I forced her to do something she didn't want to. Gods on Olympus, I violated her. And she lost her job because of me. Her life has been put in chaos, she felt physical pain, and I do not want to cause that again." Tears fell freely from more than just one pair of eyes.

"Mica." Slate held no judgement in his voice. He took the cards, shuffled them once and handed them over.

"I hurt my friend today. I caused her pain. I moved instinctively for the sole purpose to save myself- when the smoke poured over me, I reacted. I didn't think of any others. My selfishness hurt my friend, my sister." Her voice failed.

Slate took the cards again, shuffled and handed them to Amber. She whispered her words in a deep, resonate sound that echoed in the room unlike any others. "My untapped power is endless. With this new connection, I have dreamed of what is possible, and it terrifies me. I have the option to bring about a world I don't recognize." She pushed the cards away quickly.

Whoa. I had no idea what she was going through. We really needed to talk about what happened on the mountain, what happened when Amber stayed up all night, and what happened at Bonnie's, and soon.

Slate still didn't judge. He took the cards and shuffled, then handed them to me.

I shuffled just once and set the cards down. "I accept my heightened intuition, but I reject the fire. Unless it's needed to save Jade, I reject it." I pushed the cards toward Slate. Reaching up, I found my face wet with tears. Relief washed over me. While I had felt safe in the cavern of Gaia, I had not been able to call forth fire since. I realized now, I was terrified of it. You don't hand a blow torch to a three-year old. Who was I to handle something with the awesome, destructive power of fire without a manual? I wasn't the one to figure out a book of shadows on this topic.

Slate exhaled slowly for a long time as he shuffled again. Then he laid both hands on top of the deck of the Gaian tarot cards, and called quietly to the sacred four corners and to spirit. He spoke words of gratitude to Gaia, added a plea for Beverly, for her loved ones, and finally, for the demands of Lady Justice to be served.

He used poetry and prose. He sang, whispered and danced his words around the room. I fell into a deep relaxation as he worked his unique magic to soothe us.

Slate's voice was soft as he finished, looking around the table. "Do you remember what you said about the grimoires? This isn't the time for the finding of magical items, but for creating them." We all nodded. "You talked about the lucky ones who stumble across something already written out, or built with blood, sweat and tear, all the answers laid out before them. But I want you to consider something." His voice remained smooth and even, but I could tell things were about to shift.

"Each of those heroines in the story still had to give something of themselves. Heart. Courage. They had to face the great obstacle of self before they could claim the prize, and only then could the great quest begin."

He looked at me. "That means heart, courage is a built-in part of the equation. It is not up to you to say I want one gift and will not claim the others." Then he looked at us all. "The heroes could not say they would take up one of the tasks and leave the others for another time, or for another person. You commit to the quest, or you don't. You take up the ring and give every ounce of your being to getting to the fiery mountain, or you turn around and go back to the Shire."

He began to shuffle. I watched as he lost himself in the repetitive motion, his eyes glazing and his breath stretched, each exhale longer and thinner. A slight breeze rose up from the floor. I wanted to look around to see if I had left a door opened, but I couldn't tear my eyes away from his hands.

The motions grew faster until it seemed his hands did not move at all and the cards shuffled constantly on their own accord. And then Slate looked straight forward, seeing nothing. I watched the dark rings of his eyes grow in the candlelight until there was nothing else, no color to be seen. Two, empty orbs.

Then those orbs filled with a fiery malachite green. I held my breath.

With a flick of his hands, a card shot out to his left, to Crystal, and landed directly in front of her. He did the same around the table, each card landing perfectly in front of the reader. The wind that came from nowhere swirled around us, and the quiet sounds of drums on the CD we had playing in the corner rose above that.

Slate opened his mouth and a voice came out, but it wasn't his. I gasped as all the heat left my body. He didn't move his lips or tongue, and the sound seemed to be alive, moving through the room. "The challenge is to be accepted, or to be denied. Risks exist on both paths."

Slate's soulless eyes looked directly ahead to Amber. "You want to reach for the light without looking at the shadows it creates. You cannot allow fear of your own darkness to shape you, for you give it power when you do. Rise with both the light and dark revealed. Are you truly saying you will not go after the cruel people who rape my lands and vilify all life? Will you not step forward with this new gift and reclaim the world as it should be? Remake Eden, the gardens of Babylon, the Fertile Crescent?" The voice expanded to a roar.

Amber closed her eyes and shook her head violently. "I cannot do that!"

He turned his head to face Crystal, a deep, angry sigh moving through the room. "Daughter of six tribes, did you truly expect that people would bow to your will with no struggle? Who are you to force anyone to do anything? But that is exactly what your gift can do. It has brought evil men to great power, my child. You are the first in millennials to have this gift. The world waits to see how it can be reshaped, as it needs. It has ever been a bringer of pain. Are you up to the challenge of changing its very nature? Can you reshape what has been forever deformed? Will you not accept this power and change the hearts of the leaders in this capitol, to reshape this land in the ways of Gaia? Will you not be the first woman of power in this land?"

Crystal's reply came in a whisper. "I will not force people. I will not."

The voice moved to Mica, angrily swirling about her until her hair was released and flying all around. The candles flared high. "Water child. Only a passionate soul can tame the waters, call it from the very air you breathe. You can rid the world of every evil doer that exists, freezing their very bones. Every murderer, every rapist, every child molester- do you accept this great power that only you can wield?"

"I do not. I do not want it. Take it back." Mica had tears streaming down her face.

And then I watched the energy move toward me. *The voice of Gaia, angry and endless.* The wind rose up against my ankles and I felt it all over my skin. The voice energy circled me and at the drum crescendo, she spoke.

"Mist," the word was warm against my neck, seeming to enter my ear and move through my head. "You saw the fire cleanse the world, open it for new life, worthy souls left to bring forth a new era. Accept this gift and cleanse this world. Accept this gift and bring the world anew. Accept this gift." The last was a demand, howling through the room. The windows and door flew open and a fierce wind screamed at us until we covered our ears.

"No!" I shouted above the roar.

Then everything went silent. The doors and windows slammed shut. The candles went out. The music stopped.

Slate's face softened. He smiled, gentle, controlled, a knowing nod. *Good,* the voice whispered, stretching the word.

We watched the patio door open wide and a blurring movement vanished through the doors. Just before it closed we heard the words, '*An' it harm yenoan...*'

Slate spoke then, his voice normal, his eyesight returned. "And it harm ye none." He nodded again. "You passed the test." He took great gulps of air and moved a shaking hand through his hair. "Oh," was all he could add.

The cards in front of each of us had somehow remained in place during the storm of wind. They suddenly turned over by themselves.

I reached for my card. "Guardian of Fire."

"Guardian of Wind," Crystal lifted her card.

Amber turned hers so we could see. Guardian of Earth.

Mica waited a moment, then she reached forward as well. "Guardian of Water."

Slate stared at the deck in front of him. "Look." We saw a card on top that did not match the others. The back was a pure deep black without design. He picked it up. "Guardian of the Witches." He turned the card to face us. It was an art nouveau-styled card with four women clasping hands in the center over a black cauldron- the cauldron similar to what Mica had made for Crystal. The arms of the women in the picture wore large pieces of tribal jewelry, each with stones and crystals and spikes. Behind them, two men stood, hands clasped and free hands holding long spears. Guardian of the Witches was printed at the bottom in script.

Slate gasped, looking closer at the back of the card. He turned it to face us. There had been nothing on the back of the card a moment before, but now the four sacred elements translated into art-nouveau graced it corner to corner.

The patio door burst open and Liam stood there, disheveled and holding take-out bags. "Oh, sorry. But I was attacked by a windstorm that came out of nowhere." He walked into the room and dropped the bags on the table then looked at each of us. "You look worse than me. As a matter of fact, you look worse than you did when you left the *Eighth*. What the heck changed?"

We looked around at each other, eyes wide, hands shaking. "Everything." We all said at once.

I DRESSED QUIETLY so as not to awaken the household. We'd stayed up until three in the morning, so Slate and Liam crashed in Jade's room while the others took sofas or air mattresses. It was only seven, but I'm usually down in the café by this time so my internal system woke me. Stupid internal system.

Nic, Tammy and Jason had the crew well organized and everything under control so I filled a pump carafe with Wild Mountain Blueberry coffee then another with a kona blend. I grabbed a bag and raided the pastry rack, then threw in a few sugar packs. Next, I headed to the cooler and grabbed a new container of cream. Then I grabbed a second bag and stole several of the tiny pastry soufflés- egg whites with spicy turkey sausage and craft cheeses or similar varieties. I could feel Nic's eyes follow me as I moved about the kitchen and prep area. He never said a word after our first greeting and I gratefully made a hasty retreat to the back stairs.

I'd planned on taking a cup out to the patio and turning the small heater on full blast, but when I reached the living room, Mica was deflating her air mattress while Crystal and Amber were folding blankets and putting the furniture back in place.

"I'm sorry, did I wake you?" I placed my armload of supplies on the table then went to the kitchen to grab coffee mugs, plates and napkins.

"Who can sleep?" Amber groused and plopped onto the sofa, dropping her head on the arm.

"Finding sacred caverns, using hidden powers, and then getting a full freak-out test by the gods? It's all in a week's pay, right?" Mica's eyes were framed with dark circles and her cheeks look drawn. She had one of my shawls wrapped around her hair.

I watched Crystal pour a good helping of cream into her cup before adding sugar and then the blueberry coffee last, to mix it all. It sounded like a strange brew, but it was our most popular flavored coffee. When you add sugar and cream, it tastes like pie in a cup. I thought we all could use a sugar boost this morning.

"Shall I start the kettle, Amber? Would you prefer tea?"

She shook her head and poured a cup of the kona blend. "No, I think I need this."

Crystal pulled her long straight hair over one shoulder and crossed the room to the patio. She opened the door and then closed it immediately. "That chill decided to hang around."

As I watched her, an idea came to me. "Hey, Cris, have you done any more scrying on Beverly?"

She shook her head. "Not with any luck. That vision under the full moon had more clarity than anything I've ever done, though, so I shouldn't be surprised that it's not easy to duplicate. However, I had hoped to have a simple emotional clue or something." She shook her head. "Things have really changed. I'll have to practice- different liquids, different moon phases, candle light."

"So, you are moving forward?" I took a sip, enjoying the heat from the mug as I wrapped both hands around it.

"Yep, just like I said last night, like we all agreed.
"   I nodded. "I just wanted to make sure a good night's sleep didn't bring you to your senses."

She managed a soft giggle. "I'll let you know once I've had a good night's sleep."

"I hear that." Mica grabbed a spinach soufflé and ate it in three, large bites. She then grabbed a French pastry and took more time with it. I wrinkled my nose, but there was no arguing it. The soufflés were made by the *Axe & Stovepipe*- good, comforting food. Gulp it down. The pastry came from Mitchel's bakery and deserved worship.

"Mica, what happened at Bonnie's?"

She narrowed her eyes at me. "We still haven't talked about that? Good grief, I feel like we must have talked for four days straight. But yeah, I guess that was just yesterday afternoon. Sheesh." She used the linen napkin to clean her hands thoroughly and then poured a cup of coffee.

"You saw where we parked, right across the street? As we walked to the driveway to reach the porch, I saw flames suddenly shoot up inside the cottage window. "She pointed at me. "I saw it start. And if we hadn't left when you told us to, we would have missed that. I told Amber to go and get Bonnie and I rushed to the back."

Amber poured herself more coffee. "It took a moment for me to explain who I was and what we'd seen, but Bonnie believed me immediately and went to call the fire station. I ran to join Mica just in time to see her standing in the house next to a sofa on fire."

Mica continued. "When I got there, the front door was unlocked. I know we locked it before we left. I ran inside and saw the sofa on fire- nothing else, no curtains or wall segments." She smirked up at Crystal who was standing and leaning against the fireplace. "Because, you know, sofas just burst into flames all the time."

Mica spread her arms wide. "Then it seemed like the flames decided to move toward me. I don't know how to explain it, other than perhaps a wind from the opened door blew it. I could see Amber out of the corner of my eye, but all I could focus on were the flames shooting toward my face." She made a face, frowning and shaking her head. "And I don't know how, but I could see that the air was filled with water and I told it to get its lazy butt over to me right now!" She hit the table with her pointed finger on the last two words.

Then she looked up at Amber. "And I realize, now, sitting here thinking about it more fully, that I pulled water right out of you as well, dear friend." Her eyes filled with tears. "I am so sorry Amber. So very sorry."

"You mean," I said as I put down my cup and leaned forward to rest my arms on my thighs. "You're telling me that when we found you soaked to the skin, some of that was Amber water?"

"Oh, ew." Crystal's face scrunched tightly.

Amber burst out with a seal bark and started clapping her hands, loud and slow. Then she pointed at Mica. "That will teach you. Ha!" She kept laughing.

Mica frowned as she sat up straight. "I didn't think of it like that. That is kinda, yeah, ew."

Once I caught my breath, I turned to Amber. "And you grabbed a hose?"

She nodded as she gulped down more coffee. "Yes. Beverly has one of those nice garden reels right out front. I grabbed it and turned it on and wet the floor a little. Not too much- I don't think they'll have any damage. But I did see it happen. And Mica," she smiled warmly. "It was pretty impressive. When you pulled the water vapor out of the air, the room filled with a greenish/blue hue, as though a shock was needed to separate the water, or solidify it, or whatever happened. It was lovely. It was very, oh I don't know, fitting. You know, aqua colored."

"Watch out Aquaman." Crystal laughed.

"Oh yeah, Khal Drogo is Aquaman." Mica smiled wickedly. "This just got a million times better." We all had our own private, happy thoughts for a few moments before I grudgingly brought us back to reality.

"We need to find Beverly, my galère'. It's a been a week. It's been five days since Mica saw her suffering." I looked over at Mica as she stood to stretch. "Have you had any more dreams?"

"No, but we do have something. Amber?"

Amber walked over to her purse and pulled out a key. "Oh yes!" Crystal ran over to her. "I'd forgotten you had a key." She turned it over in her hands. "It looks like an old house key. Does it belong to Beverly or Bonnie's home?"

"Nope." Amber said shortly. "We managed to check both spots. Here's how we found it, and, I think, heard an arsonist's getaway." She wiped her hands and sat back on the sofa with her coffee refilled. Knowing how she became animated when she talked and used her hands, I realized how drained she must still be.

"Bonnie came running out to us, but we already had the fire out. And then the trucks pulled up, so she went to the front to get them. Right then, the small dogwood next to me began to bend and sway as though a storm had sprung up. But no other trees moved."

"Nada." Mica added.

"We walked to it, and then it stopped completely. But one behind that began to shake. And then again, the same pattern repeated until we found ourselves at the back of the property by a small alley." She put her coffee down to make circling motions with her hands, and I smiled. "And then some leaves began swirling over one spot like crazy. I walked over and could see a key."

"But then we heard a car take off quickly, right around the corner." Mica joined in. "Amber raced off after it and I grabbed the key."

"Do you think it's the person who set the fire? Why would they hang around?"

Mica shrugged. "I don't know. Perhaps to see if the fire took. Perhaps to look for the key if they realized they'd dropped it?"

"Or," Crystal began with a cynical look, "it was simply a neighbor heading out, late for something and that key has been there a long time. It looks old."

"But certainly not neglected." Amber jumped in. The key was clean- it had been recently dropped.

"So here's what we know," I began. "Fay, from the historical Lincoln home is uncomfortable about Beverly's disappearance. Her aura changed at the mention of Liam seeing it, and spiked when Cris suggested something was missing."

"Which suggests," Crystal began, "that whoever took her knew Beverly had something on her when they took her, but not afterwards. Something is missing."

"Meaning Fay is involved? Do we really know that?" Amber's voice was thoughtful.

"It was a tremendous aura change. She was upset by the kidnapping, which would be normal for anyone working there. But she had a very definite reaction to Crystal's suggestion that something fell from Beverly's purse. Why would she do that, unless it mattered to her?"

"True," Amber agreed. "And then her cottage was set on fire, potentially."

"We need to get a confirmation from that. We can check in

with Beverly, and bring those plants by, today." Mica said.

"And Fay also had an obvious reaction to the tourists' questions about the Dana Thomas House. Even without seeing her aura, we could tell she was uncomfortable." Crystal pointed to Mica. "Do you have your sketchbook- maybe we should be writing these things down."

"You need a dedicated journal." Slate and Liam walked into the living room, yawning. I don't know how they looked so fresh after just a few hours of rest and wearing yesterday's shirt and slacks. "I'll be right back," Slate said as he headed for the balcony doors in the sitting room.

Liam sat next to me on the sofa and grabbed a mug. He turned the decanter around to read the removable title tag- Wild Mountain Blueberry. He set it down and reached for the other one, then paused. Giving me a sheepish grin, his hand returned to the first decanter. I really don't understand what kind of masculine shame there is in drinking a flavored coffee. There must be some kind of a 'bro-code' that said real men drink plain coffee, black and extra strong.

"Where's he headed?" I asked.

"We went to the *Eighth Circuit* directly after work and still have our briefcases in the car. He must be grabbing a legal pad or something."

I shook my head. "He does know I'm a real business woman, right? I have office supplies, right here."

Liam laughed. "You'll always be his big sister working several odd jobs at once to keep him in school."

It was true for a time. When our parents died, I received enough money from the insurances to pay off the house, but if I wanted to get Slate through school long enough to earn a law degree, it meant working to pay the bills and putting aside a huge segment of the insurance money. It still surprised me how much our lives had changed when I started working at the farmers market just two days a week in the summer, selling coffee from an old horse trailer that we'd remade into a certified kitchen. Any work I could do with Jade in tow was gold- no childcare costs made all the difference in the world.

I smiled as Liam chose to dive into the soufflés and leave the pastries alone. Childish, I know. But it made me happy.

Slate came back in a few moments, rubbing his arms from the cold. We repeated the details they'd missed and Liam starting writing things down as we continued discussing events so Slate could grab some coffee. Then he stopped. "You know, you have to turn that notebook into the police. You should have done it yesterday."

Sometimes I forget that they are lawyers and have to do things all legal and such. "True," I said slowly, stalling for time.

"And, when you break into the Dana Thomas House, Slate and I can know nothing about it. Nothing at all."

We all looked at him in surprise. Slate laughed. "Well, we know it's what you're going to do. You had both Fay and Lauren respond strongly to the mere mention of it. And what was the other home, an orphanage? You said Lauren responded horribly to it."

"Yeah, it was a pure white. I know, everyone sees a white light when they die, and it looks heavenly. But when she blanched, it was like all colors of life fled from her. It was just evil." I bit my lip. "And yes, it was about the orphanage, so we'll have to-"

"Aaaand, what can you tell us about the orphanage," Liam interrupted as he gave me a frown. "What's the connection?"

"It's another mystery." I smiled at everyone. "In the turn of the last century, things were still in turmoil. The civil war had ended just thirty-five years earlier and people were trying to figure out the new society. The only orphanage in the city wouldn't accept black children."

"What?" Crystal put down her mug and stared at me. "Not possible." She spread her arms wide. "This is the land of Lincoln. This is where the Illinois regiments trained under Grant himself. The very first soldier to give his life to free the slaves came from right here in Springfield. We sent a quarter of a million soldiers into the army from Illinois- all of them willing to lay down their lives and die to end slavery, and thousands of them did! What did they do it for, if not to shelter children?"

I raised my hands to block her anger. "Whoa, sister. I'm there with you, but we can't turn away from the ugly that existed right here."

"The race riots that happened *here* resulted in the formation of the NAACP."

"Yes. Here. It was able to start here with support from the local people." Crystal took a deep breath. "Sorry, that just took me by surprise. It makes no sense, buy you're right- we have to claim the issues that existed here as well. It wasn't all in the south. But to turn away orphaned children?"

"What's the history, Sis?"

"A woman named Eva Monroe came to Springfield and started an orphanage for African American children, plus a place for the elderly. But in those days, and without any training, she was struggling. In the end, it has a strange connection to the Dana Thomas House and the mystery of how much, if any, input was given by Wright.

"You see, at the same time that Susan Dana Thomas hired Frank Lloyd Wright to remodel her home, her mother, Mary Lawrence, stepped in to help Eva Monroe. She paid off her debt and razed the old house which was said to be haunted. Then she had a new building created using some of the same material from the remodel. The roof and windows are the same style found in some Wright homes." I shrugged. "So, did he help design that one as well?"

"And now the preservation offices own it too, and Lauren Ryan, who heads those offices, doesn't want the workers to start before Wednesday." Amber tapped two fingers just below her ear absentmindedly as she spoke.

"Mist, you said you think you know the name of the three people who were hired to work in February but never showed up- do you have those names?" Slate was writing furiously. I wondered if we'd ever be able to read it as his penmanship was like a self-made code.

"Here." Mica grabbed her purse and found her notes.

Slate started writing but soon stopped. "Well I'll be..." He looked up at Liam. "I just interviewed this woman recently- Marta Wend." He nodded as Liam's eyes grew wide. "She told us she had received a job offer two months ago. You know, we ask about any lapse in employment. She said the start date had been pushed back several times and so she started searching again when they didn't return her last call." He sat back.

"I remember this clearly as she had taken excellent notes- the dates and times she'd called them, when they returned the calls, etcetera. She had a little note-book and showed us. I thought it showed excellent skills and she's at the top of the list. We need to check on all these names."

All eyes turned to Liam. He rolled his own. "Just because I work for the state doesn't mean there's a magical machine that connects all the departments and I can look up everything by the push of the button. But you know who can? The police. We need to get this notebook to Pete- he can find this out." Liam stood up and stretched.

"We'll do that. I'll tell Pete that you guys found this while on the tour and wondered if it might be connected. I'm sure stuff is dropped there all the time, so he might dismiss it." He frowned. "I'll think of something to give it a bit of weight so he'll look into it."

"The notebook doesn't have the names, though." Crystal pointed at him.

"Let's give him Marta Wend's name, Liam." Slate pointed at him. "He owes you more than one legal favor- ask him if he'd run a subtle background check on previous work. If she was hired, she should be in the system, right?"

"Okay, let's go home and get cleaned up. Then I'll call him and make him work on a Saturday. That'll use two favors. And I'm presuming you guys are going to stay home and catch up on sleep. That's all I want to hear."

We all yawned in unison.

"There ya go." He gave me a quick peck goodbye and they

left by way of the balcony.

"I can't see why the two houses caused them to react?" Mica drummed her fingers on the coffee table and slid off her chair to sit on the floor cross legged.

"And to react with such force." I agreed with Mica. What was the connection?

"Lincoln Home. The Dana Thomas Home. The Lincoln Colored Home. The only thing connecting them is the preservation office, and officially, even though it works with the Lincoln park, that's not under their full control."

"What else could it be?" Amber stood up to stretch.

I did the same but found the need to pace around as I talked. "We know people were offered jobs in February at the Lincoln park. But they haven't started yet, and it's the end of April. What if, what if they're on the payroll already, but someone else is collecting the money? Embezzlement?"

Crystal stood up to pace as well. "It has to be something that Beverly stumbled upon. We found that she's debilitatingly shy. She has her home with her sister, and she has the people at the senior citizen home, and they love her."

Mica rose. "Bonnie said she puts on a separate personality and does her job. Could this be a real separate identity? A split personality?"

I shook my head. "The lady at the senior center, the dancer, said that Beverly hated her job. It was exhausting for her to work there lately. She was afraid if she didn't go in each and every day, she'd never be able to go back. That doesn't sound like she was checked out and a different person was in control." I stopped suddenly.

"But why 'lately?' She has worked there for decades." I tapped my fingers on together. "We need to find out when Lauren Ryan took the reins. I think she found out something and started asking questions."

Amber shook her head. "No, I don't think she would ask questions, she's too shy. I think she would simply start digging."

"Dang, we need that notebook back." Crystal made a fist and

hit it into the other palm.

"I wrote down anything that was out of the normal pattern. It was only the two things." Mica stretched over to the table to grab her sketchbook she had shown Slate. "The segment that we talked about, and then in the back, there was a series of a bunch of numbers. They had no rhyme or reason, so I didn't bring them up. But I wrote it down, just in case."

"Numbers?" Crystal moved forward. "If the topic is embezzlement, numbers would be involved." She looked over Mica's notes.

"And then there's the key." Amber brought it forward and laid it on the table. "That's an old key, not something to a safe-deposit box or anything."

"It's definitely a door key." We all looked at the large, ornate, metal key. It was clean and showed no signs of having been discarded.

"Well, we are looking with interest at two old homes." I put my hands on my hips. "It's not breaking and entering if you have a key, right?"

"Yes, yes it is," said Crystal. "Still, I would love to go with you to see which door it opens, but we need to find out when Lauren Ryan started and see if we can get any more information on those other names. I'm the research queen, so I'll head to the library and start searching."

"I'll go with you, Cris." Amber added. She gave Mica an apologetic look. "I'm still drained and I'd rather sit in the library turning newspaper reels than climb through windows or across rooftops."

"We're not cat burglars," I laughed. "But that's a good idea. Mica and I will go and see if the Dana Thomas House or the orphanage have a door to go with this key." I frowned. I'd really rather wait until dark, though." Then I shook my head. "But I just don't know if we have time. We'll have to use our talents, I think."

"Well if you start a fire, I'll be there to put it out." Mica smiled as she headed for the door. "I'll head home and get cleaned up. Let's all meet at the library in two hours. It's just up the road from the Dana house- we can split up and then meet up again, there."

CHAPTER ELEVEN

We met at the large public library and made our way through the metal-detectors. There was no attendant, so I always wondered if it was just for show. After the world trade towers were brought down by terrorist, the state capitol added enormous, cement flower stands in front of every public building so cars can't enter the glass doors, and several had metal detectors added as well. I wasn't sure if this was a part of that change, but it seemed a waste of space and money.

"Do you have a plan?" Amber's voice was quiet.

"Oh, I most definitely have a plan. I plan on doing everything possible to avoid jail." Mica sank deeper into her seat. "I would suffocate in a cage."

Amber shivered. Thinking of her claustrophobia, I was glad she wasn't taking this risk.

"I think we can avoid jail. All we need to know is if the key fits. We won't need to enter the buildings." That didn't sound real even to me.

"Yeah, that's the plan," Mica whispered slowly. We all snorted.

"Oh wait!" I leaned forward, speaking louder than intended. We drew a few eyes from the patrons at the next table.

"Trying to stay under the radar, Mist." Crystal gave me her classic scowl, but I saw humor in her eyes.

"Sorry." I smiled at them. "But I have news. Would you like to lecture me or learn what Slate called to tell me about their visit with Officer Pete?"

"They went there already?"

"They're men. They can get ready by the time I've just warmed up the water for my shower."

"That's sexist," Amber snorted. "But in my case, it's also true."

"What. Did. They. Say?" Crystal spoke softly, but with a cacophony of impatience.

"We were right." I practically screamed the whisper at them. "Pete was actually working today, so they got lucky. When they arrived, they showed him the notebook. Which, by the way, he barely looked at. Without knowing what we found on Beverly's calendar," I began, but Mica interrupted.

"And what your aura reading showed." She smiled.

"That too. Without any of that, it really doesn't have much information. But, the 'coincidence' of Marta Wend interviewing with Slate," I made quote marks in the air, "they didn't need our magic to start digging. Slate asked if he could do a quick perusal of her name, saying they would do a formal background check, but if there was something that would rule her name out now it would save them a lot of man hours."

"Is that legal?"

"I'm pretty sure everyone who works for them signs an agreement to have a background check. I'm not sure why Officer Pete owes Liam favors, but I'm glad he does because he checked her name at once. And, my friends, he said she's been employed with the Historical Preservation offices since February. She's in the system and on the payroll.

"Naturally, Slate told him what she had said, and he mentioned her detailed booklet. If she keeps her finances in the same neat order, there should be little time wasted in proving that she has not received said salary and benefits." I slapped the table as loudly as possible with one finger, which turned out to be a lot louder than expected and we all cringed as people turned to look at us again.

"Mist, you suck at subterfuge. I think I should take Crystal with me." Mica pushed my hands into my lap.

"Mist," Crystal began, ignoring Mica. "Did they say what the police will do now, today? If things are moving forward with an investigation, Beverly might be in critical-level danger."

I frowned. That was true. "You're right. Slate just said that Pete was going to go to Marta Wend's home after he did a little more investigation. That should give us a couple of hours."

"You two get going, and we'll see if we can find anything on those last two names. We know the other two people on the February list are probably going to come up with Marta's name, and I think we can presume the lovely Lauren Ryan is involved, so I'll do a little digging to see if I can find anything else on her and have Amber look up the last two names.

"You two find a lead on where Beverly has gone." She pointed at us firmly.

"And please let it be a good lead, a lead that says she's still alive." Amber added quietly. We all shared a grim nod and left the table.

"How are we going to get close?" Mica and I had parked the car two blocks away from the Dana Thomas House and were walking at a slow place that was murder- I wanted to run there.

I held open my hand and showed her a pinprick of light. "Look. It's back. If there's a lot of people around, I'll start a fire in the trash bin across the street."

"What if there are no trashcans?"

"Paper in the gutter."

"What if there's no paper in the gutter?"

I looked at her with a frown. She nodded. Unfortunately, our once proud and beautiful small city seemed to be taking an all-too familiar path downhill in some of the sections surrounding downtown. I absolutely hated that people cared so little about their hometown that throwing garbage out into the street didn't bother them. I liked to believe that it bothered them a little, and maybe they just needed a gentle reminder to do the right thing. Or a big citation. Whichever worked.

We needn't have worried. Even though a sign on the door said the place was closed, and the yard had construction equipment on it (covered in leaves and obviously unused) we found a dozen tourists walking around the house and looking through the windows. It was clear from the smudges on the windows that they weren't the first to do so.

"That's a sight you don't see often." I agreed with Mica. Generally, the docents at these historical sites are like rabid guard dogs. Seeing people wander around freely was a bit off-putting.

But it is a glorious house. Many of the enormous windows of the prairie style home are stained glass masterpieces. No side of the house is just a flat, boring wall- copper eaves, multi-level roofs, repeating arches over the doorways, and surprising walkways between sections that just beg to be explored.   And so we did.

At the front entrance, a few children were sliding up and down the stone benches in the entrance way, just lost in their own, musical sounds. The front door was blocked by two adults, the parents I'd guess, trying to look inside. There was one child determined to climb the brick pillars that framed the door, and it looked like she just might do it.

Mica grabbed my elbow and pulled me forward. There was no way to check that door with this many people roaming about.

We made our way to the side and followed a long, low brick wall. It opened beyond to an obvious walkway, and beyond it was a wall of glass- one of the tells of the prairie style. I often dreamed of designing a home with a long hallway that ran along full-length windows looking out to bring the natural world in. I briefly pictured Slate holding a séance and getting Wright to design me a little wing or something.

It was easy to get lost in beautiful dreams walking around the house. It seemed every turn brought delight and reflected the trees and grass and sky on multiple surfaces.

When we reached the side, the house jutted out in several

segments. A couple was walking ahead of us so we slowed.

"Look, Mica." I pointed to a small side door. It must have been a servant entrance as it wasn't as ornate as the others and somewhat hidden as it required walking down four steps. Right beside it was a walkway leading up about four steps to a beautiful, carved doorway. We waited for the couple to continue and then as nonchalantly as possible, we moved toward the door. Subterfuge turned out to be impossible as I slammed into the wood, only then realizing we'd actually been running.

"We suck at this." Mica pulled the large key out and put it in the lock.

"Alarms?"

"I've been looking for cameras but haven't seen a thing. Yes, I'd presume the doors have alarms, right?"

"What do we do?" I asked her. Her eyes were wide and she shook her head helplessly. I took a deep breath, trying to find my center. "We think of Beverly a moment, that's what." We closed our eyes and then I placed my hand over Mica's. "We'll go down together."

She turned the key. I could feel the lock give. We were so surprised, we just stared at each other a moment. Then we heard children's voices coming around the house.

Without thinking, I opened the door and pushed Mica through, following on her heels and shut it as quietly as possible. We both took a step away, walking backwards. Then I leaned forward and locked the door.

It was just in time- the door rattled as someone tried the handle. "Timmy, quit that! You'll set off an alarm." We stood frozen until the voices from outside faded. Slowly, we turned to face the hallway. We moved forward and found ourselves in the opulent dining area. Normally that would be great- it's quite the sight. But the large windows on the end with the breakfast nook meant all those people trying to see something might actually get to see us getting hauled away.

"So much for not coming inside." Mica pulled me to the floor, and we started crawling under the long table set for royalty.

"Notice something?" I asked as we crawled between twenty-six or so chairs. I'd caught a glimpse before Mica pulled me down of the alternating height of the chairbacks, but from this view, they all looked the same.

"What?"

"The table. It's still set. You'd think, if any renovations were set to occur, they'd store the china and linens first. Each setting has to have at least four plates."

"I was too busy looking at the barrel ceiling. I want one of those."

I snickered as we reached the end and I pointed off to a little room ahead. "Shall we also get you a gallery for your musicians to hide in while they woo your guests, m'lady?"

"I don't think I'll need that. We'll get surround sound. Unless we get a wandering guitar-player to move in as well."

"What are you talking about?"

Mica laughed. "You need more artist friends, my dear. It's a well-known story. A wandering guitarist was begging for food and going house to house in the neighborhood. When he reached this house, Susan Lawrence scooped him up and brought him inside. She hosted recitals that asked for free-will donations, which she gave entirely to him."

"Are you serious? She and her mom just brought a strange man off the streets to live with them? Alone?"

Mica snorted. "Alone. Ha. Between the maids and the cooks, it was like running a small hotel."

"Still, weird."

"What if John Mayer came to your door with the offer to exchange a meal for a private concert? You wouldn't snatch him up?"

"Maybe Kenny Shepherd, but I'd send Mayer on down to the neighbors."

"Well, we can't design a house to snare guitarists. There must be a law against that somewhere. But I do want the private bowling alley in the house."

"It's not a real one, you know. It's called something else. It's like bowling for rich, weak people who want to gather round and howl with laughter. You know, that kind of thing."

Mica snorted again as we escaped the table and dashed to the next room. This space was away from any outside view, so we relaxed.

"So much red stained wood." I loved the furniture, but it was over the top in the goal to match.

"And something else," Mica paused.

We found ourselves moving toward the basement. Though we now stood upright, we walked as though the ground was about to explode beneath us.

"If by something you mean nothing than yes. For a work zone it's remarkably free of work materials." I nodded.

We were struck with an acrid smell that grew stronger with each step. "Gods, did a sewer line break?" I gagged. We were by the duck pin bowling alley at this point. I saw something on the lane at the other end and we made our way to it.

"Don't touch anything," we said to each other. Squatting down, we looked at remnants of rope. I drew a pencil from my purse and lifted up the ends.

"These look like they've been chewed through." As we stood back up, the stench seemed to grow. Mica covered her mouth with her shirt and then moved toward a simple door. She opened it with her shirt covering her hand and closed it at once.

She made her way back to me, stifling a cough. I was very glad not to have been the brave one who followed the smell. Quietly we headed back to the other end of the room. "It appears the water has been turned off. That was a bathroom that needs a desperate flushing."

"Ew." I wrinkled my nose.

"Also, I saw something in the corner, Mist. A purse. An elephant purse." We crawled our way past windows and looked upstairs as well. Besides a few interesting closets that held bolts of period fabric, there was nothing unusual and we made our way back to the servants' door. A crack of thunder shook the house just as I placed my hand on the knob. We both jumped, as did the small child apparently sitting on the other side of the door who also let out a good, solid scream.

That was close. Mica mouthed the words and I nodded in agreement. Too close. We listened to the voices fade as more thunder rolled. I hadn't thought to check the weather. After a week of nice conditions, we should have been prepared for some spring storms. They can get nasty and it's just a good practice to check weather-dot-gov before leaving the house from April through May.

As rain threatened, Mica opened the door and we raced outside, quickly locking it behind us. We ran all the way back to the car as the wind howled. Only a few drops fell.

"It would seem someone had to stay there during the renovations." I said as I buckled my seatbelt. "And I would suggest that he/she chewed himself/herself right out of the ropes that bound him or her. Sheesh, that was a mouthful. Let's just presume it's Beverly from here on out."

"The question is, where is she now?" We looked at each other. "Lauren reacted to the mention of the orphanage the most." I spread my hands wide. "Full on white-out. It seems most likely."

"Should we call the others?"

"Well, if we've learned anything for every horror movie ever made, everything falls in the crapper when the women go someplace alone and no one knows where they are."

Mica wrinkled her nose. "Please don't mention a crapper. That poor woman," she added softly.

"I wish we could just call the police- and I'm thinking it might be the right thing to do anyway. We know the purse is in there. I mean, if she gets hurt before we find her, then that means we put her life at risk to protect ourselves. If we told Pete that her purse was here and we think she's in the orphanage, they'd be there in minutes."

Mica nodded. "Yes, but let's be clear- we're here because of our gifts, and our gifts are to be used for the long haul. Every clue has been magically shown. Well, except for Liam seeing them at the Lincoln Home. That was amazing luck. We have to find a way to do these things and keep that completely under the rug."

My gut feeling was to agree. The police had nothing to go on without our work, and we needed to see it through and be ready for whatever came next. "There's nothing wrong with an anonymous tip, is there?" I smiled at her. "Are there pay phones around these days?"

"Yes, and cameras."

Crap. Of course there are cameras. Everywhere except at important, historical homes.

Mica called Crystal while I drove, racking my brains for a solution. What would we find at the old orphanage? Anything? Nothing? If Beverly was there, was someone watching her?

"Wait." I turned to Mica. "Why would they keep Beverly? Or go to the trouble of moving her? If she stumbled across their scheme, and it's bad enough that they needed to kidnap her, why keep her around this long? She must have something they want. That, or she's dead already." "Those numbers," Mica said, nodding. "They must have something do with the money. They didn't look like account numbers, or bank routing numbers to me- it was a mix of letters, symbols and numbers."

"Like a code?"

"Maybe," she replied. The she smacked her head. "And there were five lines. One for each person, of course."

"Do you have Liam's number? See if he can get Pete to look those up."

"How will he do that and not give us away?"

"That," I said with a smile, "is a problem belonging to two lawyers, one for whom I worked my tushy off to put through school and owes me big time."

Mica punched my shoulder, none to gently. "Family owes you squat and you know it."

"Yeah, yeah. I know." A sudden flash of light erupted overhead followed almost immediately by thunder that shook the car. "That was close. Are we expecting a huge storm system? I was hoping this might be a simple spring rainstorm?"

"Well, looking at the daylight line moving away, I'd suggest this is a full thunderstorm." She pointed to the eastern sky where the line of light was quickly fading as the dark clouds surged forward, chasing it away. Then she frowned at me. "This is your fault."

"What? I'm not a weather witch. You're the one pulling water out of thin air."

"No, but you clearly stated today that you wished we could visit the houses in the dark. And now," she gestured forward to the window. "Now I see nothing but clouds and I swear it's getting darker every block you drive."

True, I had said that. And this was one of those storms that literally changed day to night. I looked at her with a wide grin. "Dope."

"When you visited Lauren at the historical agency, did she look strong?"

I glanced over at Mica. "You can take her."

She laughed. "No, I mean, well yes, I could take her if needed, but did she look strong enough to drag Beverly quickly to a van?"

"Oh yes- who dragged, and who drove, or was it one person?"

"In other words, is there another person involved? Did Liam say if a man was dragging Beverly?"

"Yes, he did. I kind of forgot about that this week." I nodded. "We definitely have another person involved.

I turned onto twelfth street and we parked a block away. The area was not in good shape. The storm had pushed in and people abandoned the streets to take shelter indoors. Like normal people. I sighed. I was once normal, or fairly so, just a little on the woo-woo side.

The wind was blowing with that angriness found on the prairies as we neared the house. There were no lights. The one street lamp on the block was at the other end and provided little assistance. We ducked our heads as leaves swirled in mini-cyclones, showering us with their dust. My eyes burned as they hit.

Mica pointed to the front door. I shook my head and gestured that we walk around it one time. We had barely turned the corner before she slapped my arm and pointed to a side door that looked exactly like the servants' door at the Dana-Thomas house. We moved forward, the rain starting to fall regularly now. We were spared getting drenched by a long overhang.

Mica put the key in and, once more, a lock turned for it. She looked at me and took a deep breath before entering. As soon as we closed the door behind us, the thunder roared to full throttle. The windows in the old house shook. Lightening gave us glimpses of where we stood- a short, side entrance, probably once leading to a kitchen garden, or work shed. We walked up the short hallway and followed it to the back of a large living area with high ceilings.

Boxes covered almost every inch. I tried to see what kind of shape the house was in- I knew the previous owners had tried to refinish it but couldn't manage the funds required. The walls were in various stages of repair. Some had wallpaper ripped off cleanly, others showed strips of it. The floor was wooden and cleaner than I'd expected.

We moved through the room slowly, needing to wait for lightening to show a clear path and taking care not to touch anything. The house supports groaned as the wind intensified. Each rattle of the windows threatened to shake them lose. I glanced at Mica, worried by the threat of tornadoes. It was the season. It seemed hard to believe this old house had weathered over a century of violent midwestern storms. A loud moan was followed by the sound of something crashing above. A large tree branch must have fallen and scraped across the roof.

I felt the cold tingling sensation across the back of my neck of being watched and turned sharply to face the hallway. Waiting for the next burst of light, I crouched down and pulled Mica by the shirttail. When the space was illuminated a second before the thunder roared, I swear I saw movement going across the living room toward the front door.

Mica grabbed my arm and pulled me behind boxes stacked up in the opposite direction. She must have seen it as well. Still, the hair on my arms rose and I could feel eyes on me from the hallway. I pulled out my phone and gestured for Mica to do the same. I pointed for her to aim her light to the living room while I did the same to the hallway.

Just as we moved to stand, the boxes we hid behind fell over on top of us. My head took a brunt hit from the sharp corner of a heavy box that fell away. I gasped but didn't scream. I felt Mica's hand on my foot, pulling me back and out from under lighter boxes. She suddenly jumped up and clapped her hands. The room filled with the aqua colors Amber had described, but instead of water forming from the vapor in the room, a window slammed upward and water tore through the open space.

We heard a masculine voice cry out in surprise. I turned to move farther away just as flash of lightening showed a woman standing behind Mica with her arms raised over head. She held a large object and was about to bring it crashing down on Mica's crouching form.

Without thinking, I drew my arm back, palm opened, and thrust it forward. Hot light shot from my hand and hit the woman in the chest. Light surrounded her for just a moment. It was Fay, from the Lincoln home historical park! Mica swirled around, jumping aside just as the lamp in Fay's hands fell to the ground and Fay fell backwards. I didn't wait to see if she was okay- I grabbed Mica's arm and dragged her up as I dashed forward to the hall on the other side of the living room.

What had I done? What was that? It wasn't fire, but there had been heat. Mostly, though, it was light. How would that knock her down? What else was in it?

A large man suddenly lunged into the space, blocking our view. He was as tall as Mica but had twice our girth combined.

I felt Mica grab my arm at the elbow, so I grabbed hers as well. We rushed forward, surprising him and hitting him right in the neck with our clasped arms. He fell with a loud grunt. I jumped up, holding my left wrist with my right hand and threw all of my weight into my elbow, landing right in his enormous gut.

He didn't scream as the wind was knocked out of him, but in a burst of light we watched him writhe in pain. I looked around, not seeing Mica for a moment and panicking. All pretenses at moving quietly were gone so I screamed. "Mica!"

"Here, I'm here." Her voice was near the fallen body of Fay. Another blast of lightening showed her rising up, holding her phone. She shown it around the room, then screamed as she pointed to the front door. "There!"

I almost didn't hear her. The thunder that accompanied that last lightning bolt followed immediately- it was a close hit, either the house itself or the tree that had already lost a limb. I looked toward the light and thought I saw a woman jump away, but I couldn't be sure.

I was more focused on the noise. The thunder hadn't stopped. It rolled rhythmically and sounded like a train was about to crash through the front door. Realization dawned and I grabbed Mica.

"We have to get to the cellar, now!" We raced to the hallway just as the house shook and then made a violent shift. I almost lost my balance as I started opening doors to find the cellar. The first door was a mistake- it was a bedroom and a tree limb was crashing through the window and wall. I jumped back, pushing Mica down the hallway ahead of me.

She wrenched open the door at the end. "It's over here." I started to rush forward but felt a sharp pull on my hair yanking me backwards. I tried to turn to see what I got caught on. Instead of a jutting piece of wood, I found myself staring into the face of Lauren Ryan. She raised a gun and gestured me away from the door.

Then she pointed it at Mica. "You two, back in the living room!" She had to scream over the sounds of the wind. The wall next to me shook with the force of many hits. I didn't think the outdoor wall could withstand another hit. Trees must be flying liked crazed, evil witch-monkeys.

Mica stepped with care, holding onto the walls at times until she reached me, passing Lauren just as the wind entered the hallway. The house shook with a violence that made it hard to stand and I realized the living room was now opened to the elements somewhere.

"Go back to the living room!" She screamed again as she moved down the hall. Mica and I glanced at each other. That wouldn't do. But before we could think of anything, the roof right over our heads screamed and the noise of a great tearing of wood filled the house. It sounded like boulders rolled across the floor above us and as we looked, we could see the ceiling thrum up and down.

Lauren looked up as well, her back now to the basement stairwell. Without saying a thing, Mica and I rushed forward and both slammed a foot into her stomach, sending Lauren down into the darkness below. As the ceiling roared its final warning, we raced through the doorway.

I tried to close the door behind us but the wind was too strong. As I struggled with it, the dark sky opened to us as the second floor flew away. The flashing light showed what I had feared, a wall of black, spinning air was claiming the house.

"Leave it!" Mica screamed at me as she made her way down the stairs, her flashlight leading the way. We stepped over the crumpled body of Lauren at the bottom. I saw the gun and grabbed it, then chased after Mica to get away from the stairs.

Above the roar, I heard screams and the sounds of people falling down the stairs. Mica shown her flashlight and we saw the fat man and Fay pulling Lauren deeper into the basement.

In a split moment, the thunderous wind shifted direction and the cacophony lessened with a suddenness that left me confused for a moment. Then I lurched forward, the gun pointed ahead of me. "Don't move a muscle." I hoped I sounded menacing, but it didn't sound like it to me. Seriously, I think

I was ready to shoot if needed. The image of Lauren pointing a gun on Mica as a tornado was about to claim us still vividly clear.

With my other hand, I pulled out my phone again and clicked on the flashlight app. "Do you see her?" Mica pulled her light away and I could hear her exploring the basement behind me. Closer than expected, she called out to me.

"Mist, she's here!" I glanced over my right shoulder, not wanting to give our captives any advance. I only needed a glance. It showed me everything. Mica was leaning over a pile of rags on the floor. I saw a skeletal bare arm reach up to her, wavering and falling back. It was Beverly.

I smiled. She was alive.

CHAPTER TWELVE

Jasper carried a tray into the small tasting alcove and patio, latching a rope across the opening behind him and adjusting the sign which read PRIVATE PARTY. I was surprised by how packed the place was on a Sunday afternoon.

But people wanted to gather and talk about the events of Saturday. Not one, but two tornadoes had hit the town. One on the eastern edge, destroying a few barns and repositioning the topsoil in several fields.

The other was on the edge of the historic district. It had bounced down the street, tearing up the road and phone lines and the old orphanage before taking a sudden leap back into the sky. And of the course the other thing everyone wanted to talk about was the brave little mouse of a woman, Beverly Keys, who'd uncovered an embezzling ring at the state historical preservation agency.

Plus, the fact that she had been tortured, starved for a full week and given only water had all the tongues wagging as well. And yes, once again, our names were in the news.

"Thank the gods she's tougher than she looks." Mica raised her glass as I frowned at her. Seriously, we were going to need to run some telekinesis tests. Or telepathy. Or whatever gave everyone on the planet access to my thoughts.

"I'm shocked she's pulling through. A week with no food—that's beyond cruel." Crystal sipped her warm mug of cocoa—

mo and sighed deeply. We were all feeling the stress of the last week, and to a woman, we all felt guilty for not moving faster.

Liam drummed his fingers on his glass. "I think," he began slowly, and paused before nodding with intent. "Yes, I think we have to consider, and seriously consider bringing Pete into this. If he had known the details we had earlier, it might have shaved a few days off of her pain."

Slate grabbed his arm briefly with a smile. "I'm way ahead of you. I asked him to stop by today. He's taking a personal interest in the investigation and is at the hospital interviewing the three pieces of crap himself."

I frowned. "What? They haven't been arrested?"

"They are, yes, for sure. Their attacks on you and finding Beverly in the remains of that house were more than enough reasons. I meant interrogation, not interview."

"Yeah you did," Mica said before taking a long drink from her wine glass. Amber rubbed her back for a quick moment, and then handed her the basket of onion rings.

Mica was strong, but she was obviously having trouble digesting everything. While I kept the gun pointed at Lauren and her cohorts, Mica spent long moments with Beverly, trying to ease her pain. She'd finally had to race up the stairs to allow her phone to connect with the police. But she'd come back down immediately and hadn't left Beverly's side, even holding her hand in the ambulance. I too was still feeling the shock of seeing someone starved and weakened beyond recognition. Beverly had called to me once she was loaded in the ambulance and the police had taken control of Fay, a conscious Lauren and her boyfriend Ethan. When I got over to Beverly, her hand was rail thin and shaking. She looked twenty years older. I didn't think it was possible for someone to change that much in a week.

Fortunately, my car was okay, and even though the road was not in drivable condition, I followed the ambulance through the mess. When we crawled out of the basement, it looked like we'd entered another realm, one where a bomb had been dropped. The house only had a few pieces standing- the chimney and the east wall. Everywhere I looked, trees were broken, twisted, uprooted and spread all through the area. The street was filled with patio furniture at one point, like some giant had pushed a broom through a few backyards and just left them piled in the road.

I called Bonnie from the car and she met us at the hospital, arriving before we did because of our slow process. I know, you're not allowed to drive and talk on a hand phone in Illinois, but I didn't think anyone would stop me right then.

The police were great- Pete arrived with the ambulance and allowed me to leave after a short discussion so I could get checked out at the hospital and be there for Beverly. There was a moment of tension with another officer when I turned and he saw the gun in my pocket, but Pete took it as I explained things, leaving out the trip to the Dana Thomas House. I also over-emphasized how Lauren's mention of the orphanage made us curious to check the place out. Of course, we were shocked at what we found.

"How are you feeling, sweetie?" Crystal nudged me with her shoulder.

"I'm good, just a slight headache. I'll be perfectly fine once Jade gets home this evening."

"And she's so proud of her mother." Slate smiled at me. "And I am, too. Proud of you all."

"Maybe next time we can solve a mystery on a week where the gods aren't testing things out on us, ey?" Mica raised her onion ring. We offered a full table, fried-item salute in return. Jasper had been spoiling us rotten. We'd had so many free drink rounds offered by the patrons that Jasper soon converted them into food orders for us. Apparently, we could eat and drink for a few months.

"Hey," Jasper spoke softly at my right side. "There's a police officer here who wants to talk to you? Shall I tell him you'll go see them tomorrow?"

I looked up into his blues eyes, admiring how his chosen earrings complimented them. He really did look like a pirate. "Thanks, Jasper, but it's fine. He's actually a good friend of Liam's."

"Who is?" Liam looked over at the sound of his name.

"There's an officer here named Pete. He wants to know if he can pass the rope." Jasper pointed behind to the event sign.

We all laughed. Jasper left and brought him back quickly, which was a feat in itself considering how packed the place was again.

"You changed," I began, surprised. "I thought you were at the hospital?"

Pete laughed deep in his throat. "Yes, but I'm not going to come and have a drink at a bar in my uniform. That wouldn't set the right tone."

We all shuffled around the tall table to make room for him, pushing forward the baskets of warm foods.

"Can you tell us anything?" Amber asked.

"I can tell you everything. And, off the record, thank you. I don't think that woman would have survived one more day. The doctors said just a few minutes ago, though, that she is doing great. And on the record, thank you. You guys did your community a great service."

Jasper rejoined us carrying a beer for Pete, and we all shuffled once more. "Thanks," Pete took the glass and reached for his wallet. Jasper held up his hand. "This is a private party-you saw the sign. That should allow you to enjoy the free food and drinks without it being a bribe."

"That's true!" Peter reached for a slice of spicy quesadilla. "Though the truth is, I feel like I should be paying for it. You guys made incredible headway in a very short time."

"Not short enough," Mica moaned. She shook her head sadly. "We almost lost Beverly because we weren't fast enough."

"Weren't you out of town? You told me at the Lincoln house on Sunday that you were leaving until midweek?"

We nodded, and he continued. "So, you came home Wednesday night, right? And by Saturday you had uncovered that people were hired, but not hired, getting paid without receiving money, figured out where they were supposed to be working, who created the whole mess and then saved a woman's life. By Saturday." He chewed loudly. "Yeah, that's pathetic.

"Come on, ladies. You did incredible work in a very short amount of time. Crystal," he nodded to her with his fork as he dug into a mini apple pie. "That link you found where Lauren Ryan told a reporter about delays in construction at the Dana-Thomas house? You were right-the contractor was hired on one of the dates in the notebook. And the numbers in the back of the book turned out to be a simple code our experts were able to decode. It was the ID and password for five separate files that Beverly created, hiding the banking information right under Ryan's nose."

"That's why they kept her, isn't it?" I reached for the shredded chicken nachos platter. The waiters just kept bringing something new every time I finished a bit. At this rate, someone would have to roll me across the lawn to my house next door.

"That's it exactly. It looks like Beverly figured out the embezzlement scheme, and took a very pro-active response to stop their access to the funds. Everything is funneled through her- I really don't know how Lauren expected her to miss this."

"I bet she didn't." Liam said. "From what I understand, Beverly is painfully shy, to a debilitating degree. Lauren probably presumed she would never be able to go to the police. She didn't even tell her sister, as I understand."

"But she wanted to, Pete." I looked at him solemnly, not wanting him to think Beverly hadn't done all she could. "She came to my café every single night trying to get up enough nerve to speak. She seems to have a very selective form of social disorder, and she was doing what she could. She probably thought, because of what happened in Chicago, we could solve this without getting her involved. But once she chose to block access to the money, I guess it was too late."

"Yes, that's exactly what she said." Pete started, but Mica interrupted him.

"She's able to talk?"

He smiled warmly. "Yes, she talked to us for about ten minutes today. Just enough time to make sure we could charge those three to the full extent of the law."

"How exactly did Fay get involved in this? She's not in the office, it just seems unlikely that she would get a hint of things."

"Fay is Ethan's sister. And boy, did she turn on the others to get credit for helping first. It was her brother's idea- Fay would cover the employment shortage in the Lincoln site for six months, and they would all split the money. Few locals take the tours, so if the employees and volunteers don't speak out, no one's around to really notice the change, except in complaints. And those would only last a few months before things would go back to normal. It was actually the perfect setup for something like this- short time frame and not too much missing money.

"What's interesting is that Ethan didn't know about the other two dates- one for the construction work, and the other turned out to be for the Adams Wildlife Sanctuary. I don't know how you figured that out just by the date, Crystal, but once again, someone was hired to start on the first of the month and was told to wait."

Crystal opened her mouth to speak, pointing at Amber, but she shook her head vigorously. Pete didn't see as he was looking down at his plate. It had been Amber who found that date, because we had names to match. She found an article in the college newspaper where a student was giving advice on how to interview and find jobs in the environmental field that might be outside the norm. Paul Shimms mentioned that he had an interview right in town with the historical preservation agency and was offered a job right away.

However, there was no way to tell Pete that because he didn't know we had found the names on the calendar. This was getting complicated. Liam was right- we needed to bring him in on things. But how?   "Pete," Mica began. "You were saying that Beverly blocked the money?"

"Yes, on Sunday. She said she couldn't stand by and see them take any more money out, so she hid it. She was determined to try and get help the same day and didn't think they would find out since it was a Sunday. However, while she was on the patio, Ethan showed up with a gun and shuffled her out, holding her in his car for a long time. Fay waited in the park across the street. Beverly pretended to faint so she could throw her notebook away. That's what Liam saw, and it probably saved her life. If they'd found those notes, they wouldn't have needed to keep her around.

"They took her to the Dana-Thomas house, first. You wouldn't believe the state of things there. With the construction, there is no running water and she was there for several days. They beat her, starved her, and then said they were going to take her out of the state. They blindfolded her and drove around for hours, then just took her to the old orphanage. They thought that if she believed she wasn't near her home, she would crack. But she didn't.

"And with that," he wiped his mouth and took one more sip of his beer, leaving half. "I must bid you farewell. I have a wife and two kids who haven't seen me this weekend. And the kids head back to school tomorrow."

"Oh, we were hoping to talk about something else." Liam began.

"If it can wait, let's do it in a few days, okay? I really want to spend time with the kids."

"It can wait, no problem. Tell Katie I send my love."

"Will do." He pushed down and stepped over the rope. "And hey, guys? Merry meet, and merry part."

"And merry may we meet again!" We replied automatically and then burst out laughing. Okay, then. We wouldn't need much of a talk after all, it seemed.

We didn't stay much longer. Jasper loaded us down with a few dozen to-go boxes, and we thanked people for their generosity, shook hands and took a few selfies with the happy patrons of the *Eighth Circuit*. Liam and Slate were waylaid by some friends so we said our goodbyes with promises to resume our normal Thursday morning gathering now that spring break had ended. The rest of us headed over to my house.

It was time to talk about the cavern at Mount Shasta.

Since it was still daylight, we made our way to the base-ment. I collected some water bottles from my place and a few candles, but most of what we'd need was already down there.

The entire space had been converted to a dance studio. The floor has springs and two, adjacent walls have mirrors running the entire length. The lights are a combination of overhead bright lights, wall sconces and recessed lights just inside the per-imeter molding in the ceiling. One of the side walls houses a series of shelves to hold supplies, plus there's a full bath nes-tled in beside the shelves. I also had a water cooler built into the shelves, added surround sound speakers and overhead fans. The space even has a designated heating and cooling system. It looks as beautiful as any dance studio in the town.

Mica teaches tribal belly dance classes here, plus two Nia dance classes as well. I'd invited a yoga teacher to use the space for her teen class- Jade went for free so I considered that a good trade. She also offers scholarships to low-income teens and I want to support her work- since she doesn't have to pay to use the space, she can allow more teens to join for free. We advertise in the café, and she's created a solid group and a safe place for teens.

I looked around the large room. I would hate to give this up for storage if we expanded into catering.

Mica grabbed yoga mats while Amber and Crystal grabbed the meditation cushions. I sat the candles in the center and placed a water around for everyone as we settled in. We just shared the space for a while in silence, each of us gathering our thoughts.

"You already know most of my experience," I began. "I feel so bad that I left you all. I don't know how to explain it- once I threaded the flames, I had to know them. I had to... to meld with them."

"You didn't leave us," Amber said. "I walked down next and never saw you. And I didn't see anyone enter afterwards, so

I presumed it was the same for them."

Mica and Crystal nodded.

"I'm not sure how to move forward with this. How do I tell Jade? Do I tell her anything? Nothing?"

"You'll need to make sure she knows everything, and soon. She can't go into the world unprepared, Mist. For heaven's sake, she's half-Sidhe, she can pass unseen where humans and fae simply can't. That makes her powerful, but," Amber paused, shrugging. The others shared a glance.

"Vulnerable." I supplied. "If she can go someplace unseen, she can be taken the same way." I buried my face in my hands, wanting to put her in a castle with no doors and chop her hair short. But these thoughts grew hazy as soon as I thought them. Anything connected to Aiden seemed impossible to hold in focus.

"I don't think you're meant to protect her, Mist, as much as prepare her." Crystal's smile helped calm me. "And we, her magical aunties, will be here for you both." They all agreed.

"You know full well I don't believe in coincidences, Mist." Mica stretched her hands forward and cracked her fingers. "We found the sacred cavern just when you need to start protecting Jade? Not a coincidence. And that's why, my galère', I'm selling my home."

A chorus of exclamations went up around the circle. Mica had a beautiful loft that screamed artist's residence. She'd painted murals all around the building, and it was such a big hit that the city wanted her to do more. She was a staple of the downtown arts community.

"I know I'm like an anchor of our arts scene," she began. I just rolled my eyes at the mind-reading and let it go. Then she shook her hands at us. "But this! This is changing, this is growing into something we've never seen before. I want room to practice without drowning my downstairs neighbors. And all the talk we had about me opening an art and dance studio, perhaps living overhead, really has me thinking. However, I don't think that's where I want my focus to be.

"We don't always have to make our lives bigger, we just need to strive to make things better." She gave her head a shake, which caused her hair to move like a wave. "I need something else." She leaned forward like a spy about to share state secrets. "I need a witch's lair." She laughed as she sat straight again. "And it's right next door to you." She pointed.

"Me? You're moving in to the house for sale next to me?" Amber rocked side to side as she smiled. "Yay me! That's so cool- we can have a secret entrance to each other's yard and have practice sessions."

"Yes, water and earth. I see a lot of mud in our future." I smiled, but I felt an immediate spike of jealousy. What a great idea. It would be wonderful to live in a neighborhood with friends who were really family. And with the galère'? A true witch's hollow?

Mica smirked at the mud joke. "Funny. But serious, I think it's something to consider, guys. My experience in the cavern was completely off track, and I think it was a sign to grow in a new way, to shape a physical community."

We all waited for her to collect her thoughts. "Have you guys ever heard of Lumeria?"

"That's a mythical continent, like Atlantis, right?" I'd heard stories about research by evolutionary scientists for land bridges, but once they figured out how tectonic plates worked, that work was abandoned.

"Yeah," Mica said sigh. "I think I was there." She breathed out slowly. "I know, I know. That's as far out of the realm of reality as you can get. It's probably closer to say it was someone's dream, a memory that Gaia let me experience.

"I headed down the stairs and found I was walking upwards! I was standing in a large town square made of mostly stone, like one of the large plazas in Italy. The ground was completely covered in white paving stones, there were enormous fountains also made from white stones, and buildings that were rather square with lots of spaces jutting out in unusual ways. They all had balconies. And yes, made of the white stone as well."

She threw her hands up as though frustrated at trying to capture the reality of the space. "Yet it was green, and alive."

"Where was the green?" I was trying to visualize it.

"The green came from living walls of plants, from hanging baskets that were stacked one on top of another and went up the sides of the buildings, three stories- none were higher. I felt connected to nature because the sky seemed so enormous, the view unobstructed with wires or phone towers or tall buildings. Water and plants were everywhere, and the art- oh my gods on high, everything, I mean everything was designed for balance and beauty." She sighed happily with her eyes closed. It did sound like an artist created the town square.

"I looked around and felt the need to see more, so I chose a path leading out of the square. After a few turns between the buildings I found a large set of stairs leading to what looked like another square. The stairs were at least a hundred feet wide and there was a smooth, curving segment right in the middle. It would have been perfect for a wheelchair to gently climb the hill.

"At the top, it did indeed turn out to be another square. But in this one, there were far fewer plants and no homes surrounded it. Instead, there were tons of tall, rock platforms and tables and seating areas. I saw people sitting around an empty firepit, discussing and arguing with loud voices and waving hands. But no anger.

"I was drawn to a platform that was about as high as a bed. It was long, and had plants growing in the center. I watched as a tall, black man lifted one hand to the sky in a fist and stretched the other to the plants, his fingers extended. Water formed near his fist and poured down into the plants. A wrinkled woman who looked to be over a hundred smiled and laughed happily, then she tended the plants, pinching and patting soil. She had brown skin and grey hair and wore the most beautiful dress of silk I've ever seen- it seemed to dance with every move she made.

"A tiny girl, maybe five, I'm not sure, was standing on one

side and she raced over, her long blond curls bouncing everywhere. She threw her hands up in the air and I watched the pollen lift off the plants and settle down, again and again. The others clapped and encouraged her and she danced around. Then a young, Asian man walked close. He made a fist with his right hand and covered it with his lift palm, then moved down the full length of the plant bed. A warm energy glowed from underneath, and the plants shot up about two feet in just a second."

"Oh, I want to do that." Amber's face was a mix of delight and longing.

Mica laughed. "Everywhere I looked, people were testing out their talents, trying to figure out puzzles and equations and truly enjoying themselves. The space was filled with people of all ages working together, different races, different accents..." Her voice trailed. Mica sighed deeply again.

Then she shrugged. "And I want that. I want a place where we build on our work, call to others who are like us- not just the earth-based practices, like I think Pete and Tammy are, but those who can work the earth energy, like we do. If there are others like us. True witches."

"Have you," I started, but then paused. "Have you already purchased the house by Amber? Hear me out a second, please. She hates her house. You want to create a neighborhood, or a place with a teaching square-"

"Yes!" She interrupted.

"But, Amber's house is on a normal street with all those starter castles popping up. With the housing market over there completely changed, I bet she can sell the house for the land alone. And while the house needs removing, sorry honey." I glanced apologetically at Amber, who nodded in agreement with a smirk. "The land and the greenhouse area would probably bring you a sizable profit.

"Have you thought to look for a place that would be private land? They broke up that corporate farm just south of the city, and it has lake segments." I looked around the space. "And now

I'm also looking to get kicked out of here by Nic's dreams of expansion. That's three homes. They won't be white rock as that would be hella expensive, though."

"Well you're not leaving me out!" Crystal said with a little jump on her cushion. Since she was sitting cross-legged and couldn't stomp her foot, it looked like a butt-stomp instead.

"It's just a thought," I tried to placate her.

"It's an excellent thought! "Amber's voice was loud and echoed in the bare walled room. "Now that I've had a few years with the greenhouse, there are a dozen things I'd like to change. And you're right about the land value, Mist. The real-estate agent who sold it to me said the developer who did those large homes wants to buy it and break it into a space for eight homes. He offered me three times what I paid for it, which is just insane.

I was talking with the city about a tax break because they aren't suppose to raise the taxes on old homes like mine when new, expensive homes move in. It's looking to be a battle though, and I think it's because I'm young. So, I'm open to the idea. You know that parcel of land you're talking about is right next to the ecology farm ran by the Dominican Nuns, right?"

"Oh, you mean the pagan Christians?" We all laughed. They were truly unique, and the events at the sustainable farm make every witch's heart happy. They even rented their event space to the Modern Shamans for breathwork workshops.

"Yes. And my vision in the mountain might be helped by creating a safe space. In it, I was working from home and I had to fight for every lesson learned. I seemed to be surrounded by vile people and it was just one, big battle." Amber gestured to me.

"This seems like a safety net that I need, Mist. I know it doesn't sound like me, but in my vision, I was angry and bitter by middle-age, and I had a choice- to just wipe out segments of the idiots I was surrounded by or to, oh." Her voice choked and she pulled back slightly, the words coming from a deep place. "Or I would have to, to leave this planet." She bit her bottom lip for a moment. Her eyes shown. "It was one or the other."

"Are you saying kill or be killed? Whoa." That seemed like a cruel vision for the youngest of us.

"Not exactly. I mean, yeah- by the end it was feeling like that. At first it was just seeing the awesome power of my sacred element. I explored the entire earth without worry." She pulled back with a laugh. "As a small woman in a big world, I get tense just walking down a dark street. I think that's going to change in the next few weeks."

"I had a similar vision," Crystal began, her voice barely a whisper. "I think we were fighting the same battle. To me, though, it had the feeling of a specific group of people, or perhaps even one person. Someone was trying to stop our practices, throwing roadblocks at us, and it was a person, or people, who should really be on our side.

"That's why I didn't voice support for telling Pete more than we need to." She shrugged. "Women, just like us, with family and friends, women who were doing good things in their community were dragged out of their homes and thrown into the river, bound and weighed, by those people who called them friends just days before. Or they were placed on tables and physically assaulted before being tortured with fire and cutting devices. Or they were burned alive.

"This happened. This was a reality and while yes, it was hundreds of years ago, I want you to remember that just a few days ago, a gay man was dragged down the back streets of a Texas town. We have men enticing children to run away from home and putting them into slavery in Chicago, selling their bodies. This is our world."

She leaned forward intently. "I want to change that, my sisters. But we have got to do it carefully. We must protect our identities. That is what my vision told me. There is nothing out of our reach, but we need to stay as unseen as possible."

Whoa. It's easy to forget that horrors still exist in our world, and to the lives of those people involved, those terrors are just as bad as anything from our history.

"So, I'm in," Crystal continued. "But I request that we pick a place, carefully. I love those nuns too, but we all know they have no power. Even though they've made the place self-reliant and they receive zero money from the church, anything can change with one sentence from the leader at the local cathedral-those women have no power.

"I agree, their work is wonderful, but we've all heard them say they have to keep a low profile. With one word from that horrid Bishop in town, they can be sent away or even be forced to close the farm. I think if we moved in next door, it would draw attention, to them, and to us."

I had one of those intuitive bombs go off in my head. "Yes." They all looked at me. I suppose I should expand on that. "My intuition just yelled at me. What she said." I pointed to Crystal. "This is a fantastic idea, and it's exciting and has endless possibilities. But this isn't play time, and there is still great evil in this world. I suggest we move forward with our hearts opened, but our eyes opened even more."

"So, we're agreed then?" Amber's voice was quiet, but her smile was screaming. "We're going to find a place to build our own little witch's farm? With greenhouses?"

"And a fountain filled, teaching square?" Mica smiled.

"And event spaces, with cottages to rent? Plus a main house, perhaps, with separate suites?" Crystal was already making lists.

"And a coffee maker. What?" They all frowned at me. "I have simple needs. Coffee maker and fire extinguishers. And maybe I'll make Nic the general manager of *the Axe & Stovepipe* so I can focus fully on the, the, um, any ideas on what to call it?"

"Witch hollow?" Amber suggested.

"That won't draw attention." Crystal frowned at her. Amber frowned back without hesitation until Crystal smiled.

"I like 'Witch School,' but that would be just as bad." Mica joined the frown line.

I laughed. "Guys, we haven't even found the right space. I have a feeling that when we find the land, it will tell us its name. What we need first is a divining rod," I joked, but Mica perked up immediately. "Oh my gods on high, Mist! I found a stick a few weeks ago that I couldn't pass by. I've been sanding it, playing around and trying to figure out why it called to me. I think it might just be our divine rod."   "Divining rod, not divine rod." I looked at her sideways.

"I thought they were called dousing rods?" Amber pinched her nose as a sneeze tried to escape.

"That too," Crystal said, slapping her hand down. "Stop that. You'll blow your eyeballs out." Amber stuck her tongue out at Crystal, then laughed as Crystal tried to pinch it.

"Um, I guess we're done here." I rose and started to clear things away. "Jade should be home in an hour." Gods, I missed her. It was the first time I hadn't seen her in more than a full week since girl scout camp five years ago.

"I miss her," Crystal said as she rose. It took everything I had not to roll my eyes in response. We were going to have a chat with miss communications, and soon.

I walked with the galère through the café and watched them all leave. As I looked around, I saw a thriving café in full swing. Word of Nic's weekend vegan menu had spread, and I saw more than a few familiar faces from the summer farmers market.

It's hard to believe I was worried about leaving for two-and-a-half days. After a week of my neglect, it's in better shape than ever. I watched Nic laughed with a customer as he cleared their plates. Yep, I would need to run through those numbers tonight.

I frowned, recalling Jade would be returning soon and I wanted to spend the evening with her. Then a thought occurred to me. My week vacation could grow by another day, maybe two. I'll just sleep in a little, come downstairs for breakfast with Jade and then spend a few hours in my office while Tammy ran the morning. She was usually the first one in and deserved to be made a morning manager.

Wow. One week ago, I really hated the idea of leaving for a few days. Now, I was ready to walk away and leave the keys with my crew. But financially we were strong. Slate insisted on repaying me half of his tuition as that was money from our parents meant for both of us. And then there's that nagging idea I've had for about six months of opening a tiny, drive-through only extension on the west side of town where all the new growth was located. At this rate, Starbucks would do it if I didn't, so why shouldn't it be a local, mom and, um, just mom business?

Back upstairs, I finished tidying up and checked the fridge for juice. Jade couldn't get enough of the stuff. I think she's half hummingbird.

No, she's half something else and you know it!

My hand shook the metal handle as I jumped away from my own thoughts. Where had that come from? My right fingers stretched to reach my neck and stroke the chain of the necklace. I tried to focus on what I'd just been thinking. But once again, a haze covered my thoughts and I saw no need to push it. If anything, I wanted to run from my thoughts. There's so much to do.

I went to my bedroom and picked up the beautiful book Amber made for me. *Grimoire.* Shuffling empty pages, I saw no sign of the ornate patterns she'd mentioned. I wasn't exactly clear about this requirement thing either, but I hoped stitches wouldn't be needed.

Laying across the queen-sized bed on my stomach, I traced the outline of petals and stems with my finger. Amber claimed to have no artistic abilities, but this was pretty impressive stuff. I rolled to the head of the bed and reached out to grab a pen from the bedside cabinet. Opening the book, I wasn't sure what to write.

"Why not start with just your name?" I spoke aloud to calm my nerves. I had a sudden case of the chills. But how to write my name? Even that seemed monumental. According to Amber, her book came alive with magic and she just traced over the designs it created. It.

The book. Gaia.

My hand shook as I placed the pen at the top of the page, just off center.

I exhaled as I wrote the letter 'M' but then quickly reclaimed that breath as nothing showed on the paper. I moved the pen to the corner of the page and started to rub it quickly back and forth to get the ink going before I caught myself.

"No scribbling in the sacred book, Mist." I wish we had a cat or something so I could at least pretend I was talking to someone. Maybe I should do this in Jade's room and talk to her birds? Laughing at myself, I grabbed a notebook from the side table.

The ink worked the first time. "I guess you just needed a little start." I tried writing but again, nothing showed.

Sitting up, I held the book in front of me. Perhaps the light might show me things I needed to trace.   Nothing.

"Oh wait- not Mist. Amethyst." I tried an A. But still, nothing. The pen refused to leave a mark on the page. Whatever payment was required, I had yet to meet it.

I put the grimoire inside the drawer of the side cabinet and pulled out a regular notepad before closing the drawer with a gentle push. Moving my head to the pillows, I held the simple notebook up to the light for a moment. "Geesh, nada." I pulled my knees toward me and sat up a bit straighter, dragging the pen back and forth across the top of the page, making lazy loops.

"This isn't right." I pulled the grimoire back out and placed it on my knees, opened. "Listen, book. I have no intentions of giving you a blood offering." I made a large flourish of loops, but nothing showed. "Aw, come on. Aren't we suppose to work together?" I scribbled connected 'Zs' but the ink remained stubbornly inside the pen.

With a loud sigh I tossed my pen down. What did the book need from me? Why didn't it come with instructions?

There's something to be said for those who find ancient books of magic. All the hard work has already been done. "Writing one is a whole, other ballgame." I absentmindedly traced my fingers over the edge of the page, picturing our bocce ball court turning into a water polo court. Are those even called courts? It's a pool. It's...

"Ow!" My pointing finger jerked on the right side as I scraped the paper at just the needed angle to get a papercut. As I pulled my hand away, a tiny drop of blood fell to the page.

The paper absorbed it all. I turn the page over and back. Nothing. It was clean and bleach-white. "You do want a blood offering! What a sicko. That is so lame. Not to mention cliché, don't you think?

"Here." I rubbed my finger across the top and saw blood smear for just a second before it was absorbed as well.

"I guess we're at least talking now." But how to use this? I didn't have a spell to put in it if I wanted to, but if I did, would I have to write the whole thing in blood? Ew. This could get disgusting, fast. What if different spells require different types of blood: dead-man's blood; animal blood; menstrual blood; blood of a loved one...

"Ew." I said it out-loud this time. "You heard me, book. That's just sick. I'm not going to start investigating on types of blood for you." Even as I said it, I rubbed my finger across the top again and smeared it once more.

The blood was absorbed but this time it flared brightly for a second before disappearing. A sharp letter "L" shown in the middle for a moment and faded.

I hate to admit it, but I sliced my finger on the edge on purpose. I held the cut against the page and the light flared from beneath my flesh. "I can't believe I'm doing this." I sighed. "Was that an 'L'?"

Once more the letter flashed in the middle of the page. "You love the blood?" I really hoped it didn't reply. It did. Fortunately, I took it as a negative as it flashed a short, straight line. Surely a yes answer would be something more, well, just more, right?

"Oh, good. So... we are communicating, yes? Wow, okay. Witch stuff happening. That was an answer?" This time a small explosion lit up the center of the page, like the tiniest fireworks display ever made.

"Nice," I laughed. "But... the 'L' means something, yes?"

The answer was another explosion of two-dimensional fireworks in red. "So, how do you know I need to focus on something with an 'L'? I mean, what are you? Exactly. Um, please."

The letter 'U' sparked for a second.

"You're me." Fireworks. "Great. I'm insane." I tapped the edge of the book for a second. "Aw, screw it." Leaning over, I reached for the phone by the bed to call Amber, (and yes, I'm one of those weirdos with a landline.) My hand paused, though. Next to the phone is one of my favorite pictures. It was taken at Jade's graduation from Middle School ceremony and showed Slate and Liam on their knees pointing 'rock-star' fingers above them where Jade was hanging upside down from a tree. Yes, in a dress, but she had the dress caught between her thighs. I appreciated the skill in that.

"Liam." I said out loud, sitting back upright. Fireworks. "Really? Liam? What about him?" The page stayed blank.

"He's pretty dope, book. Slate loves him. That's gotta count for something, ey?" Nothing. I sighed. "Liam." Fireworks. Placing the book down next to me, I got up and began to pace around the room. "Okay, Mist. The book is somehow an extension of you, at least, according to the book. And if I was a demon book that'd be what I would say. But Amber made this, so if she made me a demon book, it was by accident. Are you a demon book?" I paused in my walking and pointed to the bed.

Moving close, I leaned in to see the straight line again. "Well, that's what I would say, if I was you. And I guess I am. So, am I trying to tell myself something I've forgotten? Ugh." Plopping down in a chair, I looked out the window. From my room, I had a south view of the town.

"South view," I whispered. "South view. Oh, gods of old, Liam lied!" Jumping up, I ran to my car.

CHAPTER THIRTEEN

As I bounded out of my car at my old home, I heard their raised voices. I know, I know. A sister shouldn't eavesdrop on her brother's private arguments. But the timing was too coincidental. "A woman could have died, Liam!" Slate's voice wasn't loud, but the anger was intense. "I made sure Pete knew everything I did. There's nothing more I could have done."

"This goes against everything you've ever said, everything for which you stand. Liam, how could you do such a thing?" The pain in Slate's voice brought tears to my eyes. I wanted him to know he wasn't alone so I rushed in the house without knocking. I found them in the office just off the front entrance.
"Mist?" They turned together.

"What are you doing here?" Slate asked me but I looked at Liam as I moved into the room.

"You lied to me, Liam." He dropped his head and ran his tongue just under his lips as he sighed. His hands came to rest on his hips.

He looked exhausted, more exhausted than I'd ever seen him. "You're right." His voice wasn't much more than a whisper.

"Tell me you had nothing to do with the attack on that woman." My voice broke. I didn't realize how much it would cost me to actually say that out loud.

"No! Oh gods, no, Mist. I swear. I swear it."

"Maybe we'd better start from the top." Slate motioned to a chair near the bay window as he plopped into the leather chair in front of the desk. Liam took the seat behind the desk, sitting heavily. "How did Liam lie to you?" Slate emphasized the last two words, making it clear Liam had also lied to him.

"The telescope." Liam groaned and dropped his head into his hands as his elbows reached the table. "Yes, that's right." I was fighting tears. "I know I had it locked to the south to see the moon pair up with the Leo constellation. The moon and the star, Regulas, should be close this evening. But the scope was locked in to the Lincoln Home. I haven't looked at it closely in quite some time." My voice grew strong. "You knew she was getting kidnapped, didn't you?"

"No. I swear it, Mist." He sighed. "Let me explain. Please, let me explain to both of you." I shared a look with my brother. His eyes told me everything. This was dead serious, and might be the end of them. Liam stood up and moved to the front of the desk. He leaned back on it with his arms crossed, his shoulder's slumped. I watched him take tiny breaths- not quite panicked, but obviously he was at an emotional stress-point.

"It's my job. You know the promotion to public relations has been a... challenge." That surprised me. He'd been promoted more than a year ago and I thought it was going well. The state's EPA had never looked so good.

"Actually no, I didn't know that. You've been a bear to live with these last weeks but before that, I thought it must have been running smooth." Liam nodded to Slate with a tired motion.

"For the most part, yes. But the reason it runs so smoothly is that I'm able to snuff out every fire before it reaches the canopy." He grunted a rough laugh. "And working for the state of Illinois, there are a lot of fires." He glanced up at Slate and then away. "By fires I mean rumors. It's a horrible environment on that level. I don't know if it's a hangover from previous days of chaos," he paused in an obvious reference to the number of Illinois governors who now reside in prisons, "but it is real, and the damage they do is substantial."

Slate pulled his head back a little as his eyes narrowed. "I don't see you as the sort to put up with rumors."

"I don't. You know me too well," he replied with a weak grin.

"Liam, what do rumors in the EPA have to do with Beverly? She's in historical preservation, not environmental protection."

He shook his head. "It's never just one state office, Mist. Anything headed here in Springfield has the potential to ruin other departments. It's not as nasty as the Chicago of old, but it's damn near close. Careers have been ruined, entire projects- good projects that benefit the state- have been waylaid because of things that start out as rumors."

Slate shook his head as he crossed his arms. "I haven't heard a single thing against the EPA since you've been in office, Liam."

"Don't you think that strange, Slate?" Liam could barely meet his eyes. I watched as he glanced at Slate again and then stared at his shoes. "I've had to stay ahead of it. At least, I told myself I had to stay ahead of it. That's why I did what I did."

"And what, exactly, is that?" I leaned forward.

Slate made a motion to me with his hand. "That's what he was just telling me when you arrived. Why don't you start from there, Liam?"

He nodded. "I was telling Slate that we can't get married unless he knows what I've done. He thinks I'm perfect, but I'm not."

"You're like the head Hardy-Boys of ethics, Liam."

"No, no I'm not. I knew that Beverly was going to be captured." He brought his hand up almost immediately. "Not that exactly- I didn't know who or what, exactly, was planned, just that something was going down at the Lincoln Home on Sunday night."

"How?"

Slate answered. "He'd just told me that when you pulled up. It seems my high-ethics leader here added a bit of spy-ware onto the emails of state agencies in Springfield."

My eyes flew wide. "Oh, gods of old, Liam. That's serious!"

He waved his arm and moved to look at out the doorway. "Not really, no. I violated nothing. In my position, I have access to all government agency emails that will be made public in one year. I just decided to look at them a little earlier."

"What do you mean?"

"Rumors are a disease in government agencies. I mean debilitating, time-consuming and they cost the tax-payers untold millions. I thought the best way to fix what my predecessor did wrong was to stay ahead of the gossip that takes root.

"I designed a pretty sophisticated piece of software that allows me to see all emails with key words I input. And it's only the text of the emails- I receive no IP information, no sender or receiver identification. It's just the email body, which will be open to the public anyway in one year. "But yeah, with this I've been able to squash every potential threat as soon as it starts to take root."

"Beverly." My voice was short. I was tired of waiting for the connection.

Liam nodded, turning back to face us. "I heard a rumor that the state is so strapped for cash that historical monuments are going to be made available for private events. Specifically, they're going to rent out Lincoln's living room." He raised his hand as I started to ask a question. "Let me finish. Something like this doesn't seem important, but I know that the EPA is going to ask for an increase in fees for environmental impact statements from public corporations. We already have one of the most expensive systems in the country- any increase in fees will be met with resistance.

"And a rumor that we're desperate for money means the EPA requisition won't receive a fair hearing."

"But aren't we strapped for cash?"

"This is Illinois government agencies- of course we are. But it would tip the scales unfairly. I doubt they'll get the increase anyway, but-"

"Bev. Er. Ly." I thumped my chair's armrest.

"Yes, yes." He cleared his throat and began again. "I heard the rumor. I went to my program and I keyed in the words 'meet' with all its variables to cover 'meetings, gatherings,' etc, plus 'Lincoln's home.'"

"And you got a hit?"

"I got a hit," he answered me. "It showed me the body of a message that said: 'Bring her to the Lincoln Home Sunday, seven, sharp. No cameras there." He lifted his hands for a brief moment. "What was I to do? That sounds like suspicious activity, but I couldn't go to the police with something so vague. I didn't know it was a 'bring her against her will' kind of thing. So, I did the only thing I could think to do that would have a valid excuse- look at the house at exactly that time from your telescope and make sure nothing illegal was going down." He sat back down at the desk. "But it turns out, something illegal was going down."

"How could you not tell the police, Liam? Surely they could have traced the email."

He shook his head. "Nope. To keep my conscious clear, or at least in a livable range, I made sure the program retrieves zero private data information. It's the body of an email only, and then all information used to gather is instantaneously forgotten. It doesn't even know how it gets it, basically."

"You can't know that," I said softly. "You're not a computer genius."

He shrugged. "Actually, I am. You'll have to trust me on that- it was a brilliant piece of programming."

"Was?" Liam looked at Slate.

"Yes, was. I got rid of it- all of it."

"Well that won't make you look guilty." Slate ignored me. "But still, you took the risk that no one could do more with it. You should have told Pete, Liam. Beverly almost died." The pain in Slate's voice was powerful.

My heart ached to hear my little brother in so much pain. "You should have told us, Liam. Or told Pete. It turns out, Crystal and I knew about an email sent by Lauren but she used the wrong email account."

"Gods," Liam put his face in his hands.

"Though, I wonder why she didn't delete it from her account once she realized her mistake?"

"She might have. But then again, deleted messages that have already been sent get tagged as a red flag- she probably avoided an investigation by ignoring it."

"Hiding right out in plain sight," Slate supplied.

"Yes," Liam agreed. "I'm sorry. I'm so, so sorry." I wasn't sure who he spoke to as he looked down at his feet.

I felt the need to leave. These two needed to talk. "For the record, it's nice to know you're not perfect." I gave Liam a soft smile. "Ethically, you don't have a leg to stand on. We the people don't need Big-Brother watching our every word, even if we do.

"And while I admire that you just went after the information and never the people involved, it's still sketchy stuff. I don't know how you guys are going to work through this, but I know you don't need me here." I picked up my purse from the floor and turned my back on them both with a wave. If I didn't look away, I'd probably try and scoop my little brother up and race from the room. But since he's two-inches taller than me, I doubt we'd get far.

They mumbled something as I left. I was worried, yet relieved. Some little part of my mind had seen that things didn't add up. For a while there, I was scared Liam was deeply involved. I knew he wasn't perfect, I mean, no one is, but he always came off as trying to shoot for a perfect score. But this kind of stumble, while human, might be too much for their relationship.

CHAPTER FOURTEEN

"**A**re you sure this has to be the last time?" Amber whined with a nasal sound as she rested her head on the hot-tub's rim.

"It is a bit early," Mica added from her corner. She too rested her head and didn't bother raising it to speak.

I scowled.

Crystal chimed in before I could speak. "If you ladies want the job of coming out here under cover of moonlight for its upkeep, Mist might be more agreeable."

"No thanks," they both said.

"Ha," Crystal barked. "That's what I thought. Let her be. If she wants to end our one bit of pampering early this year, it's her call."

"Hey." I reached over and flipped her wet hair into her face.

"Just kidding, Mist. I agree- life is getting a little full." We all grumbled sounds of agreement and spent several minutes enjoying the dark night sky.

The moon was new and absent, letting the stars have their turn to shine. "Any luck writing in the grimoire, Mist?" Amber looked over at me as she reached for her glass and took a sip. Yes, a sip. Since receiving our gifts, she was doing everything in moderation and taking tentative steps forward, as we all were.

"Nada. It won't even respond to questions now." *But had I even tried*? I frowned, trying to remember. Absentmindedly, I stroked my chain necklace. There's just so much else to work on right now. Didn't I need to tell them all about Beverly?

Mica shivered visibly. "Can we not talk about your blood-eating book, please? That gives me the heeby-geebies."

"Sorry. Of course. Did I tell you that Bonnie called me?"

"Keys? No, what did she have to say?" Mica sat up this time.

"When the doctor gives her okay to return to work, Beverly will be taking over Lauren's job at the preservation offices."

"Now, that's good news." Crystal tilted her wine glass in my direction.

"And it gets better. They looked over the records of Lauren's time there and rehired anyone Lauren fired, including-"

"Oh, that's such a relief!" Crystal almost cried. "Cheryl gets her job back."

"With back pay, it seems. Since it was just a few weeks ago, and right in the middle of the whole scheme falling down, the state wants to play it safe and not give Cheryl a reason to sue them for wrongful termination."

"I'm glad that has a tidy ending. Once they can link those idiots to the fire, everything will be wrapped up."

"Do they know about the key?"

We'd decided to just keep that under wraps. Mica shook her head before turning to me with a weak, half-smile. "How are Slate and Liam doing?"

I sank further into the foaming water until it reached my chin. "They are doing the work. They're in counseling. We'll see. Plus, Liam told his superiors what he had done. Technically, there was no breech as anything sent by agency email is open for public scrutiny. If Lauren hadn't been so careless and used her private email, that would be different."

Crystal raised her glass. "To a beautiful fact- the bad guys always make a mistake."

"The bad guys always make a mistake," we all echoed, raising our nicely aged cabernet.

"They can't be happy with him, though," Amber continued.

I jerked upright, frowning. "That's the weird thing- it's made

Slate and Liam somewhat uncomfortable. He wasn't reprimanded at all. They shrugged it off."

"What?" Crystal sat up straight, her reporter instincts going into overdrive. "How is that possible?"

I shrugged. "That's the question. Slate thinks Liam should quit his job immediately because they'll want to use this against him at some point. It's Illinois politics. If someone can hold something over Liam's head..." I let their imaginations fill in the rest.

"Crap on a stick," Mica said.

Crystal wrinkled her nose. "Lovely image, that."

"It certainly changes my image of Liam," Amber said as she swirled the wine under her nose.

"I'm actually glad to learn he's not a saint," Mica laughed. "Galère," she began in her perfect, Parisian accent, "means a gathering of misfits, not Mother-Theresa- wannabes.. Those two are almost prude's with morality issues at times. Aren't they the reason we can only buy beer and wine on Sundays?"

"You can't put that all on them, but yeah. They supported the idea."

"How are you two related?" Crystal laughed.

I raised my glass and looked at her right over the rim. "Because he was smart enough not to push for the wine as well."

"I didn't ask how is he still alive," Crystal snickered. We shared a loud laugh and I didn't shush them as usual.

For some reason, it felt like this would be our last gathering of the Naked Wine Club on the rooftop of the *Axe & Stovepipe*. True, it felt like that every year when I shut it down, but this time it seemed like something more. We have so much to work on, now; so much to figure out. How often will we be able to escape for an evening like this? I realized what I was really asking though, is what does the future hold for the galère?

While the memories of my time with Aiden were now as cold and distant as half-forgotten dreams, the work we were doing with our sacred elements was clear, though the others seemed to be advancing faster than me, all of them writing their positive outcomes into their grimoires. Mine though, remained out of reach. A stubbornness washed over me. I started to stroke my necklace but at the last moment, reached for my wine glass and once more, raised it high. "To the grimoires of the galère- I will reach mine again, I swear it."

"To the grimoires!" Everyone sat up straight and raised their glasses to the stars, daring any to defy our determination. If Mother Earth chose us for a purpose, we were going to meet that challenge by all of our witchy means.

THE END OF BOOK ONE

The Orphanage

Eva Carroll Monroe checked her reflection in the window of the hat store. Her left hand straightened the broach that held her stiff collar in place at her throat. The lace edging framed her round face nicely, and every strand of black hair was in place under her simple hat.

It wasn't broad, as the new styles she saw on display, but it was clean and well-maintained. She would love to indulge in a foot-wide piece with plumes and floral adornments, but the price of the hatpin alone was enough to stop any such a fancy. She had mouths to feed; many mouths.

Eva took a deep breath, her hands smoothing her corseted dress in determination as she looked across the street. The dress, and she, were ready to be seen. The new Savings and Loan building soared ten stories high with its large, white stones standing out in sharp contrast against the gray of the day. "Now if only my heart would listen," Eva whispered as her hands rested on her chest for a moment.

She released the breath once she realized she'd been holding it and took the time to take several more to steady herself. She refused to enter the bank looking frazzled and out of sorts. She may not be a woman of wealth, but she was a woman of considerable pride.

A short, white lady walked by and gave her a small smile and nod of the head. She returned it in kind, exactly as it had been given. She'd learn long ago not to presume anything about racial prejudices, not even here where Lincoln had lived and worked. While the city was filled with the children of abolitionists and veterans who had watched their friends die in the fight to end slavery, racial tensions had been growing and the town, in truth the entire state, was still trying to figure out how to move forward after the civil war.

There was talk up north about the Brotherhood of Teamsters prepar-

ing to go on strike. That would kick up a hornet's nest of problems, she worried. The state had passed regulations for factory inspections more than ten years before, but corruption kept that money from ever being put to use. And the teamsters had had enough.

"Focus on some good news now, Eva," she spoke outloud, hoping her own voice would calm her as well as it did so many small children each day. Good news… good news… She smiled. The miners. Yes, that had been some good news after a tragedy effecting so many homes in the area. Their union had won the labor disputes, but not before eleven miners were killed.

"You'll have to do better than that, Eva." She stomped her feet in an effort to shake off her nerves. She wished she was back at the orphanage, even falling down as it was. It was familiar. And it should be. She owned it. Her hand smoothed the outside of her purse. "But not for long," she whispered to the winds.

Good news… good news… It really was hard to think of anything, what with the times being what they were. Labor unrest was everywhere. Over six hundred people had died in the Iroquois Theater in Chicago and scuffles over racial tension in Springfield seemed to spring up every day.

So, instead of looking for good news from the city, she looked into her own heart. Eva closed her eyes and pictured the many children and elderly who made their home with her. She smiled as she recalled Anna singing while she bathed a few toddlers in the washtub, a smile on her toothless face that would light up the night. 'It's just so good to be useful again.' Anna said that to Eva at least once a day since she'd joined them last month.

Renewed for the moment, she made her way across the street, careful to keep her hem clear of the horse manure and dust. The roads could *use some attention. She looked up to the sky. "But I would appreciate if you would hold on the rain, just a bit longer." She whispered the words but knew God could hear them. He had listened to her prayers and brought her here today, after all, even though it broke her heart. But she would be humble before the Lord and do what was right for the children. Four, tiny and scared faces flashed through her mind and she smiled at the memory.*

They'd all looked so scared when she led them, her first orphans, into the dilapidated house five years earlier. But their faces had soon smoothed into actual smiles as the elderly woman named Mary greeted them from her chair, her arms wide. Mary just had that way about her, that kind of blessing to soothe away all worries with her voice and her smile. Where would she be without Mary?

Eva knew, though, that the skill had been crucial to Mary's survival on a Kentucky plantation where she had been taken ten years before the war's end, leaving all of her family behind in Georgia, sold away from her children, no hope of ever finding them. Eva had taken her in when she found Mary sleeping behind her garden shed, homeless. She could no longer work and there was no one to take her in, so Eva did. And when she'd told Mary she had found four orphans and was bringing them in as well, Mary had done what little her tired body would allow to help create a home for them.

That one elderly woman became eight and those four children became twenty-nine before Eva could hardly catch her breath. The chaos of people trying to find work, migrating hundreds and thousands of miles, left the old and the young at risk. And they kept finding Eva, who took them in. Even with the help of the Springfield Colored Women's Club, the costs of taking care of so many had outdistanced her and the board members' abilities to raise funds.

"So, here I am," Eva whispered as she entered the bank. Her mind

whirled and a slight panic settled in. How could she hand over the only security she had in the whole world? How had it come to this? Eva held no grudge against Mary Lawrence, the wife of the former mayor. Indeed, Mrs. Lawrence had helped them with bedding and linen drives, donated her time and almost eight hundred dollars to the work that Eva championed, work which Mrs. Lawrence had publicly praised and helped raise even more funds with that simple act.

And when Eva came to her in dire straits, the old house moving into disrepair and almost fifteen hundred dollars behind in payments, Mrs. Lawrence agreed to help them. She would rebuild the entire house and pay off all debts, plus help create long-term goals for financial security. And Eva would be allowed to stay in the house as long as it was an orphanage, for free. She had that in writing.

All Mrs. Lawrence required was the deed.

She'd said that, even though Eva had the persistence, intelligence and greatly admired work ethics that had done so much, without formal financial training, she was ill-prepared to keep the orphanage afloat. Mrs. Lawrence had the education and the contacts needed to make it work.

'Stand humble before God, Eva,' she reminded herself, yet again, as she made her way into the opulent lounge. More than a few heads turned her way before resuming their conversations. She had as much a right as anyone to be in the building, and she lifted her chin as she made her way across the cool, tiled floor. Mrs. Lawrence saw her from a seating area and rose to walk over and embraced her. Eva appreciated this public statement that reflected her own thoughts of a moment before.

"I can imagine how difficult this must be, Eva. I want to thank you for doing this. I feel confident that with your incredible tenacity, and

my accountants watching over the books, we'll end the stress you must have born these last years. I'm in this for life, Eva. We'll make this work." She smiled warmly, her wrinkled face always hinting of laughter barely held in check, and Eva felt the tension leave her body.

She stifled a laugh, wondering how Mrs. Lawrence would feel being compared to Mary, a former slave from Kentucky who shared her name and that same, stress-releasing talent. As they waited to be called back into the offices where she would sign away her sole piece of property, Eva sent out a prayer of gratitude that the children and the old ones would not be turned out into the streets. It was what she had asked for, and she would not be persnickety in how it came about.

She followed Mrs. Lawrence a few moments later, her shoulders lifting high. She'd done it- she raised her siblings after her parents died, and each one could read and write and was gainfully employed. She provided a home to abandoned children so they would never have to face what she'd faced, and she gave elderly people a purpose when society told them they had none.

A tear burned in her eyes. Mrs. Lawrence might see it as sadness, but Eva knew it for what it was- success. She'd made this world a better place, and she would keep making it better with every day the Lord gave her.

She smiled, free and wide and impetuously reached out to briefly clasped Mrs. Lawrence's hand. The older woman turned to her, surprise across her face, but as soon as she saw Eva's expression, she broke out into the threatened laugh and grabbed Eva's hand with both of hers. It was fitting that the gray clouds parted and allowed some light to fall onto the bank, briefly. The warm sunlight broke through the darkness and fell through the window onto Eva. She looked up and took it as a sign.

"I'm ready," she said, taking up the pen. "Let's build a brand, new orphanage!"

FROM THE AUTHOR

True history is mixed throughout the journeys of the members of our galère. Abe Lincoln did loan a friend money to build a house, and that house was indeed uplifted and dropped in the middle of the road for a month before moving to its new home and new life as a coffee shop. The architecture, rumors and sights are all based on things that the little city once lived but has now forgotten.

In book two, you'll learn a little about Springfield's importance in the Civil War as we follow the life of a ghost for a short while. You'll meet more members of the galère- human and otherwise. Mist has a major transformation and the witches start to claim their powers. It's broken into two parts, with a side story in between for book three.

Thank you for going on this journey with me! Grab your good-vibe stones and let's give them a jolt.

GOOD VIBE STONES

Amethyst- Turn negative energy into positive; overcome addictions; new beginnings

Amber- Cleansing; happiness; protection
from negative nellies

Mica- Lets one see the entire picture to
offer clarity; vision quests

Crystal (quartz)- Amplifies the qualities of others;
enhances higher *spiritual* connections and information